The True Adventures of
Charley Darwin

Other Books by Carolyn Meyer

The True Adventures of
Charley Darwin

Carolyn Meyer

Harcourt
Houghton Mifflin Harcourt
Boston • New York • 2009

www.hmhbooks.com

Library of Congress Cataloging-in-Publication Data
Meyer, Carolyn, 1935–
The true adventures of Charley Darwin/Carolyn Meyer.
p.   cm.
Summary: In nineteenth-century England, young Charles Darwin rejects the more traditional careers of physician and clergyman, choosing instead to embark on a dangerous five-year journey by ship to explore the natural world.
1. Darwin, Charles, 1809–1882 — Juvenile fiction.   2. Beagle Expedition (1831–1836) — Juvenile fiction.   [1. Darwin, Charles, 1809–1882 — Fiction.   2. Beagle Expedition (1831–1836) — Fiction.   3. Voyages around the world — Fiction.   4. Natural history — Fiction.]   I. Title.   II. Title: True adventures of Charlie Darwin.
PZ7.M5685Tr   2009
[Fic] — dc22   2008017451
ISBN 978-0-15-206194-4

Map created by Stephanie Cooper
Text set in Apollo
Designed by Jennifer Kelly

First edition
A C E G H F D B

Printed in the United States of America

The True Adventures of Charley Darwin is a work of fiction based on historical figures and events. Some details have been altered to enhance the story.

For three generations of adventurers

Joseph Smrcka (1927–1996)
Alan, John, and Chris Smrcka
Erin, Joe, and Sophie Smrcka

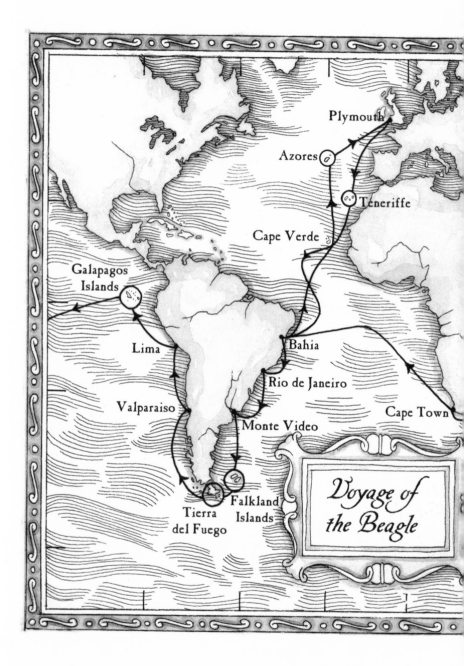

Plymouth

Azores

Teneriffe

Cape Verde

Galapagos
Islands

Lima

Bahia

Valparaiso

Rio de Janeiro

Monte Video

Cape Town

Tierra
del Fuego

Falkland
Islands

*Voyage of
the Beagle*

Keeling Islands

Mauritius

King
George's
Sound

Sydney

Hobart Town

H.M.S. BEAGLE

MIDDLE SECTION FORE AND AFT

1832

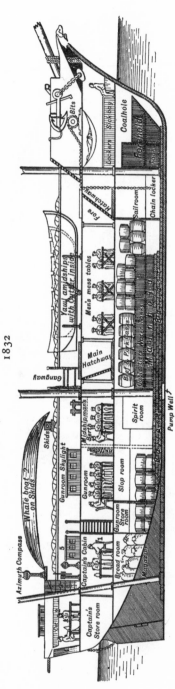

1. Mr. Darwin's Seat in Captain's Cabin
2. Mr. Darwin's Seat in Poop Cabin with Cot slung behind him
3. Mr. Darwin's Chest of Drawers
4. Bookcase
5. Captain's Skylight

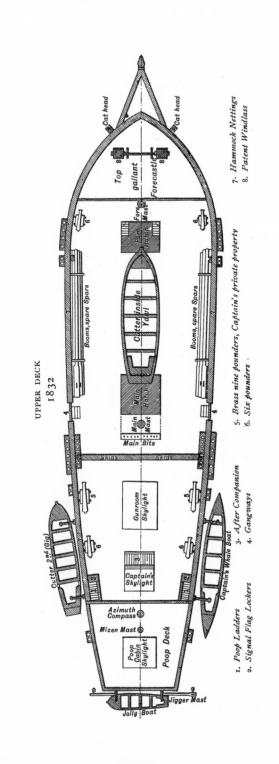

UPPER DECK
1832

Cat head
Cat head

Top gallant Forecastle

Fore Mast

Fore Hatch

Booms, spare Spars
Booms, spare Spars

Cutter inside Yawl

Main Hatch

Main Mast
Main Bits

Skids
Skids

Gunroom Skylight

Captain's Skylight

Cutter 2nd (Gig)
Captain's Whale Boat

Azimuth Compass

Mizen Mast

Poop Cabin Skylight
Poop Deck

Jigger Mast
Jolly Boat

1. Poop Ladders
2. Signal Flag Lockers
3. After Companion
4. Gangways
5. Brass nine pounders, Captain's private property
6. Six pounders .
7. Hammock Nettings
8. Patent Windlass

The True Adventures of
Charley Darwin

PART I
Charley

Chapter 1

Shrewsbury School: 1818

ODD, ISN'T IT, how a trivial thing can turn out to be a matter of greatest importance in one's life. In my case, it was my nose.

I considered my nose rather ordinary, perhaps a trifle too large for me to be thought handsome, but entirely suited to its purpose. However, because of *my nose* I was nearly denied the greatest adventure of my life. The man responsible was Robert FitzRoy, captain of a small sailing ship, who argued that a man's character could be divined by studying the contours of his head and the features of his face. Based on the size and shape of my nose, the captain believed I lacked sufficient energy and determination to endure the arduous sea voyage he planned to make round the world.

How did it come about that Captain FitzRoy, a perfect stranger, should care so deeply about my nose? And what was his decision and the results of it? To answer those questions and others that may arise, let me begin at the beginning, long before I ever heard of the captain or of his ship HMS *Beagle*.

I WAS BORN February 12th, 1809, in the town of Shrewsbury, county of Shropshire, England, and christened Charles Robert Darwin. For the first few years of my life my family called me Bobby. My father, Dr. Robert Darwin, practised medicine. My brother Erasmus, called Ras, older by four years and two months, our four sisters, our parents, and I lived at The Mount, a great brick mansion built high on a hill above the River Severn with a view of Shrewsbury Castle's ancient red sandstone walls.

Facts are unchanging, but memories are mutable — sometimes sharp, sometimes out of focus, sometimes shadowy or absent altogether. From the early years of my childhood I can summon only a few blurred images. I offer this brief list:

Paddling in the sea on the north coast of Wales with my younger sister, Catty.

Gathering beetles and shells and pebbles and various plants for my collection, my older sister Caroline complaining of the odour.

Sitting on the riverbank with Ras whilst he patiently taught me how to spit a worm on a fishhook and answered my endless questions; I idolised him.

Walking with my mother to the small day school taught by the Reverend Case and being frightened by a dog barking in the street.

Standing uneasily by my mother's sickbed as she whispered something to me, and being brought to that same room days later to see her laid out on the bed in a black velvet gown, my brother and sisters weeping inconsolably and my father's face contorted with grief. I, too, wept, but without realising all that I wept for. Oddly enough, I remember nothing about her funeral. Mostly I remember her absence.

I was eight and a half years old and no longer called Bobby. I was now Charles, and sometimes Charley.

The images become etched more clearly when I reached the age of nine. At the beginning of the summer quarter my father enrolled me at Shrewsbury School, across the road from the old castle and less than a mile from The Mount. I could have continued living at home whilst attending classes, but Father thought it best if I boarded at the school.

"Your mother and I made this decision some time ago," he said sternly when I begged to stay at home with Catty and continue my schooling with Caroline as my teacher. "We both felt that you would pay more attention to your studies there."

And so off I went, desperately unhappy but trying to be brave.

Ras had been toiling away at the school for four years when I arrived. He may have rather enjoyed it at the outset, being away from our sisters and not having to endure lessons with them any longer. He pointed out that all of our boy cousins had been sent away to boarding school.

Only girls got to stay at home. "Believe me, Charley, it's better than being all day with the sisterhood" — his name for our sisters.

But he had serious complaints about the school.

"Eat up whilst you can, Charley," advised Ras, a tall, thin, rather frail lad who looked as though he ought to take his own advice. "You'll get little enough to put in your stomach, and what you do get isn't fit for a dog. There's a sign by the headmaster's gateway with his initials, SB, on it. The letters stand for 'Stale Bread, Sour Beer, Salt Butter, Stinking Beef — for Sale By Samuel Butler.' That's the headmaster's name. And try to smuggle in an extra blanket. You could read your Latin grammar through the nap of the thin shroud you'll be issued. No use having Father go to Dr. Butler for it. He refuses all such requests."

Maurice, the groom, drove me to school on my first day, informed one of the masters of my arrival, carried my trunk up to my bed, and left me there with a handshake and a pat on the shoulder. "Ye'll be all right now, Master Charley," he said, and hurried away. I struggled not to cry or behave in an infantile manner, though I longed to run after him and plead to be taken home.

Then I met Garnett, the boy with whom I would be forced to share a bed. I told him my name. Garnett had looked me over cannily. "Like to fight?" he'd asked, and I said that I'd never been in a fight in my life and was sure I would not like it. He smirked. "I'd have thought by the look of that nose of yours you'd already taken a few jabs. You're thick as a stump, Darwin, and you look strong enough," he said. "We could make a good fighter out of you, if you'd a mind."

Self-consciously I covered my nose with my hand. "But there's nothing to fight about," I said, hoping I was right but already guessing I might be wrong.

It did not take long for me to learn to loathe the school. It took a little longer to plan my escapes.

At the end of each day the boys lined up stiffly in the school refectory for the calling-over. One of the masters read out our names, starting with the oldest students, the sixth formers, who were then dismissed, and ending with the youngest. I'd been placed in the lower third form.

"Darwin!"

"Here, sir!"

Once my name had been called and the lower third dismissed, I contrived to slip away by the servants' side door and bolted across the wet lawn and through the unlocked iron gates to freedom. I prided myself on being a fast runner and hadn't far to go — ten minutes if I gave it my best, trotting along the old town walls, across the Severn by the Welsh Bridge, and up the hill to The Mount. Spark, our black-and-white pup, was first to greet me. At the sound of his joyous barking Marianne, twenty years old and the eldest of my sisters, set down the needlepoint canvas she was working. Caroline, sixteen, laid aside the book she'd been reading aloud — one of Miss Jane Austen's novels during that autumn of 1818 — and gasped, "Charley! What on earth —?"

Susan, the fifteen-year-old sister I sometimes called Granny, frowned her disapproval. "Charley, you ought not be here!" she scolded. "You're breaking the rules, and you'll get caught and punished, and Papa will be furious."

During our mother's lingering illness Caroline had made herself into a kind of substitute mother for me and Catty, younger by a year. Caroline was tall and serious as a judge, thick black hair pulled into heavy plaits, and she had sat with us every day at a low table in a corner of the nursery at the top of the house. She'd taught us our letters and numbers, supervised the practise of penmanship, and patiently rehearsed us in our Bible verses and the prayers we were expected to recite faultlessly when she took us each by the hand and led us off to worship at St. Chad's. This church was the only building I had ever been inside that was not square but round, and for that reason alone I found it interesting. We'd all been christened there. Father, not a churchgoing man, didn't accompany us on Sunday mornings.

I was a pensive boy often lost in my own thoughts, and that dreaminess exasperated my sisters. "Charley is clearly bright enough," I'd once heard Caroline remark to Susan, who replied, "Yes, but he is intolerably lazy." Catty was quicker than I was, though not much more interested in her studies. She preferred to amuse herself with dressing her dolls and feeding them flower petals from Father's conservatory. Ras, we all knew, was the brilliant one.

Now, as I appeared unexpectedly after my escape,

Catty threw down the speller Caroline had assigned her and flung her arms round me. "Charley! I'm so glad to see you! Is the school truly horrid? Do you hate it? Oh, I do wish you were still at home with us!"

"It doesn't matter if he hates it," Susan said severely, glowering at me over her spectacles. That's why I called her Granny.

The school was every bit as dreadful as Ras had promised, but I put on a brave face and squirmed out of Catty's embrace. "I wish I were still here, too," I admitted.

I'd loved rambling round The Mount in all kinds of weather, sometimes letting Catty ramble with me, on foot or on our ponies. We'd spent hours together by the river, perched in the crooked branches of the old Spanish chestnut tree I'd named Borum, sending messages to each other by means of ropes and pulleys in the code I devised. The tree where an owl nested I called Owlo, and I'd invented names for members of the household: Nancy, our nursemaid, was "Pea-spitter," and Father was dubbed "Squirt." I don't know how I came upon those names, but I do know that Father, for one, would not have been amused. Now there was no opportunity for rambling or for perching in trees, and I missed this world with an ache felt in my bones.

"I'm afraid you're too early for tea," Marianne said, placidly threading a needle with a length of rose-coloured wool. "You know we always wait for Papa."

"I know." Father seldom got home from his evening medical calls before eight o'clock, and by that hour I had to be back at the school and in my dormitory or suffer dire consequences. If Father had found me at home, the consequences would have been dire as well.

Nancy rushed in, clucking her tongue, and rushed out again. "Lad's like to starve to death," she muttered when she'd returned with a plate of teacakes, and I'd gobbled up two and stuffed two more in my trouser pockets.

There was not much time between calling-over and locking up at Shrewsbury School — no more than an hour — and though I stretched my visit home to the last possible moment, I knew I would have to run fast to reach the school before I was shut out. A glance at the gold clock on the drawing room mantel warned me that the time had come to wrench myself away. I was bestowing one last belly rub on Spark when I heard the crunch of Father's carriage on the gravel drive leading to the front entrance. Caroline hurried me to the back door. "Dear Charley," she murmured. "Be off with you now, and quickly!"

I began to run, my feet skidding down the path to the river. I could picture the scene I left behind in every detail:

Father heaves himself out of the smart yellow phaeton recognised by everyone in Shropshire and hands the reins to the groom. He is a large man — immense, in fact. Well over six feet tall, he'd stopped weighing himself some years earlier, when he reached twenty-four stone, exceeding three hundred pounds. His bulk fills the doorway. My sisters rise to greet him, smoothing their skirts, offering smiles.

"Good evening, my dears," he says. His voice is surprisingly high and light for a man of such size. A stranger might have expected a low growl. He allows each daughter to kiss his cheek.

"Good evening, Papa," says Marianne. She pronounces it Pa-pa; to say Pa-pa or Mam-ma, with the accent switched back to front, is what people of the lower classes call their parents, not well-bred young ladies like the Darwin girls.

And so it goes, down the line in order of age, the kiss planted on his smooth cheek, the greeting, the smile for Pa-pa. Last comes Catty, his pet and well aware of her special place as the youngest.

On I ran, panting, ignoring a little pebble in my shoe, too worried about coming late to stop and fix it. The Severn wrapped round Shrewsbury as though tying a parcel. Fog curled up from the river and clung to my skin like silk.

Father settles into his favourite chair, built specially for him with adequate reinforcement and covered in deep red plush velvet. The manservant kneels to remove his boots and presents his slippers, warmed and ready. Marianne rings the bell, calling the parlour maid to bring the tea. It is Caroline's honour to pour from an elegant teapot into five delicate cups. The teapot, cups, saucers, and cake plates are all from the Wedgwood Potteries, owned by my uncle Jos. We all remember they were Mamma's particular favourites.

I pounded across the Welsh Bridge and plunged, panting, through the dark, narrow streets and over the worn cobblestones of the town centre. Shrewsbury School loomed ahead, a bleak grey stone presence. Fear drove me. I'd shaved it a bit too close, lingered at home a bit too long. Suppose I found the iron gate barred, the door locked and bolted? Darkness had closed in, the fog thickened to a drizzle.

Determination turned to desperation as the hour hand of the clock in the tower of Old Market Hall moved tick by tick towards my doom. I'd be flogged and ordered into the Black Hole Garnett had told me about, left in the cold blackness of the narrow cell for hours, perhaps even forgotten for days, as he swore had happened to others. Expulsion and the horrified embarrassment of my father would surely follow. The thought filled me with dread. I kept a little prayer ready for when disaster loomed: *Heavenly Father, I most humbly pray to Thee — help me run faster!*

My prayer was answered. In the very nick of time I reached the servants' entrance and found the gate and the door still miraculously open. In the distance the clock began to strike. Seeing no sign of Old Philip, the verger in charge of locking up, I scrambled undetected up the dark stair to the fetid attic that smelt of urine. Some two dozen unwashed boys slept two to a bed on seldom-laundered sheets. There was only one window with a row of washstands lined up beneath it. I fell, wheezing, onto the bed I shared with Garnett.

A year and a half older and far more knowing than I in the ways of the world and Shrewsbury School, Garnett was waiting for me, eyes gleaming with malice. "What've you brought me, Darwin?" he demanded. Garnett knew about my little escapes — this had not been my first — and threatened to report me if I failed to buy him off. I fumbled in my trouser pockets and produced the mashed and crumbled remains of the teacakes.

Garnett's lip curled in disgust. "You've got to do better than this," he said. "Next time, pray, bring a meat pie — if you know what's good for you."

I nodded, and Garnett bolted down the scorned teacakes, crumbs falling on our shared blanket. From the trunk at the foot of the bed I pulled out a thoroughly abused book on Roman history and carried it to the passageway where the other boys sat at long tables, studying or pretending to study, and took my accustomed seat. I opened the book. The words swam before my eyes.

I'd rather have been searching for newts in the pond of the old quarry. Or squatting on the bank of the Severn with my fishing pole. Or tramping across the fields that stretched beyond the old town walls. Or lying beneath the dining room table at The Mount, rereading my favourite book, *Robinson Crusoe,* and imagining myself as the shipwrecked Englishman surviving against all odds on an island inhabited by fierce cannibals.

I replaced the history book and took out a mousechewed book of Latin grammar. It was impossible to concentrate. My mind kept drifting back to The Mount.

Caroline calls the parlour maid to close the heavy

draperies and add a half-scuttle of coal to the grate —
more than that would be wasteful. Catty scratches Spark's
ears and sings softly to him. Susan reaches for Miss
Austen's novel to take her turn reading aloud. Marianne's
needle darts in and out, finishing the petal of an elaborate
floral design. Father dozes in his chair, snoring softly.

The prayer bell rang and we leapt to put away our
books. Speedily changing from trousers and waistcoats
and jackets into nightshirts, we knelt by our beds, hands
folded, eyes squeezed shut, lips moving. "God bless Father, Ras, Marianne," I murmured, going down the list,
ending with "and bless Mamma in heaven. And Garnett
and the others," I added for good measure, in the forlorn
hope that a blessing would make him more congenial.

Old Philip shuffled along, snuffing out the candles,
and Garnett and I finished our amens at the same moment and piled into our miserable bed, each struggling
for a share of the shrunken blanket. Quiet settled over
the restless boys, coughs and mumbled prayers and curses
eventually giving way to snores and an occasional sob,
and I lay there thinking sadly of home.

SOMETIME IN THE HOURS past midnight one of the boys
announced in a low voice pitched to wake all but the
soundest sleepers, "Time to raise the Doctor, lads!"

It was an amusement in which Garnett usually par-
ticipated heartily. That night I tried again to refuse — I
believed I'd taken enough risk for one day.

"Come now, Darwin, what sort of coward are you?"
Garnett demanded. "Leaving the dirty work to others, is

that your game?" Continuing to revile me, he at last succeeded in enlisting me.

We left with a dozen brave boys in stocking feet, sworn to carry out the deed. Boots in hand, we crept stealthily out of the attic dormitory and down the long hall to a spot known to be directly above the headmaster's quarters. We pulled on our boots and at a signal from the ringleader energetically performed a brain-rattling dance on the wooden floor, producing enough racket with our stomping to wake the dead and certainly to rouse Dr. Butler, till now sleeping soundly in his feather bed just below.

The ringleader judged how much time was needed to thoroughly disturb the headmaster, how much more time for us to yank off our boots, race back to our beds, dive under our blankets, and squeeze our eyes tight shut. Feigning sleep, breathing hard, we awaited the arrival of the headmaster, face purple with rage, spindly white shanks poking out from beneath his flannel nightshirt like the tines of a fork. He appeared from below so quickly that he seemed to have been waiting for the attack. His fury was cold and narrowly focussed. For whatever reason — it wasn't clear why — Dr. Butler singled out Garnett, dragged him from our dank bed, and hauled him down for a flogging. I was left behind and quaking, my heart thudding dangerously in my ears. Garnett did not return for the rest of the night. I slept poorly, worried and guilty.

The next morning as we were lining up for chapel, Garnett appeared, looking exhausted and proud of it. I avoided meeting his eye and instead searched anxiously for Ras in the crowd of big fellows, the upper school boys. The sight of my brother, lank hair falling over his pale forehead, immediately cheered me. He raised one finger to the side of his nose, acknowledging that he'd seen me. Were it not for the reassuring presence of Ras, nearly fourteen years old and beginning his fifth year at Shrewsbury School (*How does he bear it?* I often wondered), I was certain I could not survive the beastly place another day.

Chapter 2

The Mount: 1818

MY FIRST LAWFUL HOLIDAY away from school fell at Michaelmas, the end of the summer term. On September 29th, a Tuesday, we were released from captivity immediately after morning chapel with a warning to return for calling-over on Friday evening: three nights and four treasured days to eat at my family's well-provisioned table, sleep in my own clean bed, and ramble to my heart's content on my father's estate.

"We're free men, Charley!" Ras crowed as we strode joyfully through the iron gates of the school.

We walked along swinging our arms, breathing in the fresh, sweet air, and discussing what we'd do with the hours that stretched gloriously empty ahead of us. I tried not to think that in four days we'd be back in shackles, forced once more into the hard labour of learning with only meagre prisoners' rations to sustain us. I vowed not to waste a single precious minute.

Father was not at home. Michaelmas was a quarter day on which he collected rents on his properties and attended to business matters in addition to his duties at the infirmary. As soon as I could tear myself from my sisters' affectionate clutches, I raced up the stairs and down the hall to the bedroom I shared with Ras and opened the wooden cabinet where I kept my treasures. Everything was just as I'd left it.

There were boxes of stones I'd gathered on my explorations round The Mount, some as close as the front door, others from the garden, or down near the river, or on longer walks in the countryside. I didn't know what all of them were, though Ras was good about helping me identify my specimens.

There were shells collected during summer weeks by the sea in Wales. There were coins given me by my uncle, Jos Wedgwood. I'd persuaded everyone in the household to save postage franks and wax seals from letters, which I'd pasted into an album. Plants and flowers I'd carefully pressed were neatly labelled in my own hand. I had a particular interest in most any creeping, crawling thing — bright-coloured insects, moths, and especially beetles, all pinned to pasteboard.

"It's not right to kill any creature for the purpose of making a collection," my sister Caroline insisted. This made me feel guilty but did not stop me from my sins, such as netting butterflies and mercilessly pinning them in flat boxes with labels attached.

I also had a good collection of birds' eggs, and Ras had shown me how to blow out the contents without destroying the shell. I was always careful never to take more than one from the nest, though Garnett said taking a single egg was stupid, because birds can't count, and as long as just one egg was left in the nest, the mother bird wouldn't be bothered. But he failed to convince me entirely, and I knew for a certainty Caroline would not approve.

Assured my treasures were undisturbed, I tore down the back stairs, nabbing a sticky cake on my way past the pantry, and raced out to the garden in search of good old Abberley. The gardener looked up with pleasure and surprise. "Master Charley!" he called out. "At last you've come to give me a hand!"

"I have. But only for a few days, Abberley."

"Then let's get to it, lad."

Happily I helped our elderly gardener, carrying buckets of water from the well to the hothouses where Abberley grew out-of-season herbs and vegetables for the table. Then we made the rounds, noting all the changes that had come about since I was there three months earlier. The apples were now ripe, and I bit into one and stuffed my pockets with others. When the sky darkened and the rain began to come down — lightly at first, then a downpour — Abberley and I retired to the conservatory. In this handsome structure of iron and glass adjoining the morning room, Father cultivated his rare plants. Blushing pink camellias, brilliantly coloured azaleas, yellow-throated primulas, and great bushy ferns thrived in the warm, moist climate. Nine orange trees were heavy with ripening fruit. The conservatory was Father's pride, and he'd often let me follow him round as he inspected his specimens.

"Some of these plants come from faraway countries, but many first came here from your grandfather's garden," Abberley told me, not for the first time. He pointed out the white-flowered flycatcher and the brilliant Oriental poppy cultivated by my father's father, the first Erasmus Darwin, a physician, poet, and natural scientist famous in his day. "I remember him well," Abberley said now. "Worked for him for years, I did." The gardener gazed at me with a gap-toothed smile. "You're a lot like him, indeed you are."

It pleased me to hear this, though at the time I had little notion what an illustrious figure my grandfather had been.

When Father returned early in the afternoon, he greeted Ras and me with a handshake. "Welcome home, gentlemen! I trust you will both do me the honour of dining with me today."

"Yes, Father," I said, grinning.

This was a momentous occasion: the first time Father had allowed me to eat with him at the big mahogany table in the dining room. Before I'd been packed off to Shrewsbury School, Catty and I took all our meals upstairs in the nursery with Nancy, our nursemaid, whilst Father dined with the older sisters and Ras, when he was at home; Father only summoned the two youngest, Catty and me, for a little chat at the end of the day, before Nancy put us to bed. I felt immensely proud of this new promotion to the adult world, but Catty was left, scowling, upstairs with Nancy. I wished she could have come to the table with the rest of us.

The serving maid delivered a crystal goblet of hot water to Father's place at the head of the long table. Cook sent in a large platter of thickly sliced beef and three or four bowls of vegetables — potatoes, turnips, peas — all well boiled.

"Well, well, well," Father said expansively, forking his way through a heaping plate. "Things going well with you, boys?" He patted his large stomach with satisfaction.

"Yes, Father," Ras answered, and shot me a warning look. Ras had spent the past three months listening to my complaints about the wretched school food — gristly meat, stale bread, and hard, dry cheese served in meagre portions — the smelly bed shared with a boy I half feared, and my thorough dislike of all my lessons. I understood Ras's look. He had persuaded me that grievances would do no good and only earn me a reputation as a whiner.

I managed a smile when Father's glance shifted my way. "Yes, Father," I said.

Caroline fixed her eyes on her plate. She knew I detested most everything about Shrewsbury School. I wondered if she'd dared speak to Father after one of my unlawful visits home. Probably not, I decided, or I would have surely heard about it.

When the meal was finished, I considered what I might do in the hours that lay ahead. I was surprised, then, to hear my father say, "Well, Charles, if you have no other plans just now, I should appreciate your company as I visit some of my patients. What do you say to that, eh?"

My head snapped up. *Go with Father to visit his*

patients? I'd been looking forward to a ramble down by the river, perhaps allowing Catty to come along. But this — this was different! My father had never before invited me to accompany him on his rounds. Two honours in the course of one afternoon! I'm not sure which excited me more: having time alone with my father or the rare privilege of witnessing how he practised medicine. "Of course, Father!" I cried.

We set off, squeezed tightly together in the yellow phaeton. The groom, Maurice, rode beside us to the home of a charity patient some little distance from Shrewsbury. The poor thatched cottage appeared in a dangerous state of disrepair, its walls crumbling. Maurice knocked and entered first, to be sure the sagging floor would bear my father's great weight.

"All right, my boy, come along now," Father said. My chest swelling with importance, I followed him into the cottage.

The odour of poverty and illness rose up to engulf me — not so very different, I thought, from the smell of the school dormitory. Though the floor was solid enough, the chair offered to Dr. Darwin was not. Father remained standing, head cocked to one side, nodding sympathetically as he listened to the old woman's tremulous list of complaints. When she'd finished, he began to question her closely: Was the pain lower down or higher up? Was the coughing continuous, or did it come and go? Worse at night than in the morning? Was she feverish? Were there chills? Weakness in the limbs? Once he was satisfied that he had the information he needed for a diagnosis, he wrote out a prescription.

"You must take this scrip to the apothecary and have the medicines prepared," he told the old woman. "Take the doses exactly as he will explain to you. See that you do not exert yourself, and take care to avoid foods that are chilling."

The woman thanked him several times over and gripped his hand gratefully. After enquiring about the health of other members of the family and advising the old woman's daughter on the treatment of a child's itching rash, Father placed his hand on my shoulder and steered me outside.

"So you see, my boy, that's how it's done," he said cheerfully, heaving himself into the phaeton.

As the phaeton bounced over the rutted country lanes to the next patient, I called my father's attention to several different kinds of birds and excitedly pointed out a fox darting into the brush and a young badger plunging into a stream. "Your powers of observation have grown remarkably acute, Charles," Father said, and I beamed with pride.

We were gone for hours. I thought it the best afternoon of my life.

ONCE WE'D RETURNED HOME, Father retired to the library and sat at his desk, built with a large cutout to accommodate his enormous girth. With his spectacles perched on his nose, he tended to his account books, meticulously noting each expenditure presented to him by the housekeeper. "Mrs. Clearwater has been instructed to save the receipts for every purchase, no matter how insignificant," he told me. "A good habit."

I hung about for a while, content just to be in Father's presence. I had in mind, when the time seemed right, to ask for an increase in pocket money. The Darwin household was a frugal one. Father did not approve of unwise or careless spending. I often heard my sisters complain that when the weather turned cold, he advised them to wrap themselves in warm shawls and to wear extra flannel petticoats, rather than to have a fire laid in their rooms. Still, I hoped to convince him I might better profit from my time at Shrewsbury School if I could afford occasional visits to the cake shop on Castle Street.

Whilst I was mentally rehearsing the arguments I would set forth, Father looked up from his accounting chores and gazed at me. "Sit down, Charles," he said.

I sat, wondering what was coming.

Father pulled two small books from his shelves and placed them, side by side, on his desk. "I've decided to make you a gift of two volumes that I trust you will not only enjoy but come to treasure," he said. "They are works of natural history, in which I've observed you take a keen interest, what with your collections and so forth. These books belonged to my elder brother for whom you're named. Charles was a student of medicine and died when he was only nineteen. It was a tragic occurrence — he was dissecting the brain of a child and contracted an infection."

Solemnly, he opened one of the books and slowly turned the pages. "See here, this volume concerns bodies of water, earth, stones, fossils, and minerals with their virtues, properties, and medical uses." He paused to study a number of engravings, then closed that book and opened the other. "And this volume will inform you about insects."

Father pushed the two books across his desk towards me. "They're yours now, Bobby," he said. He sometimes still used my childhood nickname when he was deeply moved. "I'm certain you'll find much pleasure and knowledge in them. Now perhaps you will allow me to continue my work uninterrupted?"

I was too surprised by the gift and by the tenderness in my father's voice to know what to say. I ran off, clutching the books, which became my prized possessions, and decided the request for pocket money could wait till another time.

THE MICHAELMAS HOLIDAY slipped by much too quickly. On Thursday I spent several hours on the banks of the Severn with a fishing rod, idly watching the float and waiting, mostly in vain, for a fish to rise to the bait. I didn't really care about catching anything. I simply liked being there by the river with the silvery water rushing by.

Then it was Friday, the day I had to return to Shrewsbury School. I remember this as the saddest of my school days, even sadder than the day Maurice drove me there for the first time, shook my hand, and left me. I hadn't known then how unhappy I would be. Now I understood it very well, and I nearly became ill at the thought.

In the morning I coaxed Catty to accompany me down to the riverbank below the icehouse where I liked to enact my imaginings of the adventures of Robinson Crusoe. Sometimes I cast Catty in the role of one of the brutish cannibals, and when she played her role well, I elevated her to the position of my man, Friday. Spark, the dog, accompanied us, playing his own part as a wild beast.

"I can't bear to go back today, Catty," I confessed. "It's such a long while till the next holiday, and I don't think I'll survive."

"Don't be silly, Charley," Catty admonished. "Of course you'll survive. And if you stayed here, you would have Susan forever snapping at your heels, telling you what you've done wrong and how you must improve, and ordering you to wash your face and not to eat another cake. There's no end to her scolding! Caroline cares only about penmanship and memorising things from the Bible such as the beatitudes and the creeds and Lord's Prayer, and then she's satisfied. But Susan will lecture you for the speck of dirt under your fingernail or the way you hold your teacup. She makes me practise on the pianoforte every single day, though I haven't the least talent for it. I would *gladly* go off with you and Ras to your school you complain so pitifully about, and I'm sure I'd have a rousing good time with your chums."

"You'd only say that till you met Garnett, who does no

one any good, and Dr. Butler, who canes you for the smallest infraction of the rules. The food is the worst imaginable. Spark eats far better than we do in the refectory."

Catty reconsidered. "Then perhaps I would not trade places with you. But you must escape whenever there's a chance, and we'll be here waiting for you."

As WE SAT at our last dinner before I was sentenced to return to the school, Father announced, "I've had a letter from your uncle Jos. The Wedgwoods have returned from their journey to the Continent — a great success, by all reports. I suspect we'll hear a great deal more about it when we visit Maer Hall at Christmas."

Maer was a grand place to visit. This news set my sisters gossiping about our Wedgwood cousins, speculating what romances might be in progress and other matters that girls liked to talk about. I was quite fond of Uncle Jos, my mother's brother — he'd promised to teach me to shoot when I was older — Aunt Bessy showed me plenty of affection, and my eight cousins were a lively bunch.

When the hour came for me to leave The Mount, Caroline did her best to cheer me. "Never mind, dear Charley," she said. "The Christmas holiday will be here before you know it, and we'll all go to Maer and have a jolly time there."

But Christmas was a very long way off, and that jolly time seemed impossibly far in the future.

RAS TRIED TO BOOST my spirits as we plodded along

on our way to the school. "The big fellows will be pleased to see you," he said. "And you get on with them, don't you?"

I nodded miserably, reluctant to admit I got on better with Ras's friends in the upper school than I did with the younger boys my own age and certainly with Garnett. Some of the "big fellows" were nearly five years older than I was, but they shared my interest in collecting things and never treated me as an inferior being. My favourite was Old Price. I often went to him when I had a question about some specimen I wanted to identify, a shell I'd found or a wildflower. I was also fond of the two Corfield brothers, especially the younger, Richard, and of a whole host of boys whose names began with W: Whitley, Wakefield, Wingfield, Warter. Oddly, that's the letter that sometimes made me stammer. Susan used to drill me, making me repeat the words "white wine" over and over, till I conquered the problem. *White wine, Warter, Wingfield, Wakefield, Whitley . . .*

After my banishment to Shrewsbury School there had been visits from Father (once) and my sisters (three times), carrying a hamper of meat pies and teacakes along with a bunch of grapes or some ripe pears and perhaps a nice wedge of cheese. When the allotted visiting hour ended and my father and sisters had gone, I was forced to turn over a share of the spoils to Garnett, who implied that some sort of physical harm would come to me if I didn't. The lesson learnt was to hide as much as possible or risk losing it all.

I had other unpleasant lessons to learn: namely the

time-honoured tradition of fagging, younger boys being required to act as servants to older boys — not Ras and his sixth-form friends who lived in another dormitory, but some obnoxious fifth formers. After my return from the Michaelmas holiday, I was on duty every evening after supper till nine o'clock. I'd no sooner sit down to my studies than one of the fifth-form boys would shout, "Fag!" I would run to the boy I was to serve, who would have thought up some errand for me: bringing him a pitcher of hot water for washing up, fetching a snack of bread and cheese from the buttery, replacing burnt-down candle stubs with new candles, carrying messages here and there. I didn't particularly mind the errand — it was often more interesting than studying — unless the boy who summoned me simply wanted to try to run me ragged as a mild sort of torment.

Now that I was in my second quarter and had done well enough in my studies not to disgrace myself or my family, I was permitted to leave the schoolyard — lawfully — twice each week for one hour. I did not use the free hours as an opportunity to run off to The Mount — I still did that unlawfully. Instead I headed straight to the cake shop on Castle Street to spend my pocket money on sticky cakes. But my appetite was far greater than my capacity to pay. I had not had a chance to ask Father for an increase in my allowance.

Then help arrived from an unlikely source: Garnett.

Garnett had been angry with me after the incident of raising the Doctor, when Garnett was punished and I got away scot-free. "Wasn't much of a flogging," Garnett bragged. "But the Black Hole — now that's something to be avoided." Though he had berated me for letting him take the blame, I thought he had forgiven me.

One afternoon during the free hour Garnett suggested we visit the cake shop. "But I haven't any pocket money left," I protested.

"No matter. Come with me, Darwin. I'll show you how easy it is to get some cakes. The trick is in my cap."

Garnett explained how it worked. His uncle, a wealthy wool merchant, had donated a great sum of money to the town of Shrewsbury with the understanding that every tradesman should give without charge whatever was wanted to any boy from the school who wore his cap in a certain way.

"Just watch how it's done," Garnett said.

He entered the shop, ordered a sack of cakes from the baker's shelves, adjusted his cap, and left without so much as a penny out of his pocket. The owner merely smiled and called out, "Good day to you, Master Garnett!"

I watched the transaction wide-eyed. "Try it, Darwin," Garnett urged. "Go in and ask for whatever you want, and as he's adding up what's owed, you move your cap just so, and walk out. It will come off fine, you'll see."

I followed Garnett's instructions, picking out three cakes and then adjusting my cap. But when I turned to leave, the shopkeeper cried, "Stop, sir! You've forgotten to pay!" Startled, I dropped the sack of cakes and fled, the shopkeeper chasing after me, red-faced and shouting. Garnett, waiting down the street, greeted me with hoots of laughter. I realised I'd been tricked. Garnett indeed had a line of credit with the shopkeeper, thanks to his wealthy relation, but it had nothing to do with how he moved his cap.

"Serves you well," Garnett said, biting into a sticky cake without offering anything to me, whilst I stood by mortified and empty-handed. "Now we're *almost* even."

There was something in the addition of "almost" that rang like a threat in my ears.

Garnett made good on the threat a few days later. He rounded up a number of his friends, all older, stronger boys. On his order two of them seized me and held me fast whilst Garnett informed me with a nasty smile, "You're in for a tossing, Darwin."

I'd seen this happen to other boys: a blanket stripped from a bed and stretched taut by a half dozen boys, the victim dumped onto it and then tossed towards the ceiling several times. If he struggled or yelled or behaved unmanfully, he was allowed to drop to the floor. I bit my lip and determined I would submit, no matter how roughly Garnett and his henchmen decided to treat me.

The blanket was secured, and I was shoved onto it. "Once!" Garnett cried gleefully. I felt myself flung upwards — not such a bad feeling — and then dropping, a much less pleasant sensation, my arms windmilling helplessly. *What if they let go?* I thought, but they held firm.

"Twice!" Garnett shouted, and up I flew, higher this time, nearly knocking into the ceiling before I dropped.

"Thrice!" The tossers outdid themselves on this one,

and I did hit the ceiling. Then I was on the way down again. One of the boys lost his grip, the blanket sagged, and I crashed to the floor, bashing my head.

I came to with a circle of boys peering down at me. Garnett had the good sense to look worried. "Are you all right, Darwin?" he asked.

I badly wanted to cry, but I didn't. I had a knot on my head the size of a hen's egg. In a way I was relieved.

"Now we're even," I said.

Chapter 3

Christmas at Maer Hall: 1818

ON THE DAY BEFORE Christmas my father, brother, sisters, and I set out for Maer Hall in the neighbouring county of Staffordshire. Father drove the yellow phaeton; I was squeezed in beside him, bundled against the cold. Ras rode his own horse, sometimes allowing me to ride pillion behind him. The sisterhood occupied the old family carriage. The journey, twenty miles through a patchwork of snowy hills and bare hedgerows, took somewhat less than three hours.

Dusk was closing in when we turned off the Market Drayton road, passed the gatehouse, and rolled down a long drive to Maer Hall. The rambling stone manor house sat high on a thousand acres, looking out over its own clear spring-fed lake now frozen hard and surrounded by sandy paths that meandered through old-fashioned flower gardens turned a wintry brown. As we swept up to the portico, Manning, the butler, who with his shock of snow-white hair looked as ancient as the seventeenth-century house, stepped out to greet us. By the time we

Darwins had managed to dismount, climb down, or be handed out, the Wedgwoods had gathered by the entrance. The four sons, Joe (Josiah Wedgwood III), Frank, Harry, and Hensleigh, were all older than Ras. Those Wedgwoods closest to my age were the youngest girls, Fanny, just twelve, and Emma, who would be eleven in May. Known in the family as "the Doveleys," the two sisters seemed inseparable, though they were very unlike. Their mother liked to refer to Fanny, who was of a sober demeanour, as "Miss Memorandum." Lively Emma was "Little Miss Slip-Slop." Both girls were very kind to me — I suspect they felt sorry for me because I was motherless — but at the time I preferred the plainer, more serious Fanny.

The males greeted one another with manly handshakes, the females with smiles and kisses. My sister Marianne pecked the cheek of Elizabeth Wedgwood, the eldest daughter whom I pitied for having a crooked back. Susan kissed twenty-one-year-old Charlotte; even at the age of nine, I could see she was the prettiest of the lot. Caroline bestowed a dazzling smile on Joe and blushed when he made an awkward bow without uttering a single word; Joe hardly ever seemed to have much to say to anybody. Ras let himself be fussed over by Aunt Bessy. "How much taller you've grown since I saw you last, Ras! You, too, Charley!" Then Uncle Jos swept us all inside, out of the cold. Catty stuck close to Father. I trailed behind, fidgeting uncomfortably in a tight collar and cravat.

Emma — Miss Slip-Slop — came up to me and stuck out her hand. "Happy Christmas, Charley," she said.

For a horrified moment I thought she meant for me to *kiss* her hand, not to shake it. I don't know why I thought such a thing, but I recovered myself, cringing at my own near error, and wished Emma a happy Christmas.

Maer Hall was decked in holiday greens. Swags of ivy and yew festooned the mantels and banisters, and holly wreaths hung on the walls. Beeswax candles brightened every corner and burnt in wall sconces, casting flickering shadows. Father always claimed that lighting so many expensive candles was an unnecessary extravagance. "A few cheap tallow candles would do just as well," he said. "One gets used to the odour." But the Wedgwoods spared no trouble or expense to celebrate the holiday.

Compared to The Mount, Maer Hall seemed as grand as a palace with its great hall and drawing room, library, sitting room, morning room, dining room, breakfast room, many bedchambers, kitchens, pantries — and conservatory, too, though not so elegant as Father's, because Aunt Bessy took little interest in exotic plants and Uncle Jos took none at all. A legion of servants looked after it all. The Wedgwoods were rich — richer than the Darwins, I felt certain — their wealth going back to my mother's father, the first Josiah Wedgwood, founder of a famous pottery. Old Josiah had amassed a fortune making dinnerware and tea services for royalty, like Queen Charlotte of England and Catherine the Great of Russia. Uncle Jos, who'd inherited the pottery and the wealth, was a quiet man who always treated me kindly. My sisters were astonished that I found him easy to talk to.

"That's because you're his favourite nephew," Susan said. "He quite frightens the rest of us with his scowling silences."

"He's not scowling," I argued. "That's just the way he is."

After the footmen had carried our baggage to our bedrooms, the chambermaids hauled buckets of hot water to each room and filled the ewers for our washing up. Servants offered platters of savouries "to tide you over till supper," said Aunt Bessy. Then it was time to leave for the service at St. Peter's Church on the hill behind Maer Hall.

We made a fine procession, servants with torches lighting the path, the ladies in velvet-trimmed bonnets and fur tippets, the gentlemen in tight-fitting trousers and tall leather boots and silk top hats; Father still wore his old-fashioned top hat made of beaver. The aged vicar, Mr. Edwards, greeted us at the entrance of the plain little church. Mumbling through the Gospel according to St. Luke, he conducted the service in a dull monotone. When it came time to sing "The First Nowell," Charlotte's clear soprano rang out on the high notes in a way that made everyone smile and shiver a little.

A light snow had begun to fall as Vicar Edwards read his Christmas homily, and when we stepped outside after the benediction, we found the barren world transformed. In hushed silence we descended with our torchbearers to the hall. Candles in dozens of windows threw out a welcoming yellow glow.

The group now included the vicar, his wife and two daughters, and Aunt Bessy's three unmarried sisters from South Wales, and the hush soon gave way to lively conversation. Fires crackled on the two hearths of the drawing room. Servants in crisp livery handed round cups of eggnog fortified with whisky. In the middle of the great hall Father stood with feet spread wide to support his bulk and declined the eggnog. "A glass of hot water will suit me very well indeed!" he proclaimed. Father never took strong drink.

A bell summoned us to the dining room. I surveyed the dishes arranged on the sideboard: platters of oysters, a steaming tureen of clear turtle soup, a sweetbread pâté in a pastry crust, an enormous salver of cold boned turkey. I counted four kinds of cheese and three tiered plates displaying macaroons and fancy cakes. In the place of honour was a great silver bowl of sherry trifle.

I had been dreaming of such a meal for nearly three months, since the end of the Michaelmas holiday when I'd returned to the shared bed and the torments of Garnett, the endless drills in Latin and Greek grammar, the calls of "Fag!" and the miserly servings of tasteless food. Now I banished all such unpleasant thoughts from my mind and blissfully ate my fill.

Aunt Bessy, an ample woman with a warm smile, rose to signal the end of the meal. The ladies retired to the drawing room where their tea would be served. Ras and

I tagged along with the men, who withdrew to the library to savour an after-dinner glass of port. Uncle Jos passed round cigars, and he and Vicar Edwards engaged in a contest of blowing smoke rings. Later, when we heard music coming from nearby — someone playing the pianoforte — Uncle Jos proposed that we join the ladies.

Charlotte charmed everyone by singing several arias from Handel's *Messiah*. Emma plumped down at the keyboard and charged through several pieces as though the house were on fire. The whole company sang several verses of "We Wish You a Merry Christmas," carried along by the bright voices of Elizabeth and Charlotte and Emma's vigorous accompaniment. The evening ended on this good feeling, and we retired contentedly to beds warmed by servants wielding long-handled pans filled with hot coals.

CHRISTMAS DAY DAWNED clear and cold. I scraped my initials with a fingernail in the frost on the windowpane before routing Ras from his bed. We found the others already gathered in the morning room, breakfasting on porridge and fancy breads and preparing to open their gifts.

Uncle Jos presided. I was happy to receive a savings bank, a pen-wiper, a set of bookmarks, and a striped muffler and cap knitted by the Doveleys. I suspected which had been made by Little Miss Slip-Slop; there were several dropped stitches in the muffler, and Miss Memorandum would not have allowed that. Catty and I were each given a new pair of skates. My other sisters exclaimed over thimbles and pincushions, hair ribbons, scented sachets, embroidered slippers, and a new novel by Miss Jane Austen.

That done, we trudged up the hill to St. Peter's again over a crust of snow that crackled under foot. After more prayers and the sacrament of the Lord's Supper, returned to Maer Hall for what I considered the main event of the day: the Christmas feast.

Three plump geese, golden and glistening, awaited carving, along with a joint of gammon studded with cloves and several brace of pheasant from Maer forest. Servants passed bowls of rutabagas and potatoes and turnips and bright orange squash and carried round steaming fruit sauces. Crusty loaves of bread were sliced and set out with crocks of butter and pots of jam. Tarts made of apples from Maer orchard, pitchers of cold cider beaded with sweat, and glass decanters filled with ruby claret stood ready. I scarcely knew where to begin or when to stop.

Just as I thought I couldn't swallow another bite, Manning carried in the plum pudding ringed with sprigs of holly. He doused the pudding with a jigger of brandy, and set it alight. A dramatic blue flame leapt up, and Aunt Bessy led the applause as she did every year. When the flame had flickered and died, Uncle Jos portioned out generous slices. Manning passed a boat of cream sauce, his white-gloved hands trembling a little.

The dinner took up most of the afternoon, but there was time enough later in the day for playing charades and whist, for entertaining neighbours who came to call, and for singing catches and carols.

And then, as darkness enveloped Maer Hall and dozens of candles gleamed, Manning announced that a supper buffet had been laid out in the dining room. For the first time in months I wasn't hungry at all.

———

"I PROPOSE a skating party," Hensleigh announced on Boxing Day, the day after Christmas. "The ice on the pool is quite thick."

The gardeners had shovelled and swept away the snow from the surface of the small lake the Wedgwoods called the pool. Armed with cotton mops and water heated in tubs, they'd swabbed the surface of the ice till it was smooth as glass. A large bonfire blazed on the bank.

We strapped our skates over our boots and stepped out onto the glittering ice. The girls moved sedately round the outer edge, whilst some of the boys raced up and down the length with loud shouts. Ras with his long legs should have been a sure winner, but he moved so languorously that the others easily outstripped him.

Not much interested in racing, I skated off alone to the far end of the pool. I was lost in thought — "woolgathering," Father called it — when I heard Catty shouting my name. She scrambled clumsily up beside me on her new skates and promptly fell in a graceless heap. I helped her to her feet, but soon she was down again, and then a third time, frustrated and tearful.

"Let's go visit the bonfire," I told her. "Here, hold my hand and I'll steady you."

Our cousin Elizabeth, back from delivering her Boxing Day gifts to the poor in the nearby village, was making her way cautiously down to the edge of the ice, accompanied by servants carrying steaming earthenware crocks of spiced cider and trays of mugs and tartlets. The sun was bright, but the air was cold as a knife, and the skaters gathered by the fire, rubbing their hands and stamping their feet. Once we'd warmed ourselves, we took to the ice again. The Wedgwood boys launched a game of crack-the-whip, whilst the girls continued to move serenely over the smooth surface. Susan, frowning with concentration, carved a wobbly figure eight and repeated the pattern till she could execute it flawlessly. Fanny persuaded Emma to try to skate backwards, without much success, and then the two Doveleys led Catty away for lessons. I went back to scout the frozen edges of the pool, hoping to discover some unlucky creature trapped in the ice and add it to my collection.

Late in the morning, after we had straggled up to the hall, cheeks reddened and noses dripping, Father announced that he must drive back to Shrewsbury to see to his patients. Caroline tried unsuccessfully to conceal her disappointment. She had just managed to coax Joe into a tentative conversation — they'd agreed to play chess later in the day — and she couldn't bear to leave now. Susan was plainly enjoying herself in this household where fires blazed on every hearth and there was no shortage of beeswax candles, though she probably disapproved of the wastefulness. Catty had found a basket of kittens to play with and was no doubt thinking she might persuade Papa to let her take one home. Ras frowned — I guessed he wanted to stay as much as I did. Only Marianne seemed willing to go back to Shrewsbury; she may have been hoping for a visit from Mr. Parker, a medical student who'd been calling on her.

"I must take my leave," Father declared, "but I shall be happy to abandon my dear ones to the tender mercies of their aunt and uncle and cousins, be it so desired by all parties."

So it was settled, and all of us gathered to wave goodbye as Father and Marianne drove off in the yellow phaeton. For the next few days the Wedgwood and Darwin cousins skated, sang, recited poems, played whist, checkers and — Ras's favourite — charades. He was especially clever at acting out book titles. I had no aptitude for the game and tried to escape. My cousin Charlotte thrilled me when she challenged me to a game of backgammon, where I could rely upon a roll of the dice and no particular wit or skill. We tramped round the pool in fresh snow and made plans to go boating when the weather warmed and to picnic on the very spot where the bonfire now crackled.

I often found myself in the company of the Doveleys. Fanny and Emma had an annoying habit of suddenly speaking French to each other, of which I understood not a single word. Emma had the grace to apologise. "I'm sorry, Charley," she said. "We spent last spring and summer on the Continent, and we were forced to speak French constantly."

"Three times a week we had to endure French lessons, singing lessons, and piano lessons, and every single day we had dancing lessons," Fanny explained.

"Mamma said we needed to acquire some polish and thought waltzing was the way to do it," Emma added. "We found it quite abominable."

The girls giggled. I was mystified.

"There was a horrid little boy named Louis who kept dragging me off to dance with him," Emma said, making a face.

"The house where we stayed for several weeks was owned by a fishmonger," Fanny informed me. "It smelt so strongly of fish that I shall not eat another piece of fish for as long as I live."

Their stories went on and on, to their amusement and my bafflement, and made me see how dull my own life must seem compared to theirs.

On New Year's Eve Father and Marianne returned to Maer in time for a late supper. At the stroke of midnight Charlotte, blond hair streaming to her waist, sat down at the pianoforte, and the family gathered round to join hands and sing "Auld Lang Syne."

Should auld acquaintance be forgot,
and never brought to mind?
Should auld acquaintance be forgot,
and auld lang syne?

There were many verses and a chorus written by Uncle Jos's favourite poet, the Scotsman Robert Burns, dead for more than twenty years. We sang every verse with gusto and ended the evening with a toast to the start of the year 1819. I had already begun to dread the day I'd return to Shrewsbury School. I thought how pleasant it would be to spend the rest of my life at Maer Hall, where life always seemed so blissful and my cousins so kind and amusing. Even when they were speaking French.

Chapter 4

The Laboratory: 1821

MY SCHOOL DAYS passed with agonising slowness. Holidays seemed to end almost before they'd begun. Nevertheless, I made a sort of peace with Shrewsbury School and the necessity of my being there. I got on well with most of the boys and made many friends of my own, no longer dependent entirely upon Ras and his crowd for companionship. But after two years I disliked my studies as much as I had from the very first week.

Fifty-four boys had started when I did; four left the first year, and soon fourteen more dropped by the wayside. We never learnt exactly why they had left, but Ras said it was usually because they had been plucked — that is, failed their examinations. Garnett was not amongst those plucked; he remained an irritant in my life, like a pebble in my shoe, though we no longer shared a bed or even a bedroom.

Latin and Greek exercises absorbed most of my time and effort, inducing an unshakable stupor. Every day

the master called upon several of the boys in my form —
I was now in the upper fourth — to translate aloud the
passages we'd been assigned. We sat on our long wooden
benches — forms, as they were called — every one of us
hoping not to be called upon that day, the dreaded fate
postponed. The next time, we promised ourselves, we'd
be better prepared.

I didn't mind the memorisation. I could easily learn
forty or fifty lines of Virgil's Latin or Homer's Greek
whilst in morning chapel and recite them when called
upon, though forty-eight hours later the lines had evaporated from my head as rapidly as the morning dew.
Translation — construing, as it was called — was a much
more difficult matter, but I managed to survive that by
dint of hard work. The most disagreeable task of all was
the composition of verses in Latin on a subject assigned
by the master.

My closest friends were John Cameron and Frederick
Watkins. Cameron, with whom I now shared a bedroom,
was small for his age but wiry and strong. He had an
enthusiasm for angling and collecting and was always
ready to set off on an "adventure," as we called our nature expeditions. Watkins was a soberer sort, less inclined to go looking for mischief, but a loyal fellow with
a love of Shakespeare. He was more gifted than either
Cameron or I in the task of composition. The three of us
gathered in one of the study rooms and, consulting a
book of rules and a collection of old Latin verses, we
patched together the required number of lines.

I worked conscientiously at the classics, rarely resorting to cribs with the correct answers used by many of the other boys — Cameron and Watkins agreed the practise was wrong — but I considered this so-called education altogether useless, a complete waste of my time and my father's money. I saw no earthly use for any of it. How much better, I thought, to be instructed in the names of flowers, or the kinds of pebbles, or the habits of birds and fish and insects. Mostly I marked time till I could get out of that tiresome place and into something *interesting,* though I had no idea what that might be.

Now I escaped into books, as I had once escaped to The Mount. Watkins and I passed many a leisure hour curled snugly in an old window seat, reading Shakespeare's historical plays and the poems of Sir Walter Scott and Lord Byron. Why could we not hear about this interesting stuff in our classes? Why discuss the *Aeneid* when we might learn to recite a sonnet by Shakespeare? I could make no sense of it.

I borrowed Cameron's book, *Wonders of the World,* and the two of us entertained fantasies of visiting faraway places.

"Tell me, Darwin," Watkins said dreamily, "where would you go, if you could choose to visit any place in the world?"

I propped myself on one elbow whilst considering the possibilities. "The Colosseum in Rome," I decided, and then quickly changed my mind. "No, let's make that the Parthenon in Athens."

"I thought you hated Latin and Greek," Watkins said scornfully. "So why would you go there?"

"Because they're interesting. And you?" I challenged. "Where would *you* go?"

"The Great Pyramids of Egypt," he said rather grandly. "And I'd go by ship and then ride the rest of the way on a camel."

Annoyed that Watkins had outdone me with a fantasy more exotic than mine, I let my imagination run loose. "Brazil," I said, suddenly inspired. It was time for our tea, and we began to gather our books.

"Brazil? Whatever made you think of *that,* Darwin?"

"Robinson Crusoe," I said. "He's always been my hero."

LIFE AT THE SCHOOL was strictly regimented. We rose early for a quick and not very thorough washing up (Susan complained that I must wash my feet — and my whole body — more often, because, she said, I emitted a foul odour), then hurried off to the refectory for a breakfast of watery porridge and weak tea. Next began two interminable hours of construing and reciting memorised lines, followed by chapel service at which Dr. Butler read scriptures, offered prayers for our betterment, preached at us about one thing and another, and sometimes used the time to embarrass, humiliate, or otherwise punish some unfortunate soul. Having survived this, we proceeded to the refectory for an unsatisfactory dinner of fatty lamb or gristly beef in portions scarcely sufficient to satisfy the hunger of growing boys.

After dinner we faced two more hours of construing and reciting, in Latin or Greek, each worse than the other. Our reward was an hour to rush out of doors for some sort of game, followed by tea — not a proper tea, like those we all enjoyed at home, but a pathetically small quarter loaf of bread with a paltry allotment of butter. The older boys, of whom I was now more or less one, rushed off to a nearby shop to spend our pocket money on sausages or baked potatoes — "murphies," we called them — or small herring, called sprats, and we brought these provisions back to our rooms to round out the ration of bread and butter.

In the evening after calling-over and locking up, we studied for as long as we could bear it with prefects — older boys — to keep order amongst us. The day ended with a late supper of more of the same bread, this time with the addition of cheese, always dry and hard round the edges, and a ration of ale. Garnett, now in lower fifth — I was catching up with him — and one of the worst offenders in ordering the fags on tiresome errands, always managed to have some ginger beer to accompany this feast.

The next day we repeated the whole dismal routine. Only Sundays differed, with two tedious chapel services instead of one.

DURING MY THIRD YEAR, Ras, who had developed a deep interest in chemistry, set up a laboratory in an unused shed at The Mount. He was nearly seventeen. I served as his willing assistant, though I was just twelve.

Our problem was money. I had not persuaded Father to increase my pocket money allowance, guaranteeing that I would remain permanently in debt to Garnett for the irresistible sticky cakes. Father was no more generous with Ras. In its early days the laboratory looked more like an empty toolhouse, which it was, furnished with a scarred potting bench contributed by Abberley and two battered wooden chairs we'd found in the carriage house. Ras thought we needed a great deal of basic equipment to begin our experiments. All of it was expensive.

We managed to scrape together enough to buy a lamp with which to heat chemicals. We had many discussions on which types of jars, what kinds of stoppers, and how many test tubes we needed. It was my idea to seek help from Uncle Jos, who agreed to send us fireproof dishes from the Wedgwood Potteries.

"We've got to figure out ways of milking the Cow," Ras said as we sat in our barren laboratory, dreaming of what it would be one day. He stroked the few downy whiskers that had sprouted on his chin.

I knew what Ras meant by "milking the Cow": convincing Father to let us have additional funds. Surely he could understand the importance of the great scientific work Ras and I were about to accomplish.

"Ras," I said, "have you ever wondered why Father is so . . . so . . ."

"Tightfisted? Is that what you're trying to say?"

I nodded.

"I think you can blame it on our grandfather Erasmus. The old man pushed Father into medicine — he didn't want to be a physician, you know — and then refused to help him when it came time to set up a practise. He had a rough go of it for a while, trying to make ends meet, so he had to be frugal. Now it's a habit, and I suppose he thinks it builds character. If he could make it, so can we."

"So we're not really poor?"

Ras laughed. "No, Charley. We're not. It just feels that way sometimes."

Ras did the "milking" — he was better at it than I was — and the Cow yielded a little, but not enough. On a visit to Cambridge where Ras expected to attend university, he found a shop dealing in the kind of supplies we needed and returned to Shrewsbury feverish with excitement.

"I tell you, Charley, they have every sort of thing — enough to make your mouth water. Jars and stopcocks and graduated tubes and blow pipes, cubic inch measures and test tubes, and Lord only knows what else besides!" His enthusiasm was contagious.

"Did you buy anything, Ras?" I asked, catching the fever.

"Oh, I did. Just look at this." Ras opened a leather case lined in plush velvet to reveal a thermometer with a hinged scale. The two of us gazed rapturously at this instrument. "I brought something for you, too," he said, and presented me with a small sack of minerals that I poured out on the table.

"Thank you very much indeed, Philos," I said. Philos — philosopher — had become my brother's new nickname.

I was pleased with these new specimens, because I'd become quite taken up with the subject of mineralogy, as I'd been the year before with the study of birds, and before that with the study of insects.

WHEN OUR FAMILY visited Maer Hall at Christmas that year — it was 1821 — Ras and I decided to try milking a different cow. Uncle Jos had always shown great interest in our scientific projects, and when he asked, "How goes the laboratory, boys?" Ras was ready with a carefully rehearsed answer.

Unable to contain myself, I rushed in. "We're studying minerals and crystals," I reported. "And we need a goniometer."

The Doveleys, sitting nearby with their pencils and sketchbooks, looked up curiously. "What on earth is *that*?" Fanny asked.

"An instrument to measure the angles of the faces of a crystal," I explained.

Fanny said, "Oh," and glanced at Emma, who rolled her eyes. When the discussion continued on scientific matters, the young ladies turned their attention again to the still life of a milk jug and pears and asked no more questions.

On his seventeenth birthday a few days after Christmas, Ras received the coveted goniometer from Uncle Jos, plus an envelope containing ten pounds, a gift from Aunt Bessy.

A goniometer *and* ten pounds! Ras was thrilled by this generous gift. "Ten pounds is a fortune! What shall you do with the money?" I asked, wondering if our aunt and uncle might do the same for me in February, when I would turn thirteen. "What instrument shall you buy next?" I knew Ras had been longing for an air pump to perform experiments in a vacuum.

But my brother had a different plan in mind. "It should be invested in improving our laboratory. First off, we need a small area to protect our instruments from dampness." He had detected a leak in the shed roof, he said; though it was patched, it continued to be worrisome. "And we must have a shelf built in front of the south-facing window, so that we can do experiments using the sun's rays."

I nodded sagely.

The money was spent just as Ras had decided, as was the money given to me on my birthday, though less than I'd hoped for. Then came a remarkable surprise. With Ras in his final half year at Shrewsbury School and presumably of a responsible age, Father decided to recognise my brother's increasing independence by giving him control over his own finances. Father handed over the necessary funds for Ras's school expenses, accompanied by the usual warning lectures. The first thing Ras did with his windfall was to go on a spending spree at Blunt's, the chemist's shop, ripping through most of his money before the third quarter had scarcely begun.

Father learnt about this reckless spending and

summoned Ras to his library, demanding an accounting. I stood outside in the hall, nervously chewing my lip as I awaited the outcome of this interview. Ras emerged pale and visibly shaken. "What did Father say?" I asked fearfully.

"He warned me that my crime must not be repeated, under pain of having all allowances cut off for the foreseeable future. This could be difficult, especially when I leave for university. Naturally, I promised not to buy anything more." My face must have shown the pain of disappointment, but then Ras winked. "Don't take it too hard, Charley. There's more than one cow in the pasture, as we've seen. There's always the possibility that Uncle Jos will come through for us again."

In the meantime we wheedled our sisters and old Nancy into donating needles, scissors, and the like, and Abberley into occasionally providing tools that could be modified for use in place of a more expensive piece of equipment. We analysed minerals we found on our walks round Shrewsbury or already had on hand, and when we'd exhausted those supplies, we raided the kitchens at home and at school for such humble materials as tea leaves, sugar, and salt to determine the composition of a substance by producing what Ras called a calx.

"It's what's left once you've burnt the mineral or metal or whatever you're studying and it's completely oxidised."

I liked the sound of the word: *calx*. "You mean ash?" I asked.

"Precisely," Ras said. He'd studied *Elements of Experimental Chemistry,* and he now passed the book along to me.

Our obsession with chemistry caught the attention of our friends. I was nicknamed "Gas" by boys awed by the experiments I carried on at the gaslight in my bedroom at the school. I blew air into the flame through a tube whilst preparing to feed various chemicals into the mix. Cameron and Watkins and sometimes Richard Corfield were my eager assistants. They always hoped for a dramatic explosion, accompanied perhaps by singed hair and a scorched shirt cuff, but no serious injury ever occurred.

Then one morning at chapel Dr. Butler, an imposing figure in his black academic gown and flat black cap, barked out my name. "Step forward, Mr. Darwin!" he commanded.

I had no idea why he'd called me, but I knew it could not be good. "Yes, sir," I replied, my voice breaking.

Dr. Butler turned from the podium, arms locked across his chest, and regarded me grimly. I had grown taller, and I was a sturdy boy, the largest of my friends, but the headmaster towered over me. I waited nervously for him to tell me what I'd done wrong. All three hundred boys waited as well.

"I understand you have taken up the study of chemistry," the Doctor said, spitting out the word *chemistry* as though it had an evil taste. "Correct or incorrect?"

"But, sir," I began, thinking I could explain it all.

"Correct or incorrect, Mr. Darwin?" he roared.

"Correct, sir," I whispered.

"And on a regular basis you conduct certain experiments that endanger your fellow students as well as the property of the school. Correct or incorrect?"

"Correct, sir." I believed I was doomed.

"You are nothing more than a *pococurante*!" Dr. Butler shouted, his face close to mine.

I gaped at him openmouthed, having not the least idea of what he meant. He advanced on me and boxed my ear hard enough to bring tears to my eyes. *"Pococurante!"* he repeated. "A careless person! One interested only in meaningless trifles! Do you recognise yourself, Mr. Darwin?"

"Y-y-yes, sir," I stammered, backing away.

"Sit down, then, Mr. Darwin," the headmaster said. "And kindly cease your experimentation." He paused whilst I stumbled back to my seat, my face burning with humiliation. "Let us pray," he ordered, and every boy's head bowed obediently.

Thus ended my chemistry experiments at school.

IN JUNE RAS FINISHED up his last examinations at Shrewsbury School. There was a huge celebration at Midsummer, the end of the term, with a great deal of singing scandalous songs and reciting irreverent poems and drinking innumerable bottles of ginger beer. The evening ended on a solemn note as the boys stood and sang "God Save the King" together for the last time, so fervently that a few tears were actually shed. Most of Ras's friends, Old Price and the group I called "the Ws," who had become my friends as well, were leaving, headed for university. Ras would go up to Cambridge in autumn to begin the study of medicine. Father had long cherished the hope that Ras would follow in his footsteps as a physician.

"Is that what you want?" I asked my brother.

"It's what the Governor wants," he said with a shrug — he'd begun calling Father "the Governor." "It's all the same to me."

That summer our family took a holiday on the seacoast of North Wales. Ras and I rolled up our trouser legs and hiked along the shore, splashing in the cold waters of the Irish Sea and searching for interesting specimens to add to our collections. This was my notion of a perfect holiday. Our sisters strolled on sandy paths beyond reach of the breakers. Even Catty, who once would have pestered to go with me, now preferred to spend her time with her sisters.

When the weather was rotten, as it often was, the sisterhood stayed inside to read and take tea. The cold and wet never bothered me — it was better than sitting in the musty hotel — and I wanted to be out on the beaches no matter how wet and blustery. Ras, too, was willing, though he had never been strong and required all sorts of precautions against illness. Father insisted he wear a flannel waistcoat next to his skin all year round to protect his chest from inflammation. Now, in addition to the waistcoat, Father prescribed a bitter tonic to be swallowed several times a day.

At the end of the holiday I watched Ras pack his

trunk for his new life as a university student at Christ's College, Cambridge. Maurice hauled the trunk down to the Lion Inn near the High Street, where Ras would board the stagecoach. After Ras said good-bye, shook hands with Father, and kissed our sisters, I walked with him to the inn. Whilst we waited, he passed on instructions to his faithful apprentice — me — concerning the care and maintenance of the laboratory. Suddenly the toot of the coachman's horn announced the arrival of the coach. There was a hurried bustle of loading the trunk and finding a seat, and the coach was off, carrying Ras to Cambridge. I walked home alone, footsteps dragging, desolate at the prospect of returning to school without the presence of my brother and his friends.

A stream of letters soon began to arrive from Cambridge. Ras instructed me to obtain additional funds by whatever means I could, to increase our collection of bottles, particularly the large, green, stoppered kind, and to have them filled with distilled water by Blunt, the chemist. I had no idea to what use the distilled water would be put, but I understood that every laboratory required some. Ras promised to buy certain supplies in London and to bring them to The Mount at the next holiday. If necessary, he would go without teatime sausages to afford them.

He was enjoying his courses. *Professor Cumming is remarkable. He demonstrated the qualities of nitrous oxide — laughing gas — which turns one utterly ridiculous when one inhales it,* Ras wrote gleefully. *If you've been*

practising as I suggested and learnt to manage the
gas lamp properly, we can make this interesting stuff
ourselves.

Impatient for the next holiday and Ras's return, I slogged through my classes with the least possible amount of effort. Even my friend Cameron was a little concerned about my apparent idleness.

"I say, Darwin, I confess that I envy you a great deal," said Cameron one night as we lay awake talking, long after the candles had been extinguished.

"How so?" I asked curiously, for I had never considered myself the least bit enviable.

"You seem so unconcerned about your studies. I, for one, must scramble to keep up with it all if I ever hope to pass my examinations and get to university, but you — you seem perfectly satisfied to do as little as possible."

That brought me upright in bed. "What utter nonsense!" I exclaimed. "Just because I ignore my studies does not mean that I am idle!"

In fact, I fancied myself quite busily engaged. The school stood near the top of the great loop of the Severn that nearly surrounded Shrewsbury. At the bottom of the loop in the fields beyond the old town walls, red sandstone had been dug out and used to build the castle and many other Shrewsbury structures. The quarry had long ago fallen into disuse, but the ponds left behind teemed with creatures drawn to still water, and I escaped there in search of specimens. I spent hours watching birds as they built their nests and fed their young, and I filled a notebook with observations about how they flew, how they perched, how they found food. I put together a large collection of their eggs, now carefully nested in cotton wool. I explained all of this to Cameron. "So you see, I'm not at all idle," I concluded.

"All very well and good, Darwin, but it won't help you pass the examinations and you may find yourself plucked."

To which I had no sensible reply, though I appreciated my friend's concern.

AT CHRISTMAS, when we were all gathered at Maer Hall, Uncle Jos presented me with a shotgun, certainly the most thrilling gift I had ever received. That night I slept with it next to me in my bed. The next day, when the others went down to the pool with their skates, Uncle Jos beckoned me. "Time for a lesson, Charley." I raced to get the gun. For the next few hours — I forgot about dinner — he showed me how to clean it, carry it, load it, and, finally, how to shoot it. The recoil delivered a painful kick and nearly knocked me over, but I soon learnt to handle it properly. We talked little. Uncle Jos used few words of instruction; his method was to demonstrate and then to let me work it out for myself.

"Good eye and a steady hand, Charley," said my uncle approvingly as he watched me take aim at a target. "And lots of practise," he added when I fired and missed.

On a terrifically cold day at the end of the year we went out shooting together, and I killed my first snipe, a long-billed sandpiper I'd sighted in a marshy area. I became so excited that my hands trembled and I could scarcely reload.

From then on I was passionately fond of shooting and began to keep lists of every bird that had become my victim. I tried to teach Spark to retrieve the dead birds for me to examine. But Spark was getting old and stubbornly refused to cooperate, so the next summer, when I was again at home, I got another dog and named him Mr. Dash. I had become great friends with Squire William Mostyn Owen, who lived scarcely an hour's ride away in the hamlet of Rednal, and soon I was a frequent visitor at Woodhouse, the Owen family estate. Squire Owen, a great shooter himself, taught me how to train the dogs; by then I'd acquired still another. Every minute that I wasn't forced to be in class, I was out shooting, or working the dogs, or collecting. Anything to be out of the stuffy classroom and in the glorious outdoors. Anything but studying.

Chapter 5

Visitors to The Mount: 1823

RAS HAD ENTERED his second term at Cambridge as I neared the end of my fifth year at Shrewsbury School. At the start of the spring holiday I rushed home, anticipating free time to work in the laboratory on experiments Ras had sent me, as well as to fish in the Severn; shooting was out of season, to my great disappointment, but angling placed a good second.

I was surprised, then, to find The Mount reverberating with the fluty voices of young ladies. Four Wedgwood cousins had travelled from Maer by carriage, and Squire Owen's two daughters, Sally and Fanny, arrived on horseback accompanied by their mother. They had gathered at The Mount for a few days of musical instruction with my sisters.

My attempt to avoid notice was thwarted when the Doveleys discovered me, and the girls interrupted their chatter to make a fuss over me. Even Mrs. Owen had her say, throwing up her hands and exclaiming, "Why, just

look at you, Charley Darwin! What a great lad you've become! Soon you'll be as tall as your father, if you are not
already!" I blushed and fidgeted, for I had reached the
age — fourteen — of extreme self-consciousness.

My sisters being otherwise occupied, the Doveleys
explained what was going on. "Caroline hired an itiner-
ant music master to give us lessons," Fanny Wedgwood
said, adding meaningfully, "though Emma doesn't think
she needs any."

"Not true!" Emma protested and turned to me. "Dr.
Darwin has gone out to tend a patient and sent word he
will not be present for dinner," she said. "Just as well,
don't you think? I believe your papa would find this all
rather upsetting."

She was no doubt correct. Father had particular ways
of doing things, and it did seem likely that the next few
days would not be going according to Dr. Darwin.

"Ah, dear Charley!" Caroline cried as she rushed by. "I
have no time to speak to you now, or even to sit down
with my guests. I absolutely must finish sewing this gown
before Señor Sor's arrival, and there are at least a dozen
other things requiring my attention." Off she flew, calling
over her shoulder, "Ask Cook to fix you something to eat."

"I do wish she'd stop scrattling about," Fanny said,
frowning.

The music instructor arrived, a dapper little man
with a thin moustache, and I was promptly forgotten. I
fled to the laboratory for the remainder of the afternoon,
but I could not avoid dining with the guests.

"I beg you to join us, Charley," Caroline pleaded. "We need another masculine presence at the table, and Papa can't be here."

Amazing, I thought; all of Father's patients seemed to suffer crises on that one particular day. "But I have nothing to say!" I protested.

"Nonsense," she said, and clucked her tongue. "Of course you do."

My sisters and their guests turned their attention to Señor Sor, whilst Miss Fanny Owen turned her attention to *me*. I was in an agony of shyness, but Miss Owen was an exceptionally pretty girl with eyes the colour of larkspur and so wittily talkative I soon felt quite at ease with her, ready to laugh at nearly anything she said. I was not at all as tongue-tied as I'd feared, and I survived the dinner without embarrassment.

That evening Mrs. Owen and the whole chorus of young ladies urged me to join them. I begged off. "I must study," I said. "Examinations, you know." It wasn't exactly a falsehood. I left my door open and their trilling voices drifted up to me as they sang.

Their lessons began in earnest next morning, sight-reading and vocal exercises and some part-singing. I'd taken an early breakfast in the kitchen, and I planned to spend the day making a long, solitary tramp into the countryside, perhaps as far as Houghmond Abbey. Whilst Cook was packing a lunch for me to carry, I loitered outside the sitting room and listened. Señor Sor sounded rather put out at Fanny Owen. She was deeply involved in one of Miss Austen's novels — she'd talked about it at supper — and paid hardly any attention to the instruction he was endeavouring to give her.

"My dear, pray put away the book," I heard Mrs. Owen say. "I shall give you a shilling if you do."

"Very well, Mamma," Fanny Owen said, accepting the bribe. But as I took my lunch and prepared to leave, I heard her say, "I've changed my mind. I'd rather read." The stubborn young lady gave back the shilling and took up her book again. *What a headstrong girl!* I thought admiringly.

The day was fine and I made good use of it, sighting a number of nesting birds and marking down my observations in a notebook I kept for that purpose alone. When I returned rather late, tired and in need of a washup, it appeared that all the girls, including the rebellious Fanny Owen, had spent the whole day with their music. But a few more minutes of spying revealed a new problem. Susan and Sally, the elder of the Owen girls, had been sitting side by side for the lessons, and that had led to much stifled laughter. Exasperated, Señor Sor now insisted the two sit separately. Minutes later I encountered him taking a solitary stroll on the gravel path that traversed the slope above the river, muttering and gesticulating. The poor fellow was trying to calm himself, so I merely nodded and passed on without speaking.

After evening tea Señor Sor again gathered his pupils. Till bedtime he played — he attacked the pianoforte like a madman — and sang. He knew a great many songs by heart, bellowing them out with such fervour that even Fanny Owen laid aside her book to listen.

"Delightful," the girls sighed, applauding. "Señor Sor does have a glorious voice."

"Tomorrow we shall perform an opera," Señor Sor announced. "In French," he added.

Early next morning I gathered my rod and a supply of earthworms and ran off to the riverbank for a few hours of contemplation whilst waiting for a fish to strike. I was competing with a kingfisher that dived in head-first and was more successful than I in catching any-thing. I never tired of this. By mid-afternoon the sky had darkened and the rain that first merely dimpled the surface of the slow-moving Severn became a downpour. Having thrown back my few small catches, snatched im-mediately by the shaggy-headed bird, I climbed back up to the house empty-handed. The young ladies were in the midst of performing their French opera, all of them roaring with laughter.

"Oh, Charley, there you are!" Fanny Owen called out, interrupting Susan's aria and bringing the production to a temporary halt. "You simply *must* come and be our au-dience! You'll find us absolutely magnificent."

She seized my hands and led me to a chair. I was wet and muddy and smelt strongly of fish, but there was no refusing Fanny Owen. And I have already mentioned how uncommonly pretty she was.

AUNT BESSY had been feeling poorly since a fall from her horse, and Uncle Jos thought a slow-paced journey through the countryside would be good for her. In June she invited Caroline and Susan to join her and the Wedgwood girls on a visit to the seaside town of Scarborough. When I visited Maer later that summer, my sisters and the Doveleys were still discussing the tour and the balls they attended.

"Public balls have gone quite out of fashion," Susan said.

"They were a great hum," Emma agreed.

"Quadrilles have made the balls so dismal," Caroline explained. "Ladies dance them as if at a funeral."

They might have been discussing life in a distant galaxy, so unfamiliar was I with the world of balls and dances. But Emma — Miss Slip-Slop — did capture my attention when she spoke of her new enthusiasm, discovered at a bookshop in Scarborough. She had taken an interest in the adventures of explorers and developed a crush on Mungo Park, a Scotsman who went to Africa to explore the course of the Niger River. He and his party had been attacked in their canoes and drowned.

"I moped for days when I learnt of his terrible fate," she confessed now. Who could not admire a girl who felt so passionately about explorers?

Towards sunset as I prepared to take a boat out on the Maer pool, Emma asked to go along, and I agreed. I was absorbed in poking amongst the reeds near the end of the pool where it emptied into the creek when I heard Emma ask behind me, "Do you still hate school so much, Charley?"

"I try not to think about whether I hate it or not," I said, my attention fastened on a water strider skating on the silvery surface. A fish rose and snapped at it.

"Well, I can surely tell you I did not much enjoy the time my sister Fanny and I spent at Greville House in London. The headmistress was supposed to teach us French, but she spoke very poorly and it annoyed her that we spoke so well."

"Umhmmm," I murmured.

"And then there was French history," Emma said, her voice like distant music rising and falling pleasantly in the evening air. "Every time a new girl arrived — there was always someone going and someone coming to take her place — the history master began at the beginning with Clovis, king of the Franks, A.D. 481 to 511. And we barely made it to Charlemagne, king of the Franks A.D. 768 to 814. Sometimes we managed to get him crowned Holy Roman Emperor before we had another new girl, and then it was all the way back to Clovis."

Listening with only half an ear to Emma's tales of her boarding school, I reached for the net I'd brought with me and leant over the side of the boat, intent upon scooping up samples of insects that lurked beneath the placid surface.

"I did quite like my music master," she continued. "But he complained that I played everything too allegro. Even the andante passages. Fanny and I were extremely glad to come home and be educated by the tutors Papa hired for us."

I was manoeuvring my net round the edgewater

when apparently Emma, curious about what I was doing, stood up for a better look — she later denied doing any such thing, but in any case she did make an abrupt movement — just as I leaned farther to capture my prey. The boat tipped. We both plunged into the water.

The pool was not deep there — barely up to Emma's waist. We were in no danger of drowning. I found my footing immediately, grabbed Emma's hand and pulled her up, sputtering. Her pale summer dress was soaked and plastered against her, and her hair streamed over her face, the ribbons hopelessly muddied. She'd lost her spectacles. I expected her to burst into tears.

Instead, Emma burst out laughing. I groped in the sandy bottom for the spectacles, wiped them as best I could, and settled them on her nose. I steadied the boat whilst she scrambled into it, dripping, and heaved myself in after her. I rowed to the little dock near the hall, where Uncle Jos, Aunt Bessy, and several of Emma's brothers, sisters, and aunts were seated on the steps of the old portico. They applauded vigorously as I handed her out onto the dock with such aplomb as I could manage. "Not nearly the fate of Mungo Park!" she said, still laughing.

"You are my favourite cousin, Emma," I said sincerely.

"And you are mine, dear Charley," she replied cheerfully, and acknowledged her family's applause with a wet and dishevelled curtsey.

I RETURNED to begin my fifth year at Shrewsbury School and found my studies as dull and, to me, as irrelevant as ever. I thought I could not bear to spend my days cooped up in musty classrooms when the whole great outdoors beckoned irresistibly. But there was a difference: I was now one of the "old boys," playing the role of well-informed friend for younger lads that Old Price and the Ws had once played for me. A new boy named Edward Edwards became a great chum when we discovered similar interests in natural science.

Our preferred destination was the old quarry. On afternoons when most other boys were in the commons, bashing one another in rugby or some other sport that left them with scraped knees and bloodied noses, Edwards and I quietly gathered up our nets and jars and made off to our refuge.

During the autumn we became adept at catching and identifying newts of various species — the smooth newt was the most common — and in various stages of metamorphosis. We learnt to determine whether it was male or female. We were eager to find great crested newts, large brown creatures with rough, warty skin, but they eluded us. Then winter came, and the newts went into hibernation. Though we still visited the quarry occasionally, we were forced to find other diversions.

Edwards was a bright little fellow with a gift for memorising Latin and Greek; he always learnt far more lines than anyone else. He was skilled at construing. And he was amazingly clever at composing those required lines, making me and my friends seem doltish and slow. He advanced rapidly through the forms and at the age of twelve had already reached the upper fourth.

But Edwards was small and thin and took a chill easily. His nose dripped and his eyes watered, and he became the target of Garnett's mockery. When Garnett called him Miss Molly and other effeminate names, I intervened as well as I could, for I was now a big, strapping fellow, taller and heavier than Garnett and his friends, and known to be strong. Though I still refused to fight, I thought I might have to.

"Leave Edwards in peace," I growled threateningly. "Or there will be the deuce to pay."

Fortunately, we got through the winter without a confrontation, and Edwards and I eagerly prepared for the emergence of the newts from hibernation. Shivering in the dampness of early spring down by the quarry, we watched the creatures awake from their winter sleep, their orange bellies and bright spots announcing the arrival of the breeding season.

Edwards could scarcely contain his excitement as their courtship commenced. "Look, Darwin!" Edwards whispered as the newts scuttled to the water's edge. "He's vibrating his tail to attract a mate!" Crouching amongst the rushes, we scarcely dared breathe as the male dropped a capsule in front of the female, and she somehow managed to pick it up and take it into her body.

"Amazing!" Edwards kept saying through chattering teeth, chilled to the bone after several hours of intense nature-watching. "That was simply amazing, wasn't it, Darwin?"

A few days later we were back at the pond, hoping to find a few females laying their eggs. It was disappointing at first — "Water's still too cold," I said — but soon the egg-laying began in earnest, day after day, as many as a dozen eggs a day deposited under the leaves of water plants. I carried a notebook in which to record the process, and soon Edwards was doing the same.

"We must be patient," I advised. "It can take weeks for the eggs to hatch. It may well be summer till they do."

Just before the end of the term we spotted the first tiny larvae. We caught the tadpoles in nets and examined them as they gradually matured, their front legs developing first, their gills shrinking as their lungs grew, changing over time from water creatures to land creatures. The newts would not be full-grown until autumn. But now it was Midsummer, and I was leaving for the summer holiday.

Edwards and I shook hands as I gathered my notebooks and other items and prepared to go. I noticed the little fellow seemed on the verge of tears. "What shall you be doing over the holiday, Darwin?" Edwards asked in a small, shaky voice.

"A journey to Wales with my brother, I hope. Doing interesting things with him in our laboratory. Visiting my cousins at Maer. What about you, Edwards?"

His lips had begun to quiver. "I do envy you, Darwin," he said, making an unsuccessful attempt to appear brave. "My father died just last year, you see, and my mother is sending me off to stay with my uncle, a clergyman in Pembrokeshire. It's possible I shan't return here for the start of the next term. I just don't know."

Suddenly Edwards was sobbing, and I could not think how to comfort him. All the time we had spent together, watching the newts, talking about newts, planning the next stage in our study of newts, we had never spoken of our homes, our parents, our brothers or sisters. I realised I knew almost nothing about the lad.

"Well, well," I said, awkwardly patting Edwards's shoulder, feeling that I was not quite up to the situation. "Well, well." But I recognised how deeply he felt his loss, as I still felt mine for the death of my mother, though I never spoke of it to anyone — not even to Ras. I wrapped my arms round the boy and let him weep till he'd run dry of tears and even allowed myself to do a bit of grieving of my own.

Chapter 6

Edinburgh: 1825

TWO WEEKS by the sea in Wales collecting specimens my sisters pronounced "fishy-smelling," long days in the laboratory pursuing my brother's scientific experiments — the sweet taste of freedom made starting back to school at the end of the holiday more difficult than ever. Ras went off again to Cambridge. My young friend Edwards did not return. He wrote to tell me he was living with his clergyman uncle, he was lonely, and he'd not yet found anyone who shared his interest in newts. I wrote back, encouraging him, but heard no more.

At Michaelmas I rode to Maer with Susan and Catty. Two weeks earlier our cousin Emma had finally agreed to be confirmed by the bishop of the Church of England. "Emma didn't want to do it, because she doesn't care for ceremony," Susan informed me on the way, "but Aunt Bessy persuaded her. Aunt Bessy says, 'It's better to adhere to the ceremonies of our church, because omitting them may make one more liable to sin.'"

Sin was a concept that didn't mean much to me, and I certainly couldn't imagine Emma likely to fall into it. Now, the solemn event of her confirmation behind her, Emma was in charge of what turned out to be a very large party attended by lots of Wedgwood cousins.

She'd organised what she called "revels" — walks on the sandy paths round Maer, rides across the heath, picnics in the orchard, boat races on the pool, and archery contests on the lawn. Emma herself was a skilled archer. "We call her the Dragoness," her sister Fanny told me when Emma swept away the competition.

Games filled the evening hours; beggar-my-neighbour required no wit whatsoever and went on interminably, as long as everyone was laughing. A steady parade of roasts and puddings and cheeses emerged from the Maer kitchens. From time to time Emma plumped down at the pianoforte and urged everyone to sing. Elizabeth and Charlotte were visible only for minutes at a time, both young ladies apparently too old for the revels. Aunt Bessy, left to chaperone, looked ready to drop from exhaustion. Cousin Harry, at the start of a law career in London, came home for a few days, and I saw from Susan's dejected expression that his attention to Jessie Wedgwood, a cousin from another branch of the family, was making her very unhappy. For a long time Susan had been hoping Harry's attention would be directed at *her*.

At fifteen, I was only dimly aware of my sisters' hopes for the future. Marianne's were settled; she had recently announced her plans to marry Dr. Parker in November. Caroline silently pined for our equally silent cousin Joe. Susan made it plain that she wanted to find a husband, but I knew of no candidates beyond cousin Harry. Catty, just fourteen, was not yet concerned with finding a suitable mate. I sensed that the revels offered an opportunity for flirtations, but I had no interest in any of it.

Uncle Jos rescued me. "Shall we do some shooting, Charley?" he asked.

How I did enjoy shooting! I was happiest when I was toiling through the thick heath and young firs with my uncle and the gamekeeper, spattered with mud, my gun broken over my arm, a gamebook in my pocket to keep a tally of my kills. There was little conversation, merely a few terse words and gestures. I'd persuaded myself that shooting was a worthy intellectual activity, because it required so much skill to judge where to find the game and to handle the dogs well.

But there was not enough time. After only two days we rode home again with only an hour to spare before I had to rush back to school.

IN FEBRUARY OF 1825, shortly after my sixteenth birthday, Dr. Butler's report of my mediocre scholarly performance arrived on Father's desk. I'd made the usual resolutions to change my desultory habits but broke the resolutions almost as soon as they were made. My grasp of Latin and Greek was weaker than ever, mathematics almost nonexistent. I'd often wondered what Father had in mind for me. Perhaps his vision of my future was as clouded as my own. Summoned to my father's library, I braced myself for the inevitable rebuke.

"What have you to say for yourself, Charles?" Father asked. He looked weary — enormously fat and suffering from gout. Short of breath, too, it appeared.

"Nothing, sir," I replied. We'd been through it all before, countless times, and I'd been unable to convince my father I was doing the best I could with subjects that bored me half to death. I wished he could understand that I was not brilliant like Ras, who effortlessly mastered whatever was required, and I hated disappointing him.

"You're not stupid, Charles," Father said thoughtfully, making a steeple of his fingers.

"I don't believe I am, sir."

"Lazy, then? Is that it?"

"No, sir. I work quite diligently, really I do, sir. But it can't be helped. The study of classics just does not —" I halted, groping for the words that would explain it all, and began again. "I'm not a classical scholar, sir. I would much rather be out of doors, observing nature, studying things that appear interesting. Or in the laboratory, especially when Ras is there, too, and we conduct our experiments and witness the most amazing results."

"That's all well and good, observing nature, etcetera. But have you considered how you intend to make your way in the world, Charles? Gathering up interesting things and conducting amazing experiments?"

"No, sir. I haven't."

Father was regarding me carefully, but I avoided his stern gaze. A thick silence settled between us.

Abruptly Father threw himself back in his chair. "Though you show no willingness to confront the subject yourself, it may surprise you to learn that I have given it a great deal of consideration. Obviously you cannot pursue a degree in law, since you have not the slightest inclination to master Latin and Greek. Despite tutoring in geometry, you are even more deficient in the field of mathematics, a lack that bars you from the study of science. Military service seems out of the question, though I do understand you've become a remarkably good shot. Have you any disagreement thus far?"

I shook my head and stared at the inkpot on my father's desk. Everything he said was true. What *could* I do that Father might think was appropriate? I had once thought, whilst out tramping over the heath with Uncle Jos, that I would surely enjoy the life of a gamekeeper — except that gamekeepers didn't actually shoot. Shooting was for gentlemen, like Uncle Jos. And Father would surely *not* approve. He would consider such a life beneath me.

"Having considered all the possibilities," Father continued, "I have decided to withdraw you from Shrewsbury School at the end of the term in June." I jerked my head up and stared at him in disbelief. Surely I'd heard wrongly. "Erasmus will finish his studies at Cambridge at that time," he went on. "In October he will enroll at the University of Edinburgh to complete the courses necessary for a medical degree. You will accompany him and attend lecture courses till you're older. I think you will each benefit from the arrangement. My plan is that you will both become physicians and continue the family tradition — your grandfather and your late uncle and I all studied at Edinburgh to prepare for the practise of medicine. What have you to say to this plan?"

I was stunned. I could hardly think what to say. I had never considered becoming a doctor. But I grasped at the piece of good news: I would be leaving Shrewsbury School a year or two early and I would be going with Ras — it didn't much matter *where*.

"Well, Charles?"

I had a sudden image of myself riding round Shropshire in a yellow phaeton, calling on grateful patients, but with plenty of time left for rambling out of doors, collecting specimens and shooting birds. "Yes, sir," I said, beaming, feeling almost giddy. "Thank you, sir."

"Off with you, then, Charley," Father said gruffly, waving me away.

I managed to walk out of my father's library in a dignified manner and to continue walking, through the front door, coatless, into a full-blown blizzard. "I'll be free!" I shouted to the whirling snowflakes. "Free! Free!" Then I rushed back inside to write the great news to Ras.

JUNE 17TH, 1825, was one of the most joyous days of my young life: I left Shrewsbury School forever, confident I would never have to memorise another line of Latin or construe another passage of Greek. Ras came home from Cambridge, and we often went walking through the Shropshire hills together. These were wonderful days, though I noticed Ras had less energy. Father must have noticed, too, for he prescribed more medications to strengthen Ras's bones.

Before Ras and I left for Edinburgh, Father decided to introduce us to his own practise of medicine. "You will doubtless learn all sorts of important lessons at the university where I did my early training," he told us. "But after my many years of practise, I assure you the best diagnostic tool you possess is this." He tapped his ear. I thought he meant listening to the patient's breathing or heartbeat, but I was wrong. "Listen carefully to what the patient tells you," Father said, "and you will be able to diagnose what ails him."

"And what about the treatment, Father?" Ras asked.

"A large dose of sympathy mixed with a small lie will make most patients feel better almost at once," he advised. "Though at times, of course, something stronger is needed."

Several afternoons a week Father took Ras on rounds at the clinical wards in the infirmary. I was despatched to visit charity patients suffering minor illnesses that didn't warrant admittance to the infirmary. At first I felt very uneasy in my new role. Why would these sick people trust a sixteen-year-old youth to treat them? But I got on well with the children from the start, and in short order the older people were persuaded that I meant them no harm.

Following Father's instructions, I wrote down as complete an account as I could of each case, listing the symptoms and my observations. Later, I read my notes aloud to him, and he suggested additional questions to ask. Once a diagnosis had been reached, he advised me what medicines to administer to the patient, and I went to the laboratory and prepared them myself.

By the end of summer I had more than a dozen patients, mostly women and children. I treated chest colds with doses of tartar emetic to help their coughs — the compound was known to be effective in getting rid of congestion, but it proved too harsh and made a lot of unhappy children vomit instead.

I truly believed I had found my calling, and Father thought so, too. "I'm certain you have everything it takes to become a successful physician, my boy," he said, laying his large hand on my shoulder. "The main thing is to inspire confidence. If your patients believe you will cure them, then you will."

RAS AND I ARRIVED in Edinburgh in October. We managed to find two large bedrooms and a bright sitting room on the fourth floor near the university and set out to explore this new world. We wandered from the ancient castle looming on a bluff on the western edge of the city down the Royal Mile to the Palace of Holyroodhouse and walked the windswept beaches on the Firth of Forth, the estuary of the river flowing through Edinburgh. When we could afford it, we treated ourselves to a night at the theatre. Once we were guests at a supper celebrating Robert Burns's birthday, where the haggis —

sheep's stomach stuffed with oatmeal and offal — was carried in with great ceremony, accompanied by bagpipers. We reveled in our independence.

Ras proclaimed the Scottish capital the most beautiful city he'd ever seen. I, who had never been anyplace larger than Liverpool, agreed enthusiastically. I wrote to the sisterhood about this magnificent city, and our sisters wrote back, describing a Shrewsbury even duller than I remembered. A year earlier Marianne had married her longtime suitor, Dr. Henry Parker, and Caroline reported, "She's taken Spark to live with them in Overton." Four of us, including Spark, were gone now from The Mount. The dog's departure seemed saddest of all.

During the six months Ras spent in Edinburgh completing the necessary work for his medical degree, I didn't try to make other friends; my brother's companionship was enough. But when Ras left for London for private studies in anatomy, I stayed on alone, not knowing what else to do.

I loved the city, but the lectures at the medical school were another story: The students were a rowdy crowd who sang, shouted, stamped their feet, and made vulgar noises to express their disapproval — "making a ruff," they called it. Most of the courses were dull beyond words. The worst was anatomy, taught in an amphitheatre with steeply tiered seats. Students looked down at a corpse laid out on a table whilst a professor droned on in a monotone and his assistant did the cutting. I usually climbed to a seat near the top, as far as possible from the cadaver, and avoided any possibility of actually practising on it.

Where did that body come from? I wondered from the safety of my perch, knowing that many corpses were stolen from graveyards. Some might be the bodies of poor souls murdered for this lucrative market. I'd heard of bodies being shipped over from Dublin in kegs of cheap Irish whisky.

As time passed, I wanted less and less to do with any of it. I began skipping classes, with the exception of chemistry — the professor was quite a showman, and his demonstrations attracted hundreds of spectators. Instead, I preferred to stay in my rooms and read. I mentioned this in a letter to Susan, who, regrettably, passed the word on to Father. I should have known better. Susan reported back, "Papa says that if you do not discontinue your present indulgent ways, your course of study will be utterly useless."

I already *knew* it was utterly useless, but I refrained from saying so and plodded on.

Then I learnt I must observe my first surgery. The cutting would be on a live patient, not a dead body.

I found a seat in the hospital operating theatre, much nearer to the patient than I cared to be. To my dismay, I saw that the person laid out on the table beneath a white sheet was a child whose leg, crushed in an accident, had turned gangrenous. The surgeon explained that the leg must be removed to save the boy's life.

The little patient was given a dose of opium, which

calmed him till the first cut was made, and then he began to scream and writhe horribly. It required the efforts of two men to hold him down. The agonised screaming continued, drowning out the sound of the saw cutting through the child's thigh bone. Blood spurted everywhere, drenching the white-coated doctor and his assistants. I believed I was going to faint. The screaming went on and on as I managed to make my way out of the operating theatre, out of the hospital, and into a driving rain, the child's cries still ringing in my ears.

I vowed I would never go back. But when I left the university at the beginning of the summer holiday, I had no notion of how to break this news to Father.

EARLY IN JULY I set off on a long tour of Wales with my two school friends, Cameron and Watkins. Carrying knapsacks, we walked thirty miles most days. We climbed Mount Snowdon, the highest peak in Wales, enduring frequent rain squalls, but when the clouds lifted we enjoyed spectacular views extending for over a hundred miles. Sometimes, when we lay on our bedrolls in the shelter of an overhanging rock at the end of a weary day, I was tempted to unburden myself to my old friends. Both of them had gone off to Cambridge, and both were preparing to take Holy Orders and become clergymen.

"I see myself in a sweet little country church someday," Cameron said into the darkness.

"Not me!" declared Watkins. "I'm for the city life,

big church, fine choir, no grubbing about for a few extra shillings from my impoverished parishioners to buy a new set of altar cloths. And perhaps I'll write a bit, too — something profoundly theological."

I marvelled at the clarity of their vision.

"What about you, Darwin? You're into medicine — where shall you set up practise? London? Shrewsbury?"

"Oh, that's still undecided," I said. "Now if you don't mind, I need some sleep."

But sleep would not come. *I'm going to leave off studying medicine,* I imagined myself telling them in the intimacy of the darkness; *I'm not cut out to be a doctor.* But in the end I never spoke of it. Instead, I simply tried to forget about it.

I RETURNED HOME determined to speak to Father about my disillusionment with the study of medicine in general and the courses of study at Edinburgh in particular. But my father had fallen into one of his periodic black humours, not the best time to bring up a difficult subject. Fortunately, I found an invitation to join William Mostyn Owen for the start of the grouse-shooting season on August 12th — "the glorious twelfth," as it was called — packed my gear, and prepared to leave directly for Woodhouse.

Catty pouted when I told her I was going. "We hardly ever see you anymore, Charley," she complained. "You're always running off hither and yon. You're not even hiding in your laboratory, as you used to with Ras —

nobody goes out there anymore. Now Ras spends all his time in London, and all *you* think about is shooting!"

Catty's outburst surprised me. I remembered with fondness the hours we'd spent together in the crooked branches of the chestnut tree. We were the two youngest in the family, and my feelings towards Catty had always been especially tender. "I'll be back in a day or two," I assured her. "I swear it."

"Enjoy yourself at Woodhouse," Catty sniffed. "Caroline and Susan and I were entertained there for a week last spring, and we never talked a word of common sense all day. It was really quite fatiguing. Mrs. Owen had twenty-nine at dinner, but the dining room is so vast that everyone was seated quite comfortably. Still, the racket was almost too much!"

Caroline and Susan had joined the conversation. "More than half the gentlemen were a little too stimulated," Susan said disapprovingly.

"In my opinion," Caroline said, "it is hardly possible for common mortals to keep their spirits wound up to the level of the Owens."

And my sisters complained a little too much, I thought. I had never heard of them refusing an invitation to visit their Woodhouse friends.

Chapter 7

Discovery: 1826

WOODHOUSE WAS LESS than thirteen miles from Shrewsbury, if one rode a straight line towards Oswestry on the Welsh border. I left The Mount at sunup, seldom keeping to the rutted roads that led from village to village, instead leaping over hedges and splashing across streams. Squire Owen's "patch," as he was pleased to call it, was larger than Uncle Jos's Maer, perhaps as much as two thousand acres. An avenue of beech trees led to the splendid white freestone mansion that sat grandly on the brow of a low rise, overlooking thickly wooded grounds, lush gardens surrounded by low walls, and fine views in all directions. Four massive Greek columns supported the great portico.

A groom took charge of my horse, and a butler ushered me into the vast hall. "Mr. Owen is at breakfast, sir, and wishes you to join him."

I had over the past few years paid numerous visits to Woodhouse and the family of William Mostyn Owen, and I felt quite at home here. I admired Squire Owen and got on well with his son, William, a captain in the Royal Regiment of Dragoons. I was of course acquainted with the two eldest daughters, Sally and Fanny, who'd visited The Mount with their mother for my sisters' musical events. The Owen girls were not at home when I arrived that morning, having gone off with their chaperone to visit friends in a neighbouring county.

There were five in our party — Squire Owen, his cousin Major Richard Hill, Hill's son John, William, and I. Though we had a late start, we put in a fine day of shooting. The early fog had lifted. The dogs were eager, tails wagging. Beaters drove the birds out of their cover in the heather with a great whirring of wings. The red grouse are extremely fast flyers and hard to hit, but my aim was deadly, as always. That evening we dined quietly and the next day were up well before sunrise. I had placed my shooting boots open by my bedside when I retired, so as not to lose half a minute in putting them on in the morning.

I'd begun to keep a tally of exactly how many pheasant, woodcock, partridge, grouse, and so on I had brought down: I tied a piece of string to the buttonhole of my shooting jacket, and every time I hit a bird — which was most of those at which I fired — I tied a knot in the string, so that later I could enter the number in my notebook. But on that day my friends decided to play a joke at my expense.

Each time I fired and thought I'd got a bird, either Squire Owen or William or one of the Hills pretended to be loading his gun, and cried out, "You must not count that bird, Darwin, for I fired at the same time." The gamekeeper, in on the joke, always backed them up. After some hours of this and much frustration on my part, they owned up to what they had done. I was certain I had shot a large number of grouse but didn't know how many and therefore couldn't add them to my tally. I managed to laugh, though I was not amused.

The hall at Woodhouse was very grand. Tapestries and paintings covered the walls, along with a number of heads of various animals bagged by the squire on hunting expeditions. A broad staircase led up to a gallery extending round three sides of the hall. Partway up the staircase split in two, one going to the left and the other to the right. A dozen or so bedrooms were situated on corridors behind the gallery. My bedroom was amongst them.

After a long day spent tramping over the muddy heath and handling bloodied birds, I was in need of a washing up, but I found a pair of laughing young ladies blocking my way, Sally Owen defending the left branch of the stairs, Fanny on the right. The sisters had returned that afternoon from their latest jaunt, and a handsomer pair of stair-guardians would be hard to imagine. Sally was of medium height with dark hair and bright eyes as black as a gypsy's. Fanny was taller and altogether sunnier, her hair light and her startlingly blue eyes clear and sparkling. The two girls were like the moon and the sun.

"Why, lookee here, Mistress Sarah!" Fanny called out to Sally as I stood at the foot of the stairs, wondering which way to proceed. "If it isn't our very scientifically minded Mr. Charley Darwin come to visit The Forest!" She pretended to hold a spyglass up to her eye and to examine my sweaty and mud-caked person from head to foot. "A rare specimen, indeed! Should we add him to our collection, d'you think? Pin him to pasteboard and put a label on him? Or lay him out in a drawer on a bed of cotton wool!"

I was seventeen, with little experience of girls other than my sisters and my Wedgwood cousins whom I had known since childhood. Fanny was eighteen; she and Sally, twenty-one, were now out in society, attending teas and dances and musicales and whatever it was young ladies did when they went to visit friends. I had scarcely seen the Owen sisters since their stay at The Mount three years earlier, when as a lad of fourteen I'd been entranced by Fanny Owen's larkspur blue eyes. I remembered how determined she was to pass the time reading a novel. Now it was Sally who seemed more bookish and serious. Fanny, on the other hand, fairly sizzled with high spirits.

I felt myself colouring furiously, and I could not think of a single clever thing to say. "W-w-won't you let me pass?" I asked, horrified that my old stammer had suddenly reappeared.

Fanny yielded. She smiled and stepped aside, dropping a curtsey as she did. I hurried past her, unable to meet her eyes, which seemed bluer than ever.

As I washed and changed, laughter began to drift up from below — a crowd seemed to be gathering. I delayed going down till it could no longer be put off. Guests had arrived from neighbouring estates, and half the gentlemen were already deep in their cups, the other half determined to catch up, just as Susan had described. Everything seemed amusing, even hilarious, to everyone else. I was unaccustomed to drinking, as spirits were forbidden at The Mount, and I felt awkward and out of place. I searched for Fanny and at last sighted her surrounded by admirers.

She must have observed my discomfort. "Come, Charley," she whispered, appearing suddenly by my side. "I believe you'll find the air outside much more pleasant."

Mutely, I followed her through a butler's pantry and a side door to a terrace. The air was indeed more pleasant and the terrace was quieter as well. But it was also quite chilly, and we had gone out with no thought of taking a wrap. I had sense enough to drape my coat over Fanny's pale white shoulders, but I did not have further sense to see that she would have also accepted my warming arm round her and even the kiss that I longed to press on her full lips. But, never having done such a thing in my life, except on Spark when he was a young pup, I did not dare.

Afraid we would be missed and I would be found guilty of something, though I didn't know just what, I urged Fanny to go back inside. Still not knowing what to do, I helped myself to some oysters from the sideboard, ate them quickly, excused myself, and retired.

That night I slept poorly, unusual for me. Our shooting party went out before the ladies came down for breakfast. Though no one played tricks on me, it was not my best day, for Fanny was too much on my mind. When we returned to the house, Fanny and Sally were nowhere to be seen, nor did they return that evening. I was disappointed, for I'd made up my mind to put myself forward — perhaps take her small white hand and kiss it.

I left Woodhouse early the next morning and rode slowly home to Shrewsbury, taking the regular road. I was expected to return to Edinburgh the following week, and I had still not spoken to Father. This, I'd decided, would be the day. But when I reached The Mount and found him still sunk in a dark mood, I felt it better simply to keep on doing what I'd been doing, to continue with my university courses and see how things worked out.

I'll talk to Father about it another time, I thought. *Perhaps at Christmas.*

THE ROOMS Ras and I had shared in Edinburgh seemed too large when I returned in autumn of 1826. I avoided the medical studies, which either sickened or bored me, and enrolled instead in natural history courses: zoology, botany, paleontology, geology, and mineralogy. Some of the material was interesting, some intolerably dull. Geology, for example, seemed dry as dust. Whilst a student at Shrewsbury School, I'd met an old man named Mr. Cotton who appeared to know a great deal about rocks. A boulder known as the Bellstone was prominently displayed in Shrewsbury and considered very unusual, for there was no rock of the same kind to be found nearer than Scotland. Mr. Cotton had informed me solemnly, "The world will come to an end before anyone is able to explain how this stone came to be here."

But now I learnt an explanation did indeed exist for the Bellstone's presence in Shrewsbury: It had been carried there by a glacier. I wondered how old Mr. Cotton would accept this astonishing news. But even this revelation was not enough to persuade me I would ever again attend a course in geology, one of the least interesting of natural history subjects I had yet encountered.

The one bright spot, and more relevant to my interests, were the lessons in the art of taxidermy I received from a black man named John Edmonstone, a freed slave, who taught me how to skin and stuff those birds I'd been shooting by the dozen. (In fact, that summer I had kept a list in my gamebook of my score during the two months of the season: a total of 177 hares, pheasants, and partridges had met their end; for reasons I've described, I didn't have an accurate count of the grouse.)

For an hour every day for two months I visited Edmonstone in the laboratory he had set up in a tenement close by my rooms. There I learnt not only the techniques of taxidermy but Edmonstone's story as well. He had been a slave on a sugarcane plantation in Demerara, part of British Guiana on the coast of South America. There he met Charles Waterton, a Yorkshire naturalist who'd journeyed to Demerara as a young man to manage his uncle's estate. Waterton had begun to explore the rain forests of Guiana and to collect specimens.

"Mr. Waterton knew all about how to take a dead bird or some other creature and just about bring him back to life," Edmonstone told me. His large hands, the colour of mahogany, moved as delicately as moths over a specimen. "I thought at first he'd done some kind of magic. He taught me how to do it. When he came back to England a few years ago, he brought me with him and told me I was a free man. So now I teach the lessons Mr. Waterton taught me. He always said there are three things you need for this work: a penknife, a hand neither coarse nor clumsy, and practise. Lots of practise, Mr. Darwin!"

It was best, he said, to begin with a bird that had not been wounded and was in perfect feather, but since all my specimens were birds I had shot, I would have to learn how to deal with a bird that usually had holes in it. For now, though, I practised on birds Edmonstone had procured, working with knife and fingers to separate the skin from the skeleton without tearing. "Now, Mr. Darwin, remove the skin in one piece over the head as though slipping off its shirt."

I progressed to removing innards and flesh and, to prevent rot and attack by insects, applying to every surface a solution of corrosive sublimate — mercuric chloride. "A powerful poison, Mr. Darwin," he warned.

"Now," Edmonstone said, "with great caution and tenderness, return the head through the inverted skin, just so."

I stuffed the body with cotton, stitched the skin in place with needle and thread, arranged my bird in a life-like position, and allowed it to dry for several days. It goes without saying that my first efforts were a good deal less than perfect, but by the end of my course of study I had become quite proficient.

These were surely amongst the most rewarding instructions I received in Edinburgh, and perhaps the most enlightening. As we worked side by side, John Edmonstone recounted in his musical accent stories of his life as a slave, the beatings by the overseers, the daily humiliations endured. I listened, rapt and appalled, and developed a hatred of the entire system that put one man in bondage to another.

I WAS OFTEN quite lonely without Ras. The city that had seemed so beautiful only a year earlier now struck me as crowded, grey, and dingy. Fanny Owen was on my mind more or less constantly. I decided to write to her, and I was delightfully surprised to receive letters in reply from both Fanny and her sister Sally. Sally's letters dwelt on gossip about dances and parties. Fanny's provided annoying details of suitable partners met at these dances and parties. She called them "the shootables" and dismissed them as "remarkably useless, as very few of them go out and dance." I was relieved that she seemed to find her partners tedious but realised I wouldn't fare much better in her eyes. Wondering if she was at all interested in the scientific matters that absorbed me, I wrote back, though I hadn't Fanny's talent for amusing descriptions, and felt tremendously pleased when she bothered to reply.

Slowly I began to make a few friends in Edinburgh. I joined the Plinian Society, a group of students interested in natural history who gathered once a fortnight to discuss the birds and sea creatures we'd found in the Firth of Forth. (How dull the Misses Owen would have thought our discussions!) Amongst the Plinians I found a few congenial young men with whom I went on trapping and shooting expeditions. The students also liked to debate such subjects as phrenology, the increasingly popular notion that character and personality are determined by the shape of the head.

I had plenty of time to read, and during this period I became more intimately acquainted with my grandfather, the first Erasmus Darwin, who had died in 1802, several years before I was born. In addition to being a physician, my grandfather was a radical thinker with deep interest in scientific matters, as well as a respected poet who often expressed his unconventional ideas in rhyme. My father spoke of his father in the vaguest terms, when he mentioned him at all. From Ras's description, I gathered their relationship was not cordial, and I was left to find out what I would on my own.

I set out to read everything my grandfather had written, beginning with two books in poetic form, *The Loves of Plants* and *The Temple of Nature*. I found these lines of particular interest:

Organic Life beneath the shoreless waves
Was born and nurs'd in Ocean's pearly caves;
First forms minute, unseen by spheric glass,

Move on the mud, or pierce the watery mass;
These as successive generations bloom,
New powers acquire, and larger limbs assume;
Whence countless groups of vegetation spring,
And breathing realms of fin, and feet, and wing. . . .

I puzzled over these lines and what they meant. My grandfather had used rhyme to describe something quite unlike Creation as I had learnt it from the Bible. As a young child I'd sat on Caroline's lap whilst she read to me from the book of Genesis, and I loved the images it brought to mind.

And God said, Let the waters bring forth abundantly the moving creature that hath life, and fowl that may fly above the earth in the open firmament of heaven.

And God created great whales, and every living creature that moveth, which the waters brought forth abundantly . . .

And God said, Let the earth bring forth the living creature after his kind, cattle, and creeping thing, and beast of the earth after his kind: and it was so . . .

And God said, Let us make man in our image, after our likeness . . .

So God created man in his own image, in the image of God created he him; male and female created he them.

But I understood that my grandfather believed all life on earth began with primeval filaments — those "first forms minute," so tiny you could see them only with a microscope — filaments that changed over time, growing more complex and developing variations passed on from one generation to the next till they reached their present form. Primeval filaments that slowly changed? How different from the fully formed and fully recognisable creatures of the book of Genesis, each one an unchanging link, from the lowest one-celled creature to the highest, man, in a great chain of being created by God! And my grandfather didn't even *mention* God.

On gloomy nights in Edinburgh with rain rattling against my windows I read my grandfather's prose work, *Zoonomia, or the Laws of Organic Life,* in which he explained his view of the animal kingdom. He had intended *Zoonomia* as a medical text, but in it he spelt out his ideas on a subject considered radical in his time and in mine: evolution.

From there I went on to read the work of Jean-Baptiste Lamarck, a Frenchman who'd lived at about the same time as my grandfather. Lamarck had studied fossils and concluded that some species of animals *had* changed — not just over generations, as Dr. Erasmus Darwin suggested, but over several millennia. I was fascinated by this idea of change in nature, but the more I read, the more I felt in my grandfather's writing the absence of a Creator. I couldn't imagine a godless universe, but it seemed he could and did. Grandfather sounded like an atheist. To a believer like me, that was troubling.

ALL THESE THRILLING but unsettling ideas were churning in my mind when I developed a friendship with Dr.

Robert Grant, a medical doctor who lectured at the university on invertebrates, animals lacking a backbone. A tall man almost twice my age with a broad forehead, intense light brown eyes, and a stiffly formal manner I found off-putting at first, Dr. Grant became my mentor and introduced me to marine zoology. He took me on outings during the cold, wet Scottish winter to rock pools at the edge of the Firth to gather tiny sea creatures. We carried them back to his small cottage by the sea — he was a bachelor — where Grant taught me to dissect them and examine them under a microscope. The growing amity began to fill the empty place in my life that had opened up when Ras left for London.

Bobbing in a fishing boat on the choppy waters of the Firth in search of specimens one chilly afternoon, Grant tamped tobacco into a pipe and began to describe his ideas about the gradual change and development of invertebrates. "Many people think the idea of evolution is shocking," Grant said. "They prefer to believe that all species were created by God and don't change. I disagree. I'm convinced they *do* change."

I looked up in surprise, nodded, and quickly looked away again, not quite knowing what to make of this confession. No one I knew discussed such things.

Grant concentrated on lighting his pipe. "I know you're well acquainted with these ideas, Darwin — you're the great man's grandson, after all," he said. "Best, though, if you keep this conversation between us," he added with a tight smile. "It would not go well for me in my professional career if my unorthodox beliefs became known."

"Of course," I murmured. "I understand." The fact that he had confided in me was immensely flattering.

Over the next month or two Dr. Grant and I spent a great deal of time together. On occasion he took me as his guest to meetings of the Wernerian Society, a natural history group open only to men with medical degrees. We often dined together, talking science until the small hours, but there was no more mention of evolution.

One day at Grant's cottage he loaned me a microscope to study *Flustra,* a simple marine animal that resembled moss found on rocks by the sea. Peering into the lens, I observed that the organism produced ova — eggs — that seemed to glide to and fro in order to become fertilised. I rushed to tell Grant, who had been studying the same organism.

"Dr. Grant, I've observed something unusual here. The ova are moving, almost as though they're dancing." I waited expectantly, thinking my hero would be as excited as I was. Perhaps I had made an original discovery!

"Interesting," he said at last. That was all. He was not nearly as impressed as I thought he'd be.

Nevertheless, I wrote a paper about my observation, and soon after my eighteenth birthday I prepared to read the paper to the members of the Plinian Society. I even hoped to have my paper published in a scientific journal.

But three days before I was to present my findings to the Plinians, Dr. Grant read his own paper on the same subject at the Wernerian Society without giving me credit for my findings or even mentioning my name — either that night or in the version he later published.

I was hurt and confused. All those expeditions to collect specimens, enduring seasickness in fishing boats and shivering in tide pools, all those hours squinting into a microscope, all those stimulating discussions — and suddenly my mentor had turned his back on me. I went ahead and read my report to the Plinians, but my heart was no longer in it. I had experienced, firsthand and painfully, the reality of scientific rivalry. I felt betrayed. By the end of April I had completed the rest of my studies of the reproductive dance of these simple organisms. But I no longer met with Dr. Grant. In fact I utterly avoided him, and he made no effort to contact me. The friendship — if it had indeed ever been a real friendship — was over.

This was the final straw in the load that had been threatening all along to end any thought I'd had of remaining at Edinburgh. Now I absolutely had to find a way to tell my father. There could be no further postponement. I went home to The Mount and steeled myself for what was to come.

It was even worse than I expected.

Father exploded. "You care for nothing but shooting, dogs, and rat-catching," he roared, "and you will be a disgrace to yourself and all your family!"

He loomed behind his enormous desk, his face purple with rage. I had never seen him like this — hardly the mild-mannered physician so beloved by his grateful patients. But his patients had never disappointed him in the ways I had.

I groped for words to make it plain that it wasn't just

shooting and dogs — though, yes, I did suppose that my collections of stuffed birds and beetles and other small creatures could be called "rat-catching."

"Father, I just don't have the stomach for it — the blood, the pain, the suffering . . ." I stopped, dangerously close to unmanly tears.

Father dropped into his chair, flinging one arm over the back. "Yes, yes, Charles, I do understand, you've made it quite clear. I thought you had a special gift for healing, but now I see that you do not." He appeared to be struggling to be calm, reasonable. "But you must have a profession, Charles — some purpose in life! Surely you agree that you must not simply lead a life of idleness and sport?"

"Yes, sir, I do agree." I did realise I must stop the shooting, or do less of it. One couldn't spend one's whole life shooting, pleasant as that might be.

"Yet you have no notion what that purpose might be?" Father's bushy eyebrows lifted, his sober grey eyes boring into mine.

I saw myself bending over a microscope, slopping round in tide pools, clambering over rock piles, writing my notes in a lovely leather-bound book, perhaps even exploring a rain forest somewhere with a man like Edmonstone to assist me. I opened my mouth to speak, hoping the right words would find their way, and quickly closed it again. My father waited for an answer, but I had none to give him. My notions all seemed completely far-fetched, even to me.

Father heaved a great sigh. "Since you seem to have no ideas, Charles, let me put one forward." I was relieved to see that he was calmer now. "I should like you to consider becoming a man of the cloth."

"Sir?"

"Go into the church. Become a cleric, an Anglican clergyman. You might very well find yourself in charge of a country parish, christenings and weddings and the occasional funeral to be conducted in a pretty little church, good gentlefolk gathered about you on Sunday mornings, waiting for inspiring words to fall from your lips, a comfortable parsonage where you'd have plenty of room for your confounded collections, plenty of time to pursue whatever interests you wish, horses and dogs, even some shooting, nothing wrong with that. A pleasant life, perhaps even a useful one. Well, Charles, what have you to say to that?"

I stood gaping at him, entirely speechless. *A clergyman?* The idea had never entered my mind.

"Think about it, Charles," Father said brusquely and dismissed me.

I *did* try to think about it. I hadn't attended divine services since I'd left Shrewsbury School, and my father had never been a churchgoer, though my sisters traipsed off to St. Chad's every Sunday and on certain obligatory holy days. Still, the life of a country parson had its appeals — a couple of my cousins on the Wedgwood side had taken that path and seemed to like it well enough.

But I worried that my beliefs were not sufficiently

strong. Did I truly accept wholeheartedly every item in the Nicene Creed, the basis of the Anglican faith? *I believe in one God, the Father Almighty, maker of heaven and earth, and of all things visible and invisible.* I wasn't sure. But I did believe every word of the Bible, strictly and literally. And since that was the case, I soon persuaded myself, I should not have any problem with the creed. I could, perhaps, bring comfort and solace to those who needed it, and be a teacher to those who desired instruction. I could help to reveal to them the beauties of God's creation. Were my beliefs strong enough to persuade the doubters? That was open to question.

But I realised it didn't matter *what* I believed or did not believe — Father had already made the decision. I would go to Christ's College at Cambridge to study for a degree in arts, the first step before taking Holy Orders. I would become a clergyman, whether I wanted to or not.

The good news was that I would not have to become a doctor.

Chapter 8

Fanny: 1827

A CLEAR MAP to my future had been laid out before me. I felt a measure of relief, but a practical problem remained: I had lost even the small amount of Latin and Greek I'd painfully acquired at Shrewsbury School and would need for my studies at Christ's College. Complaining about money poured down the drain, my father hired a tutor to cram me in the ancient languages. I would not leave for Cambridge till the following January; the next nine months would be spent at The Mount in the company of Mr. Graham, a former master from Shrewsbury School, now long retired, much withered, and cursed with a whining voice. The prospect was dreary beyond imagining.

In April, soon after the decision had been made, Uncle Jos arrived unexpectedly at The Mount. I'd gone out shooting with him in autumn and again during the Christmas holiday, and we'd spent days trudging over the heath in comfortable silence except for occasional comments about the birds or the dogs or the weather.

None of Jos Wedgwood's four sons had any love for shooting, preferring to spend their leisure indoors, and my uncle seemed grateful for my company. I was grateful for his, too. I never felt I had disappointed him, as I had my own father. I hadn't seen Uncle Jos since the beginning of the year. I was about to take an early lunch in the conservatory between tutorial sessions and invited him to join me.

"Thought of sending you a letter, but changed my mind," he said. He glanced at Father's exotic flora with diminishing interest, being more of a sporting man, and tucked into the sausages and potatoes. "Always better to say it in person. Have a proposal for you. Need to talk to your sisters, but you first. My girls are on the Continent, you knew that?"

The Doveleys — Fanny and Emma — had not been present at Maer at Christmas. It had seemed a duller place without the lively presence of Miss Memorandum and Miss Slip-Slop, but I'd forgotten where they'd gone.

"They're with their aunt Jessie, my wife's sister, married to a European scholar, peculiar sort of fellow, living in Switzerland. Thought you and two or three of your sisters might be willing to travel with a poor old fellow to fetch his daughters. Stop in London and Paris on the way to Geneva, throw ourselves on the hospitality of Jessie and her husband, take in some of the wonders of Germany and Holland with the young ladies on the way home. Make a nice little tour of it. Leave in mid-May, here by the end of July. What do you say, Charley, eh?"

I was delighted, and told him so. The question, though, was not what I had to say but what Father would have to say about a holiday when I'd scarcely buckled down to the Latin and Greek. "But you know I'm preparing to begin at Christ's College in January?"

"I'll have a word with the doctor, if that's what worries you. Tell him I'll see to it you study every day," Uncle Jos added with a wink. "Now let's speak to your sisters."

The sisterhood had just returned from a shopping expedition. Removing her bonnet and gloves, Susan declined. "I really have no appetite for travel," she said, a surprise to me. I wondered if she might have her eye on some young gentleman in Shropshire or Staffordshire and didn't want to risk losing his interest. Susan often lamented the scarcity of eligible men. "There are so few who are our kind of people and clever as well," she complained. "I never meet anyone new." It seemed to me that anything in coat and trousers from eight years to eighty was fair game to her; perhaps she'd found one.

Catty, too, declined. Her reasons weren't clear, though later she explained to me, "Uncle Jos is just too frightening. I cannot imagine spending all that time with someone so *silent*."

Only Caroline expressed pleasure at the notion of such a journey, and so the matter was settled: Caroline and I would accompany our uncle to the Continent, if Father agreed. He did without much comment, other than to extract from me a promise to devote myself for at least two hours a day to the tortures of Latin and Greek grammar, though I don't believe he thought I actually would.

*　　*　　*

ON THE DAY BEFORE we left Shrewsbury, I received a letter from Fanny Owen, posted from Bath. She and her mother and sister Sally were taking the waters and doing whatever fashionable ladies liked to do. By the time I had her letter in hand, she wrote, they would have returned to Woodhouse.

The Forest is so unbearably dull, Fanny scrawled. *Won't you please come this very instant and save us before we expire of our tedium?* The Owens were planning a celebration of her brother William's twenty-first birthday in June, "an event not to be missed." It was certain to be a "perfectly wild party," and I *must* be amongst those present. She would permit no refusal!

I dashed off a hasty reply, explaining that I was leaving at once for the Continent, sincerely regretted, etcetera — too formal, I realised, but I could not match Fanny's heedless gaiety and felt foolish if I tried.

Father saw us off the next day on the London stage, our numerous trunks and bundles and hatboxes secured in the boot. The coachman blew his horn, the four horses plunged forward, and we were on our way. With stops at posts along the road to change horses and stretch our cramped legs, we arrived in London near midnight and went directly to a hotel.

Ras met us at breakfast. He was in his final months of study at a private anatomy school, preparing to sit for his bachelor of medicine examination at Cambridge in January.

"I'll be there, too, at Christ's," I told him. "Now that I'm to become a parson."

"A parson?" Ras burst out laughing. "Oh, Charley, Charley!" he cried. "What are you thinking?"

"Why are you laughing, Ras?" Caroline demanded. "I believe he'll make a very fine clergyman."

"Perhaps he shall," Ras acknowledged. "What say you, Uncle Jos?"

My uncle gazed at me thoughtfully. "Can be a pleasant life," he said. "Plenty of time to pursue one's own interests."

"And you, Charley?" Ras pressed good-humouredly. "Your thoughts on your future?"

I shrugged. "It's Father's idea," I said.

"Ah, well," Ras said, "I understand *that*. Do you think for a moment I'd be studying medicine if the Governor had not decreed it?"

"But I thought you wanted to be a doctor," I said, surprised by his remark. "Or at least didn't mind."

"Better than a parson!" Ras exclaimed. I'm certain he was as relieved as I when the talk moved on to other subjects.

Ras accompanied us to Dover and saw us off for France. I was wretchedly seasick for most of the crossing but recovered rapidly once on dry land. Uncle Jos, Caroline, and I arrived in Paris the next day.

My imagination could never have conjured up a city as beautiful as Paris, and yet it was lost on me. I could think only about Woodhouse. A stroll down the

Champs-Élysées put me in mind of the dramatic approach to the Owen mansion, and the Bois de Boulogne paled in comparison to the wooded parklands of "the Forest." The magnificent works of art in the Louvre filled my mind with visions of Fanny Owen.

After ten days Uncle Jos prepared to continue our journey to Geneva, and I abruptly announced my intention to return to England. The decision stunned my two companions. "But why on earth, Charley?" asked a bewildered Caroline.

I had an excuse ready. "I find it impossible to concentrate on Latin and Greek as I promised Father I would. I must get home and buckle down to serious study."

I'm not sure if either of them believed such an outrageous story, but I stuck with it doggedly. "Fanny and Emma are sure to be disappointed," Caroline said.

"Please give them my sincerest apologies," I said. "Tell them I'll visit them at Maer in autumn."

The next day I boarded a coach for Calais, made the crossing with a minimum of discomfort, sent a note to Miss Fanny Owen, and proceeded straightaway to Shrewsbury. Rattling along in the coach towards home, I wondered if I had made a foolish decision. Here was my first chance to see something of the world, and I'd turned my back on it because I fancied a pretty girl. *Too late now,* I told myself; *I'll have other chances to see the Continent.*

Susan and Catty were surprised to see me and accepted my excuses with scepticism, especially as two days later I stuffed some clothes into my saddlebags and prepared to ride to Woodhouse. Before I left, Susan said, "You've heard the gossip, haven't you? The talk about Sally? And Fanny as well? No? Well, of course you wouldn't have, away all those months in Edinburgh, though I thought Caroline might have mentioned it."

"Then tell me, please," I said.

"Poor Sally has had an especially difficult time of it this year. She believed she was *this* close to an engagement to Robert Biddulph, but nothing came of it. He's dashing and handsome and rich and all that, but a cad, no doubt of it. And so Sally is recovering from her disappointment."

I thought of the gossipy letters Sally had written me, never mentioning a word of this. "And what about Fanny?" I asked stiffly, dreading what I might hear.

"Oh, *Fanny!*" said Susan, with a little laugh. "We all thought surely she would announce her engagement to her cousin John Hill by now, but she hasn't."

John Hill? I'd gone shooting with him on my last visit to Woodhouse, when he and the others had played their joke on me, and Fanny had flirtatiously led me out into the fresh air. I'd not had the slightest notion then of anything between them.

"Hill's behaviour has been extremely coldhearted," Susan went on. "He says one thing and does another, according to Sally, and so the whole thing may be off as well. I don't know in what spirit Fanny is taking it, though I do believe she's better off without him. Such a ridiculous thing, both Owen girls treated so cruelly by their suitors." She smiled ruefully. "But at least the Owen girls *have* suitors, even if both Biddulph and Hill are monstrous blackguards."

I rode off for Woodhouse wondering why this was the first I'd heard of Fanny's suitor. I wondered, too, how she would behave towards me this time, and how I would behave towards *her*.

WOODHOUSE WAS in an uproar when I arrived, everyone in a terrific rush to prepare for William Owen's party. Workmen were putting finishing touches on a pavilion erected at the far end of the gardens, and servants scurried about, arranging masses of potted plants and torches to be lighted as darkness fell. I looked for Fanny, but no one seemed to know where she was.

Her younger sister, Caro, came to my rescue. "She's picking strawberries," said the little girl. "Shall I help you find her?" I followed Caro into the walled garden. "There she is!" the child piped.

Fanny smiled up at me from beneath the brim of a straw bonnet. "Hello, Charley," she said. She selected a berry from her basket and offered it temptingly.

I reached for it, but she snatched it away. "Uh-uh," she said. "Just open wide!" She popped the strawberry into my mouth and another into her own. "Delicious, isn't it?"

I nodded, my mouth full.

"Let me help you," I said. I picked a few berries and dropped them into her basket. I wanted to feed one to her, but I wasn't bold enough to try.

"I haven't seen you in simply ages," she complained,

brushing at a red stain on her light-coloured dress. "What have you been doing? Chasing beetles, I'll wager!"

"Thinking of you, Fanny," I replied honestly.

"Really? Then come sit with me and let's have a chat." She settled in the shade of a large yew, leaned against the trunk, and stretched out her legs. I sat beside her, as close as I dared. "I've thought of you, too, Charley," she said. "Now tell me everything you've done since I last saw you."

I told her about my trip to Paris, and several times came close to asking her about John Hill, but it seemed a doltish question if there was no engagement. Surely, I thought, she would tell me if there was.

But Fanny made no mention of Hill, and so we idled away the time, lounging under the tree and gorging on strawberries in a manner that would have surely shocked my sisters. Pure enchantment, I thought. Then Fanny called an end to it and scrambled to her feet.

"We must dress for the evening," she said. "And look! We've eaten nearly the whole basketful. What beasts we've made of ourselves!"

IT SEEMED HALF of Shropshire had been invited to the party. Servants carried round an endless supply of food and drink, the music never stopped, and a troupe of acrobats and jugglers moved through the crowd. But I could not take my eyes off Fanny. Her golden hair was piled high, and she wore a gown of blue and ivory silk that brought out the colour of her eyes and was cut in such a way that showed off her plump bosom.

As I watched her, my eighteen-year-old heart beat with a fervour I'd never experienced. However, I had to be content to stand to the side as one smartly dressed young man after another stepped forward to claim her and guide her through the steps of dances that were a complete mystery to me. I would not be amongst Fanny's partners. I'd never learnt to dance well, I felt ill at ease, and I hated the whole idea. I tried to affect an expression of amused indifference.

Presently her brother William joined me, and we chatted about familiar subjects: birds and dogs and guns. The torches were lighted. Fanny was still dancing — not with John Hill, who was amongst those present but whose interest seemed centred on the punch bowl. Now her partner was a tall, dashing fellow with fair hair and luxuriant side-whiskers. She caught my eye and fluttered her fingertips in a way her dancing partner couldn't observe. My hopes soared.

"I say, Owen, who's that dancing with Fanny?" I asked her brother in the most casual manner I could muster.

"Robert Biddulph," he said. "I'm surprised to see him here, to be frank. We thought he was going to marry Sally, but he threw her over, and I'm glad, for he's something of a blackguard — gambling debts and all that. His father is in Parliament from Denbighshire — calls Chirk Castle his home when he's not at his London mansion."

I regretted ever accepting Fanny's invitation to this party. Her brother wandered off, and I began to think I might simply get on my horse and ride back to Shrewsbury. There was a bright moon, and the ride would be quite pleasant — better than staying here and watching Fanny dance and flirt with one "shootable" after another.

Then a miracle occurred: Fanny swept up and, standing on tiptoe, murmured close to my ear, "Come, dear Charley, let's run away."

I thought I'd misunderstood. "I'm so sorry, Fanny, but I don't dance, you see, and it would be horribly embarrassing —"

Fanny cut me off with a sharp little frown and a toss of her shining curls. Catching me by the hand, she instructed, "Do what I do, and we'll be away from here in a moment."

Clumsily I imitated her. In seconds we had slipped beyond the yellow glow of torchlight.

This time I knew — more or less — what to do. I took Fanny in my arms and kissed her. The whalebone stays of her corset were stiff and unyielding under my trembling hands. After one more kiss Fanny pushed me away, gently but firmly. "We must go back," she said. "Papa will notice I'm missing."

"I could wait for you here, Fanny," I proposed hopefully.

She dismissed my suggestion with a laugh. "Don't be silly, Charley!" she trilled, and darted away.

The party dragged on interminably. I felt stupidly jealous of every man who danced with Fanny, especially the fair-haired Biddulph. Eventually, though, the servants stopped offering round food and drink, the musicians put away their instruments, and yawning guests — save for those who would spend the night — began to drift away. I stumbled up the great staircase to the west gallery and the monkish bedroom I would share with another guest, a fellow named Edward Williams.

"A word to the wise," said Williams, tugging off his boots. "Squire Owen has a little trick he likes to play on his male guests. He calls the rooms off the east gallery 'Paradise' — that's where the girls sleep. But in the event that some gentleman might be tempted to pay a night-time visit to one of them, the squire lays a trap, pots and pans randomly placed all along the corridor. Any man foolish enough to think he can sneak through to Paradise is bound to set off a great clatter and give himself away."

"Has it happened to you?" I asked, snuffing out the candle. I was tired but not yet ready to sleep, too achingly aware of lovely Fanny lying amongst delicate laces and silk pillows somewhere beyond the gauntlet of kitchen pots.

"Not I," Williams said, and in minutes he was snoring lightly.

Soon fatigue overtook me as well. I was deep in a dream when a terrible clatter, followed by a string of muttered oaths, brought us bolt upright.

"Someone's caught in the squire's trap!" Williams cried gleefully, leaping out of bed and making for the door. I followed close behind.

Williams opened the door cautiously and motioned to me to have a look. Up and down the corridor heads poked out of doorways to witness Squire Owen sprawled in his nightshirt amongst the scattered vessels. He had set off his own alarm. "Forgot about the blasted things," the squire muttered. Williams and I helped him to his feet. He tottered back to his bed and we to ours, and the next morning not a word was said about events of the night before.

For the next few days I remained at Woodhouse, circling round and round the enchantress without ever again coming close. Fanny smiled and flirted whenever she saw me, but she was always surrounded by friends and admirers, and it was impossible to find her alone. Finally I abandoned the hope of another private conversation, let alone more kisses, and rode back to The Mount. There Mr. Graham waited with his arsenal of declensions and conjugations.

WHENEVER I COULD ESCAPE my tutor and Father's incessant questions about my progress or lack of it, I fled from Shrewsbury. Early in August, after Caroline had returned from the Continent with Uncle Jos and the Doveleys, I rode to Maer for "the glorious twelfth" and the first days of grouse shooting. In the evenings we sat on the steps of the portico opposite a steep wooded bank reflected in the pool. Here and there a fish rose or a waterbird paddled about. There was much agreeable conversation on interesting subjects, and when we went indoors Emma often played on the pianoforte whilst her sisters sang. I called it "Bliss Castle" and relished its peacefulness.

Emma had not entirely forgiven me for my failure to come along with Caroline and Uncle Jos to fetch them home from Switzerland. "It was cruel of you to disappoint us, Charley. We did so look forward to having you with us in Geneva. We talked of you often as we travelled through Germany, and Holland, too. Fanny was always saying, 'Wouldn't Charley enjoy this!'"

I doubt either of them believed my excuse that I had to study.

I was drawn to Woodhouse — "the Forest" — for quite different reasons than the easy comforts of Maer, and only a week later I rode there again. The Owen household could not be described as peaceful, or even orderly. One never knew quite what to expect. The uproar seemed normal. Squire Owen was an enthusiastic teller of stories, often repeating the same ones several times over. I listened patiently to oft-told tales of his military campaigns in Flanders some thirty-five years earlier, remained alert for any mention of John Hill — there was none — and hung about like an eager puppy for the scraps of attention that Fanny Owen dispensed frugally. It seemed all a great game to Fanny, though I took it more seriously. At times I doubted she cared for me at all; other times I believed she did.

One afternoon towards the end of summer I persuaded her to go out walking with me. As we rested by a meandering stream in dappled sunlight, I was wondering for perhaps the hundredth time if I dared kiss her when suddenly Fanny kicked off her shoes, rolled down her stockings and garters, hoisted her skirts above her knees, and stepped into the water. When she scooped up a handful of water and tossed it at me, I plunged in after her. There was a great deal of shrieking and splashing, but still I did not manage to kiss her.

The next morning I went out shooting with the squire and two of Fanny's brothers. At the end of the day as we stood talking beneath a large oak, Fanny joined us. Soon tired of masculine conversation, she impetuously picked up my gun and announced she meant to fire it.

We were all shocked. Women did not *shoot;* it was a man's sport, at least in part because of the shotgun's powerful recoil.

"Fanny, put down that gun," her father ordered.

"I will, Papa," she said, smiling sweetly at him, "as soon as I've got off a shot."

How charming she looked, tossing her head and determinedly sighting along the barrel! "Fanny, pray, I beg you not to fire," I pleaded. "It will surely do you injury." *What a headstrong girl!* I thought, not for the first time.

She gave me a stubborn smile, took aim, and squeezed the trigger. The shot blasted through the tree, tearing down twigs and leaves, and the recoil staggered her backwards.

"There," she said, handing me my gun. Tears glinted in her eyes, but she managed a triumphant smile. "I wanted to show you I could do it."

Fanny walked away proudly, her head high. I gazed after her, caught fast in her bewitching spell.

Chapter 9

Cambridge: 1828

THE STAGECOACH RUMBLED out of Shrewsbury bound for Cambridge. I was a month shy of my nineteenth birthday, over six feet tall, strong, in good health, and Catty had assured me that I was "handsome enough."

"Enough for what?" I'd asked.

"Breaking hearts, dear Charley," she said, laughing.

"Even with this nose?" I still thought it too large for my face.

She'd studied me critically. "You've grown into it," she assured me.

My quarters beyond the Great Gate of Christ's College included a sitting room with dark wood panelling and deep window seats, decently furnished with two wing chairs and a table before the fire, a large desk, and a grandfather's clock that struck the quarter hour. A servant looked after me and others living on our stair.

My first visitor was Ras, who stayed for two weeks whilst sitting for his medical exams. He looked weary, with dark circles under his eyes, and I observed that he was taking a number of medications prescribed by Father.

"Are they helping?" I asked.

He smiled wanly. "It helps the Governor to think so," he said.

Before he returned to London, Ras made sure I'd found companions. Hensleigh Wedgwood, elder brother of the Doveleys and always a good friend of Ras's, was also studying at Christ's. "I don't think there's the slightest possibility Ras is going to become a doctor," Hensleigh said after Ras had left. "He's just going through the motions, because it's what your father wants, but he plainly hasn't the vigour for it."

"But what will he do instead?" I asked.

"Probably nothing, if he's given the choice. He's better suited to idleness than most."

"Father won't allow it," I said. "He wants us to live useful lives."

"The doctor is well aware of Ras's lack of strength," Hensleigh replied.

Old Price, a great friend at Shrewsbury School, was at nearby St. John's College, preparing for Holy Orders; Cameron and Watkins also turned up at St. John's. Then I discovered William Darwin Fox, son of my father's cousin. We became inseparable.

"How much alike we are!" I marvelled on my first visit to Fox's rooms, crowded with all sorts of interesting items: stuffed mammals, newly hatched birds, assorted plants both alive and growing or dead and drying. I noted approvingly that the place was a mess.

We were alike in other important ways. Fox, too, was enthusiastic about shooting and dogs; he kept two in his rooms, Fan and Sappho. I regretted not bringing Mr. Dash, the dog I'd been training during the months I'd spent at home.

I was still inclined to do as little work as possible. My days began with lectures and tutorials in theology and moral philosophy, followed by a hearty breakfast in Fox's rooms. With nothing more required but a mercifully brief daily chapel service before dinner, I finished off with an evening of indolence. I saw no reason to bother with any serious studying till examinations made it absolutely unavoidable. That left plenty of time for reading, engaging in good conversation, taking interesting walks, and collecting with Fox as my willing partner in all of these enjoyable pursuits.

Since I was a young boy I'd collected beetles, but now entomology — the study of insects — became a true passion. I was always ready to drop everything and go searching for some new specimen, tearing the bark off dead trees, digging into piles of rotting leaves, and poking round stumps and logs and neglected fence posts in search of my quarry.

One day I discovered two rare beetles and seized one in each hand. Then I spotted a third kind, which I couldn't bear to lose. Without thinking, I popped the one in my right hand into my mouth, in order to grab the third. Alas, the unfortunate creature ejected some intensely acrid fluid, which burnt my tongue, so that I was forced to spit the beetle out. Only the first one I'd captured made it into the tin box and was carried safely back to my rooms to be pinned onto a board for further study and identification.

Fox and I accumulated so much equipment for our collecting trips — nets and jars and tins and an array of proper clothing, flannel breeches, canvas gaiters, stout boots, hats . . . the list goes on — that we hired a guide to help lug it all from place to place. We carried long jumping poles for vaulting across ditches. My pole once stuck fast in the muddy bottom and left me swinging at the top. I slid down and ploughed on, covered with mud and ignoring Fox's laughter.

Second to bagging beetles, my great passion was shooting. To improve my aim, I'd stand in front of the looking glass in my rooms and throw the gun up to my shoulder, making sure I was bringing it up straight. I persuaded Fox to hold a lighted candle and wave it round whilst I fired at it with a cap. If my aim was accurate, the puff of air blew out the candle. I'd been a good shot before; now I was *very* good.

Though Fox was three years older and had only a few months till he'd finish up his studies, we became the closest of friends. He reminded me of Ras, but more easygoing. There was scarcely anything we couldn't talk about. Fox awakened my interest in music, and together we sought out concerts, especially choral music, in the chapels of the various colleges that made up the university. He also had a taste for fine art. I'd paid scant attention to the gloomy paintings on the walls of The Mount, but when Fox proposed a visit to the Fitzwilliam Museum with its vast private collection, I went along.

"There is a painting you absolutely must see," Fox said as we entered the Fitzwilliam through the Greek portico. "*Venus* by Titian, the sixteenth-century Italian artist."

He led the way into a hall where one of the paintings was concealed behind a velvet curtain. He pulled a cord and the curtains parted, revealing a reclining nude wearing only a bracelet and a ring on her little finger. Her curly hair cascaded over her creamy white shoulders. She seemed to be gazing straight at me.

I had never seen a naked woman, and I was amazed that such beautiful flesh could be hidden beneath tight corsets and stiff whalebone stays and thick layers of cloth that encased the body of every girl I knew. The painting brought back the vivid memory of a summer afternoon by a stream with Fanny Owen peeling off her stockings, revealing her dimpled knees. I felt a little light-headed.

"What's the matter, old man?" Fox asked, grinning. "Is she a bit too much for you?"

"I was just wondering," I answered, "if we shall be able to find the likes of this girl who will agree to become the wife of a country clergyman and bring such a warm glow to the parsonage."

"Actually, I was admiring that little dog lying curled at Madame's feet," Fox said, squinting at the painting. "I should like to have such a pup in my parsonage, wouldn't you?"

He yanked the cord, and the velvet curtains swished shut. I made up my mind that I'd come back — alone — to gaze again at Venus. But at the moment all I could think about were the dimples on Fanny Owen's lovely knees.

"COME ALONG with me, Darwin," Fox said when I'd been at Cambridge for little more than a month. "I've someone I think you should meet — John Stevens Henslow, professor of botany. Every Friday evening a dozen or so students and intellectuals gather at his home to talk, and his pretty wife serves tea."

I'd already heard about Professor Henslow from Ras, who'd described him as a man knowledgeable about every branch of science. I liked him immediately, a soft-spoken man with a ready smile and silvery threads showing at his temples. That first Friday evening led to many more — whole evenings of talking about nothing but science!

At one of those evenings I met Adam Sedgwick, a bluff and good-humoured professor of geology. I enjoyed our conversations, though memories of mind-numbing lectures in geology at Edinburgh made me wary, and I avoided signing up for his course or even attending his presentations. Instead, I read the books he recommended and accepted his invitation to join a group inspecting rock formations in the countryside round Cambridge.

"I cannot promise to teach you all geology," Sedgwick told us when our horde of mud-spattered horsemen stopped at an inn for a merry dinner. "I can only fire your imaginations." In that he was successful.

I did enroll in Professor Henslow's botany course. He was a fascinating lecturer, and his field trips were incomparable. He hired coaches to take his students to a heath west of Cambridge in search of a pretty little toad called a natterjack. We floated on a barge down the River Cam to Ely, and after collecting a number of specimens, retired to an inn for an evening of hearty eating, drinking, and singing. I enjoyed these outings, but most of all I benefitted from the long walks and the quiet dinners alone with my new mentor. I became known as "the man who walks with Henslow."

Whilst I walked and talked with scientists and peered into a microscope, attempting to learn the secrets of the plant kingdom, I was also enrolled in the courses required to become an Anglican clergyman. That both Henslow and Sedgwick had also taken Holy Orders eased my mind. Perhaps one day I would have a life like theirs. That would surely please Father.

From Adam Sedgwick, the geologist, I began to see no reason for science and religion to lie at opposite poles. "The one explains the other," Sedgwick said. Unlike my atheist grandfather, I maintained a steadfast belief in God as creator of the universe, though I continued to have uneasy questions about my own personal beliefs. I wasn't sure I could declare my unwavering belief in the Thirty-Nine Articles of the Faith in order to receive my degree.

Article Nine, on original sin, always bothered me — that every newborn babe is a sinner and only baptism can wash away the sin. How could Henslow look at his children and believe they were sinners until the moment a clergyman poured water on their tiny heads? And at what age was a child actually capable of sin? Guiltily, I remembered an incident when I was a very little boy — too young as yet for Mr. Case's day school — and I acted very cruelly: I beat a puppy, simply to enjoy the sense of power it gave me. Though I couldn't have beaten it severely, for it did not howl, the act lay heavily on my conscience ever afterwards. And thus did my sense of sin have its beginning. But surely not *before* my birth!

When I mentioned my inner conflict to Henslow, he bowed his head and solemnly and replied, "Darwin, if so much as a single word of the Thirty-Nine Articles were altered, I should be grieved. And that includes Article Nine."

His firm declaration shook me. Given my friend's deeply held faith, I said no more, hoping I'd be certain of the answer when the day came.

I CONTINUED TO WASTE my time. I couldn't blame it on Fox; he had finished his studies in June and gone home to Osmaston in Derbyshire. We'd promised to write and kept our promise faithfully by exchanging so many letters it almost seemed as if he were still there and we were still tucking into gargantuan breakfasts every morning in his rooms.

That same year Ras decided to give up medicine, and Father, concerned about my brother's delicate constitution, agreed to permit it. Granted a handsome allowance, Ras would live in London and spend his time as he wished. Having always been almost painfully frugal with us, Father had suddenly and inexplicably swung the other way. I, too, was the grateful recipient of a generous allowance and could afford to live at university as a gentleman. But I did not believe Father would cut me loose to do entirely as I wished. I'm not sure I really wanted that, since I didn't know *what* I wished!

Aside from my studies, which with few exceptions didn't interest me, I was happy at Cambridge. I kept a hunting horse as well as a dog. An old Shrewsbury School chum, Charles Whitley, and his cousin John Maurice Herbert became close friends who shared my enthusiasms. Those two were quite willing to spend hours turning over rocks in search of a rare beetle.

Herbert, whom I nicknamed Cherbury for no very good reason, was one of the founding members of a group we called the Glutton Club. We Gluttons took supper together once a week and prided ourselves on *not* being like a certain group of men whose overly refined tastes we mocked. We ordered our cook to prepare dishes that any sensible person would avoid: a bittern I'd shot in a marsh, for instance, and a hawk, both of which were tough and disagreeable even after a good soaking in wine. Whitley showed up with an old brown owl, scarcely recognisable once the creature had been plucked and roasted. The Gluttons gathered round the table in Herbert's rooms, staring down at the owl laid out on a platter, naked and undignified in its final state, though the cook had done her best to dress it up with some boiled prunes. We raised our glasses and toasted the owl in Latin and then in Greek — my months of tutoring at last proving useful — and waited to see who would be the first to sample it.

"Since you're hosting the affair in your rooms, Cherbury," I said, "you must have the honour of the first taste."

"The deuce take you, Darwin," Herbert muttered, but he stepped forward, sliced off a bit of sinewy meat, and began to chew. He paused, chewed, paused again, and finally spat out the mouthful. "Indescribable," he said.

No one else had the courage to try. Fortunately, Herbert had had the foresight to arrange for the cook to keep a joint of mutton roasted and ready.

Shortly before the end of the term I received a gift from an anonymous donor — a magnificent microscope, vastly superior to any scientific instrument I had ever owned. I thought my benefactor must be Ras. Who else had such faith in my abilities? Only later did I discover that the microscope was a gift from Herbert. Cherbury had outdone himself, and I could not have been more grateful.

WHEN HOLIDAYS CAME ROUND, I made the trip back to Shrewsbury to resume riding and shooting and fox hunting, with visits to Maer, where intelligent conversation, music, and dining well were as much part of life as shooting. I was fond of the Wedgwoods, nearly as fond of them as I was of my own family, and enjoyed an especially close relationship with Uncle Jos. But I had no idea my sisters had the notion of doing some matchmaking on my behalf till Susan introduced the subject.

"Have you ever considered," she began, "that our cousin Fanny Wedgwood might make you an excellent wife?"

I stared at my sister, astonished. "No, I had not considered that," I admitted.

"Well, you should, Charley. Little Miss Memorandum is just as keen as you are on making lists, keeping track of all sorts of things. And she's quite devout, as befits the wife of a clergyman."

"Fanny is very nice, of course," I said, wishing to put an end to the conversation.

But Susan wasn't nearly finished with it. "And we've been thinking of Ras, too," she said. "Wouldn't Emma be absolutely ideal for him? Just think how Ras adores music, and so does Emma. They're both passionate about Paganini. So we were just saying — Caroline and Catty and I — how perfect it would be if he were to marry Emma and you to marry Fanny."

"Susan, I'm not thinking of marrying anyone!" I protested, and left Susan with her plans of matrimony for everyone but herself.

True, I wasn't thinking of marriage, but I was certainly thinking of Fanny Owen, who like a rare butterfly was always fluttering just out of reach of my net. Fanny wrote to me irregularly, usually from some place she was visiting — Exeter, Buxton, Bath. I savoured her coy, flirtatious letters, though they made me restless and dissatisfied.

We are very dissipated here, at a Ball or party almost every night, which as you may suppose I find not bad sport in its way, but all must come to an end and I fear we shall be dragg'd away to the shades of the Forest and leave Brighton in the higths of its gaiety.

On she scribbled in her eccentric spelling and untidy handwriting, referring to herself as "the Housemaid" and to me as "the Postillion," and ending with the warning, *Burn this as soon as read — or tremble at my fury and revenge!*

Whilst Fanny danced and flirted, I was immersed in other pursuits. Sometimes I didn't bother going home for holidays, and then Fanny expressed her displeasure: *I fully expected to see you, but I suppose some dear little Beetles in Cambridge or London kept you away.*

Fanny, Fanny! Was this a girl who might marry a country parson? Would I one day be able to capture this elusive creature and make her my wife?

I didn't know. And I had no idea how or when to find out.

<hr />

EARLY IN MY LAST term at Cambridge, beginning in the bleak winter of 1831, I discovered the journal of Alexander von Humboldt, recounting his five-year journey into the jungles of Brazil. It reminded me of stories John Edmonstone, the taxidermist, had told me of Charles Waterton in the jungles of Guiana. From then on, I dreamt constantly of travel. These were no longer the romantic fantasies of faraway places I had as a boy reading *Robinson Crusoe*. Now I wanted to explore and to discover.

"I've been reading about Teneriffe, and I can't get it out of my mind," I said to Henslow on one of our long walks. "I'd like to organise a natural history expedition to the Canary Islands. What do you think?"

Henslow allowed it was a capital idea, but an expensive one. He'd like to go, too, he said. "But I simply don't see how I can manage, with a wife and family and responsibilities." Henslow was thirty-five; his wife was expecting another child. I was just twenty-two.

I tried out the notion on Fox when I visited him in Derbyshire. "I've almost hatched this scheme," I told him. "I've been wishing for some time to see tropical scenery and vegetation. Teneriffe is a very pretty specimen, if one can believe what one reads." I read aloud some of the most enticing sections of Humboldt's book whilst Fox listened, head cocked to one side.

"And how do you intend to present this wonderful idea to Dr. Darwin?" he asked sensibly.

"Ras has been wandering all over the Continent since he finished his medical training, and now he proposes to live in Paris for a year! Father will no doubt allow it and give him the money to do it. How can he then refuse me the perfectly reasonable request to make a brief scientific tour to the Canaries?"

"I doubt he could," Fox agreed.

"I cannot wait to see the great dragon tree, and the sandy plains, and the gloomy, silent forest. Do think of coming with me! I'm still working on Henslow. I haven't given up on him just yet."

"Maybe you should learn some Spanish before you go," Fox suggested.

"I've already begun," I announced triumphantly. I was indeed spending hours beneath a palm tree in the botanic garden at Cambridge with a Spanish book open on my lap, my mind already in the islands.

Henslow reminded me that, even more than chattering badly in Spanish, I needed to become fluent in mineralogy. "You'll surely encounter volcanoes, Darwin, and there is much to be learnt about the island's volcanic beginnings."

I took his advice and began to cram geology, as I once had Latin and Greek. But my plan to leave in July after the end of the term was scuttled when I enquired about passage to Teneriffe and was told that ships sailed for the Canary Islands only in June. I would have to postpone my dream for a year and accepted the disappointment as an opportunity for more preparation.

Meanwhile, I promised Father I would return to Cambridge in autumn to begin reading for Holy Orders.

BY SUMMER I'd begun to think of speaking seriously to Fanny Owen. Despite my protests to my sister, marriage *was* on my mind — not as an immediate action, but as a promise, once I'd finished my studies, taken Holy Orders, and been given a parish somewhere. I was fairly certain Squire Owen would find me an acceptable son-in-law, but I was not at all certain Fanny would have me. I decided to risk it.

One hot day in July I rode to Woodhouse. The squire greeted me cordially, but I was both disappointed and relieved to learn that Fanny and Sally were visiting their cousins in Exeter. Jealously certain she was flirting with a whole range of "shootables," I rode home again. There I found a note from Professor Sedgwick, proposing that I accompany him on a geologising excursion to North Wales. "It will help you on your expedition to Teneriffe," he promised.

I accepted his invitation. Perhaps the time would be right to speak to Fanny when I returned from Wales. I resolved to ask her then.

Chapter 10

Invitation: 1831

WITH THE NEWS that Professor Sedgwick would spend the night at The Mount before we left for North Wales and that, by the bye, the geologist was a bachelor, my sisters' excitement reached an unaccustomed pitch.

"How wonderful!" Caroline exclaimed. "This is the first time you've brought us a visitor, Charley. And an esteemed professor!" She began to plan what Cook should prepare. "Something more interesting than the usual boiled beef," she decided. "We could even have a pudding with the tea."

"I wish you'd given us more warning, Charley," Susan said peevishly. "I might have had a new gown. As it is, there's barely even time to see the hairdresser."

"I'm sure it won't make the slightest difference to Sedgwick," I said. "He's a Yorkshireman and rather crusty, as one gets from spending so much time amongst the rocks."

"Poor Susan," Catty whispered later. "It's so unfair! She's twenty-eight, and she never meets any gentlemen.

She was so hoping our cousin Harry would show an interest, but I think we can cross him off. The Owen girls' mother takes them everywhere, and Sally is only two years younger than Susan and has had more suitors than I can count — and now I hear she's thinking of marrying that nice Edward Williams. Susan is afraid she'll be left on the shelf. It would be so good of you to bring home suitable men for her to meet."

I was pleased to hear about Sally and Williams, an agreeable chap with whom I'd shared a room the night Squire Owen was caught in his own noisy trap. But it hadn't occurred to me that one of my responsibilities was to find husbands for my sisters. "What about Ras?" I asked. "Hasn't he brought home any interesting friends?"

"Oh, *Ras!*" Susan said dismissively. "He's hopeless, even worse than you."

That was not to be construed as a compliment.

Until then I confess I had given little thought to the plight of my sisters. In a moment of clarity I realised that without a mother to see to their marriage prospects my three unmarried sisters might well be "left on the shelf." Mrs. Owen made sure her daughters were introduced to "shootables" once they were out in society. Aunt Bessy saw that her daughters were sent to boarding school in London and to visit their aunts, all for the sake of broadening their possibilities. But it seemed to have fallen to the Darwin sisterhood's feckless brothers to turn up some eligible men — or to watch all but Marianne, now Mrs. Parker, wither into spinsterhood.

*   *   *

SEDGWICK'S PROJECT was to examine the national geological map compiled a dozen years earlier; he thought it contained critical errors. I was to assist him in investigating an area in the Vale of Clwyd, a river valley running from the medieval town of Ruthin to the northern coast. So as not to waste a minute of the opportunity I'd been given to learn a great deal about geologising, I purchased a copy of the geological map of North Wales and began to study it.

Adam Sedgwick drove up in his gig at the beginning of August. He was in his middle forties, tall and strongly built with unruly dark hair, expressive dark eyes, and a generous mouth that laughed easily. He made a very favourable impression on my sisters — especially Susan.

Susan had managed a visit to the hairdresser, and she wore her best gown with the wide lace collar, usually saved for Christmas at Maer and other special occasions. Too bad there were so few special occasions, I thought, for the dark blue velvet did flatter her somewhat sallow complexion. Throughout the meal Susan plied Sedgwick with intelligent questions about his work and was obviously unwilling to let the man leave the table. Eventually she had to allow him to retire, though I had visions of her lying in wait for him early next morning at breakfast. I wished her success; I would not have minded having such a man of science as a brother-in-law.

Sedgwick and I disentangled ourselves from my family soon after sunrise and trotted off in the gig, taking the road to Oswestry and passing near Woodhouse on the way. Had I been able to think of a reason to stop there, I would surely have suggested it. Throughout most of the long drive we talked about fossils, and that helped steer my thoughts away from Fanny.

We left the gig at an inn near our destination and set out on foot. Sedgwick showed me how to recognise rock formations, take measurements, and make drawings before sending me off alone to look for a certain kind of red sandstone marked on the geological map. I spent the day searching but found no evidence of it. Was I making a mistake? I wasn't sure. That evening, as agreed, we met at the inn and I reported my findings — or lack of them. I was afraid I'd failed, but the professor seemed pleased.

"As a result of your work, Darwin, major changes will have to be made in the map."

When our investigations were finished, we went our separate ways. There had been no mention of Susan. With compass, map, and knapsack I walked in a straight line across the mountains to the seaside town of Barmouth, where I joined Herbert and other university friends who had gathered, supposedly to cram mathematics. Promising to see them in a month's time at Cambridge, I travelled home to Shrewsbury by coach and prepared to go at once to Maer for the first days of partridge shooting with Uncle Jos. I should have thought myself mad to give up shooting for geology or any other science.

THESE INTERESTING TRAVELS and pleasant activities helped keep at bay the reality that I would shortly return to university. Then the hard work would begin — not the scientific studies that preoccupied me, but the preparation for Holy Orders and my life work as a parson. My family — father, sisters, cousins, everyone but Ras — already imagined me in a pretty country church surrounded by a plump little wife, numerous happy children, and loyal dogs. Uncle Jos said only, "Whatever brings you satisfaction, my boy." As I rode home from Maer on a hot morning at the end of August, I entertained myself with idle dreams of Fanny Owen. There was still time, I thought, for a visit to Woodhouse. I'd speak to her of a future together.

But when I reached The Mount, I found a letter waiting for me from Henslow. I greeted my sisters and hurried up to my bedroom, as eager to read Henslow's news as I was to avoid Susan's questions about Professor Sedgwick.

I have been asked to recommend a young man with an interest in science and natural history to sail on a surveying ship on a round-the-world voyage, Henslow wrote. The purpose of the voyage, commissioned by the British Admiralty and expected to last two years, was to chart the southern coastal areas of South America, where British colonies were a part of the expanding empire. There was particular interest in finding a sea passage from the Atlantic to the Pacific through the Americas by way of Tierra del Fuego. The captain, Robert FitzRoy, wanted a gentleman who was qualified for collecting and observing, but who would be a companion as well. There was no pay; the naturalist was expected to cover his own expenses. Henslow had recommended me. Me! The letter set my head spinning.

I could not have been more astonished at the idea of such an expedition. Henslow seemed to have no doubt I was the one for the job. I rushed downstairs. Father was not at home, but I called my sisters together.

"Sit down, please," I said, trembling with excitement. "Let me read you this letter from Henslow."

In short, there never was a finer chance for a man of zeal and spirit. I believe you are that man. I advise you to go straight to London and consult with the man at the Admiralty who has been asked to find the naturalist-companion most suitable to Captain FitzRoy. Do go at once.

My sisters listened quietly and were as bewildered as I. "But who is this Captain FitzRoy?" Susan asked sensibly. "And why does he want to invite a complete stranger to be his companion on such a long voyage?"

I had no answer, only more questions of my own.

"You were dreadfully seasick when we crossed the Channel to France," Caroline reminded me gently.

"One surely gets used to it," I argued, though I remembered my misery all too well. "Certainly all seamen are afflicted at first."

When Father came home and had settled into his accustomed chair, I handed him the letter. He read it quickly and reread it slowly. "He must be mad," Father said at last.

"The ship sails in just one month," I said. I was pacing agitatedly. "I must go to London at once, meet with this Captain FitzRoy, and begin making whatever preparations are necessary."

"Surely you're not planning to accept, Charles!" Father exclaimed.

"But of course I am. It would be lunacy to refuse such an opportunity."

"It would be lunacy to accept!" Father cried. "What do you know of conditions on a sailing ship — the filth, the disease, the danger of shipwreck? This is not your pleasant little junket to the tropics — it's a journey to the ends of the earth! I'll wager others have been offered the same opportunity, understood the problems, and wisely turned it down. You've read what Samuel Johnson had to say on the subject, haven't you? 'Being in a ship is being in a jail, with the chance of being drowned. A man in a jail has more room, better food, and commonly better company.'"

"I'm certain I could manage, Father," I said, though my enthusiasm was fading in the face of his arguments.

"It was my understanding that you had agreed to a life in the church. This wild scheme will most assuredly do nothing for your character as a future clergyman. Now you intend to throw it all over for an adventure that will ill prepare you for that life, an adventure you might not survive — and to pay your own way in the bargain!" Father heaved himself out of his chair. "I cannot give my blessing to this useless undertaking, Charles," he said, and left the room.

My sisters said nothing, though they looked distressed.

I went to my bedroom and continued to pace in a deepening gloom. Dinner was a silent affair. That night I sat down and wrote to Henslow: *My father does not decidedly refuse me, but he gives such strong advice against going that I must follow it.* I understood, too, that without Father's help, I would not be able to afford it.

Next I wrote to the Admiralty, turning down the offer with the greatest regret, and next morning I posted the two letters. Feeling sorely disappointed, I prepared to leave again for Maer to make some partridges pay dearly. A visit to Fanny at Woodhouse would have to wait till I was in a more positive frame of mind.

Father came out to the stable as I was saddling my horse. He watched for a moment, his manner subdued, and then said, "If you can find any man of common sense who advises you to go, I will give my consent."

I gaped at him, confused. What could he mean?

He drew a folded sheet from his waistcoat pocket. "Deliver this to your uncle." Without another word he turned and made his way slowly back to the house.

Uncle Jos, I thought; *he means Uncle Jos.* And away I flew to Maer, the letter in my pocket.

UNCLE JOS READ the letter.

Charles will tell you of the offer he has had made to him of going for a voyage of discovery for two years. I strongly object to it on various grounds, but I will not detail my reasons so that he may have your unbiased opinion on the subject. If you think differently from me I shall wish him to follow your advice.

From my arrival at Maer through dinner and supper and evening tea, the entire Wedgwood family discussed this remarkable development. My Wedgwood cousins found the offer thrilling. "What a grand adventure, Charley!" Hensleigh cried. Uncle Jos spoke largely in favour. When the rest of the family retired for the night, my uncle and I withdrew to his library to decide how to go about persuading Father.

Uncle Jos's approach consisted of three parts. First, I was to send a message to my father at once, assuring him that I would not go against his wishes. Secondly, I was to list all of Father's objections, which I did, so that, thirdly, Uncle Jos could respond honestly to each of them. We applied ourselves to these tasks till the letters were written and ready to be delivered to The Mount.

The next morning the groom left on his errand with our letters, and Uncle Jos and I went out shooting — it was, after all, the first day of partridge season. By mid-morning we had little to show for our efforts; our hearts were not in it, our minds were distracted, and I had only one lone bird in my game bag.

"Come, Charley," Uncle Jos said at last. "Let's drive to The Mount. I want to talk to Dr. Darwin myself."

As it turned out, my uncle's intervention was not needed. "I've changed my mind, my boy," my father said sombrely when we arrived at The Mount. "After you left, I had more time to think on the honour of the invitation the Admiralty has extended and the esteem in which your professor holds you. Then your uncle's letter arrived this morning together with yours. Upon further consideration, I am prepared to give you all the assistance in my power."

"Father!" I cried, clasping his hand and as close to tears as a man of twenty-two could allow himself to be.

There was no time to lose. I had already written to Henslow and his colleague at the Admiralty, refusing the invitation, and I'd posted those letters before Father had wavered and referred the matter to Uncle Jos. Now I wrote again, this time to tell them that things had been decided quite differently: *I should be most happy to have the honour of accepting the offer.*

But what if my earlier letter had already arrived, and this splendid opportunity had been offered to, and accepted by, someone else? I was probably not the only candidate. I must act hastily — leave for Cambridge at once to discuss the situation with Henslow, ask for his advice and letters of recommendation, then hurry on to London to speak to the man at the Admiralty and, most important, to meet Captain Robert FitzRoy.

What if FitzRoy doesn't like me? I thought, throwing articles of clothing into a bag. *What if he doesn't find me the kind of person he has in mind?*

It scarcely occurred to me that I might not like *him*.

There was no time to visit Woodhouse, but I made up my mind to call on Fanny once everything was settled. If FitzRoy and the Admiralty rejected me, I would suggest a two-year engagement, till I had finished my course of study and taken Holy Orders and found a small parish, perhaps somewhere in Shropshire. But if I were accepted for the expedition, would she be willing to accept a wait of two years till I returned from the voyage? Now the two-year engagement would likely stretch to four, including my studies — maybe even longer.

I boarded the next stagecoach to Cambridge. Gazing out the window at the early autumn countryside, I thought how delightful it would be to write letters to Fanny, describing my adventures on the ship, and have her letters waiting for me when we called at foreign ports! Hers would be affectionate and witty, no longer mentioning the ridiculous men who stepped on her toes and were no good at charades. She would tell me how much she missed me, how she longed for my return. She might even tell me that she loved me.

HENSLOW AND I were sitting in his library, indulging in our shared vice, a pinch of snuff, when Mrs. Henslow handed him a letter just arrived from the Admiralty. Henslow tore it open and read, then wordlessly passed it over to me. The gist of it was that FitzRoy thought he'd found the gentleman-naturalist-companion he'd been looking for, a certain Mr. Chester.

I handed it back, my hopes deflated. "I suppose that's the end of it," I sighed. But I only half believed the captain had found someone else. I felt horribly disappointed and ready to give it all up.

But Henslow talked me out of my gloom. "Go to London, Darwin," he said firmly. "Meet the captain face-to-face. It's not over yet."

I followed his advice. The next day I reached London

and contacted Captain FitzRoy. We arranged to dine at FitzRoy's club. I was as nervous as I had ever been in my life. The slightly built man with the long arched nose, thick lashes, and sensitive mouth who strode forth to greet me did little to put me at ease. He was too handsome, too elegantly dressed, his air too aristocratic. He was also quite young — just twenty-six. He put me in mind of Fanny Owen's "shootables."

We shook hands, took a table near a window, studied the menu longer than seemed necessary, and each ordered a plain meal. Then, as we began to talk, everything reversed itself. I found FitzRoy open and kind, his manner attractive as he came straight to the point about issues that concerned him: Would I be able to endure the rigours of the voyage?

"It is not without its dangers," FitzRoy warned. "We will face rough seas and horrendous storms. You will at times suffer from extreme heat and at other times extreme cold. You will sleep in a hammock and the diet, while generally healthful, will be far from meeting your usual standards. It's even possible that we will not be able to complete the circumnavigation of the world."

"Are you trying to dissuade me, Captain?" I asked.

"Not dissuade, Darwin — forewarn," he replied. "The greatest problem, to my way of thinking, is that we shall be living in extremely close quarters for very long periods of time. Can you bear being told that I want the cabin to myself when I want to be alone? If we treat each other this way, I hope we shall suit. If not, we shall probably wish each other gone to the devil."

But nothing he said — not the danger or the discomfort or the lack of privacy — dampened my enthusiasm.

By the end of the meal we wholly liked each other. Mr. Chester, whoever he was, was quickly forgotten, if he ever existed in the first place.

But still something stood in the way of winning the captain's complete and unqualified approval. "I must tell you in all candour, Darwin, there's one thing that puts me off about you."

"And what's that, sir?" I asked uneasily, fearing again that what had seemed to go so smoothly might now go up in smoke.

"Your nose, Darwin."

"My nose?

"I'm an ardent believer in phrenology, and I hold that a man's character is revealed nowhere so strongly as in his face. I doubt whether anyone with a broad, indelicate nose such as yours could possess sufficient energy and determination for the voyage."

Was it all to end here, because of my nose? FitzRoy seemed to be waiting for me to say something to ease his doubts, all because of my deuced nose. "Well, sir," I replied at last, "I can tell you that my nose has been known to tell the most outrageous lies about me."

FitzRoy stared at me for a moment. Then he threw back his head and laughed heartily, and offered to shake hands, and told me he no longer had any doubts whatever about my suitability. "Now, sir, I should like to introduce you to my ship."

A few days later we travelled by steam packet from

London to the dockyard in Plymouth where the ship was being refitted for the voyage. "There she is, Darwin," he said proudly. "HMS *Beagle*. We sail the fourth of November."

I gaped. I saw nothing but a complete wreck, barely the skeleton of the splendid sailing vessel I had imagined. She was quite small — only ninety feet long. I could scarcely utter a word as Captain FitzRoy pointed out the changes he had ordered to improve her. Her three masts and rotten planking had been stripped away, her upper decks were being raised to give more headroom, and an iron stove would replace the open fireplace in the galley. My future quarters in the poop cabin, aft of the main deck, looked impossibly small, and now I learnt this limited space would also serve as the chart room and must be shared with two others. I listened to all this in a daze. November 4th was just over a month away. I had much to do before then — if not as much as the shipbuilders. I left immediately for The Mount to begin.

MY SISTERS PROPOSED to make me all the shirts I could possibly use, and when I suggested that I could wear each one for days on end without washing, Caroline threw up her hands in horror. I needed sturdy boots, a good rifle and pistol, a compass, a barometer, a geological hammer, a telescope, pencils, notebooks, books on geology and botany, and an expensive portable dissecting microscope that I considered absolutely necessary — the list was very long. I spent several days in London with Ras, acquiring all that I could imagine I would need. Father paid the bills, though not without grumbling that he'd already had to make good on several of my debts in Cambridge.

All that was about to change, I promised my father. "I should be deuced clever to spend more than my allowance whilst at sea," I told him, and he shot back, "But they all tell me you are very clever, Charles."

Packing for the voyage was the easy part. Soon I would face the most difficult thing, saying good-bye to dear friends and family. My sisters for the most part had rallied round, putting on a brave face — all but Catty, my closest companion of early childhood, who took the prospect of our long separation very hard.

"Two years isn't such a very long time, Catty," I reasoned. "We've been separated for many months whilst I was in Edinburgh. And we'll write often — you've promised me that!"

"A lot can happen in two years," she said. Her eyes were red and swollen. "And it's not as though you can come home for a holiday whenever you please."

"Just don't marry some hot-blooded fool without my say-so," I said, attempting to make her laugh, or at least smile, but Catty burst into a fresh storm of weeping.

"Please don't joke!" she cried. "I'm afraid you'll be shipwrecked. Remember what happened to Robinson Crusoe!"

I'D MADE MY POOR joke about marrying because the subject was too much on my mind. Working up my courage, I rode to Woodhouse, besieged by memories: *Fanny, sprawled in the garden eating strawberries. Fanny, wading in the stream, her knees bare. Fanny, boldly firing my gun and bravely enduring the recoil.*

Fanny, dressed in shimmering beige stripes and lovelier than ever, called me "dear Charley" and stood on tiptoe to kiss my cheek, something she'd never done before. I was encouraged, but as usual, it was not easy to find a moment alone with her. Then Fanny herself proposed it. "No one's in Papa's library," she said, taking my hand and leading me there.

Painted the soothing green of moss, the room smelt pleasantly of leather and tobacco. Books bound in leather and stamped in gilt lined shelves reaching to the high ceiling. Fanny sat down on a bench covered in yellow silk and patted the place beside her, smiling up at me. I was too nervous to sit.

"Charley, I hear you're going away, and for a very long time. Is it true?"

"Yes, it's true — I'm to begin a voyage round the world as a naturalist on a scientific expedition. I leave in ten days. It's a wonderful —"

Fanny rose and placed her finger on my lips. "Hush," she said. "When are you coming back?"

"Captain FitzRoy plans to be gone for two years."

"Two years!" Her usually sunny expression clouded over. "And what after that?"

"After that?" I repeated. "Well, then I suppose I'll go back to Cambridge and continue my studies to become a clergyman. And I wanted to ask you . . ." My courage faltered and nearly failed. Fanny waited, lips parted, larkspur blue eyes fixed on mine as we stood facing each other. I reached for her hands. Hers were cool, mine were damp with sweat. My collar felt too tight. I drew a breath and plunged on. "Will you wait for me, dearest Fanny?"

"Dear Charley," she began, "my family thinks highly of you, and I know Papa would be pleased if I pledged myself to you. But your future is so — so *unclear!* How can I promise to wait, when I'm not sure what I'm to wait for?"

"But Fanny, do you care for me?"

"Of course, dear Charley! But I care for a future more settled than the one you describe." There was a painful pause, and she gently pulled her hands away. "I can't promise to wait for you."

There was nothing more to discuss. I was afraid if I now took her in my arms and kissed her, as I longed to do, my emotions would overcome me, and I would say or do something regrettable.

"I understand," I managed to mutter, and turned away to hide my disappointment. "Good-bye, Fanny."

Within minutes after that scene in the library at Woodhouse, I took my leave of Squire Owen and his wife. Fanny had disappeared. I rode swiftly back to Shrewsbury, trying to ignore the dull ache somewhere in the region of my heart.

PART II
Flycatcher

Chapter 11

HMS Beagle: 1831

I ENDURED one wrenching farewell after another. Uncle Jos thumped me on the back. Aunt Bessy kissed me and begged me to take good care. My cousins promised to write. Father gripped my hand hard. My sisters wept; Catty clung to me. I felt I had to pry myself away from all this emotion, lest my determination begin to crumble, but my excitement and desire to be under way carried me through.

Leaving Shrewsbury behind, I travelled by stage to London and stayed with Ras whilst attending to last-minute errands and purchases. I wrote to Fanny, a pitiful sort of letter expressing my hope that she would not have quite forgotten me when I came back. Days later I had a reply: *Wherever I may be and whatever changes may have happen'd, none there will ever be in my opinion of you — so do not, my dear Charles, talk of forgetting.*

Towards the end of October I presented myself to Captain FitzRoy in Plymouth and found another letter awaiting me from Fanny:

You cannot imagine how I have missed you already at the Forest and how I do long to see you again. I cannot bear to part with you for so long. What a steady old sober body you will find me when you return from your Savage Islands.

She sent along a little purse she had sweetly embroidered, with an attached note, *In remembrance of the Housemaid of the Black Forest.*

I folded that letter with the first and tucked both inside the purse, which I shoved into my pocket, and hoped the *Beagle* would get under way quickly.

READYING THE SHIP took much longer than FitzRoy anticipated. At mid-November the *Beagle* was still undergoing refitting. She now more nearly resembled the ship I had expected, and work was being completed on the interior. Provisions were being stocked for seventy-four people: captain, officers, seamen, and a handful of others, including three natives of Tierra del Fuego who'd been living in England for several years, a missionary returning with the Fuegians to set up a mission in their land, and an artist named Augustus Earle who would make drawings and paintings as a record of the voyage. All of us must somehow fit ourselves into that ninety-foot ship. My corner looked so small that I feared many of my things must be left behind.

The days dragged on. Lodged in a hotel with nothing to do but wait, wishing I had stayed in London with Ras, I began to worry, and with the worry came misgivings that the entire enterprise was a terrible mistake. I experienced heart palpitations and believed I might indeed be suffering from a serious condition. I thought of consulting a doctor. But what if he told me I was unfit for the voyage? I was resolved to go at all costs, mistake or no.

By the first week of December all was ready at last, but now the weather turned against us. On the 10th we weighed anchor. Winds sweeping up the English Channel were so strong we pitched and rolled unmercifully, and I took to my hammock so sick I could hardly lift my head. We could make no headway, and the captain ordered our ship turned round. The *Beagle* headed back to Plymouth to wait out the conditions. I staggered ashore to recover. Was it always going to be like this? How would I endure it?

This depressing state of affairs persisted for two more weeks. Ras came down from London and tried to cheer me, and we spent Christmas Day together, eating a forlorn dinner at a dreary inn near the port. Memories of previous Christmas feasts at Maer with the Wedgwoods dominated our conversation. "Remember the plum pudding blazing away, and Aunt Bessy always leading the applause?" I asked Ras as the waiter set down two small, dry portions. "There won't be anything like that on the *Beagle,* not even on the captain's table," I said, suddenly unable to swallow.

Ras gazed at me across the spotted linen cloth and made a steeple of his long fingers. "Charley, are you determined to go through with this? It's scarcely a pleasure cruise, and it strikes me as miserably uncomfortable and downright dangerous. It's not too late to change your mind."

"Yes, I'm determined," I replied stoutly. "It's the chance of a lifetime." That was a phrase I had repeated to myself many times during the nerve-wracking weeks.

The next day the weather began to clear. Boxing Day would have been a perfect day for sailing, but alas, the crew had gone ashore to celebrate the Christmas holiday and most hands were either drunk or missing. Not till the following day were they rounded up. Captain FitzRoy and I lunched ashore on mutton chops and champagne, and at two o'clock the afternoon of the 27th the *Beagle* set sail. My great adventure had begun, and I recorded the moment in my new journal. There was no turning back.

THE POOP CABIN measured just ten feet by ten feet. I shared these quarters with two cabin mates: John Stokes, assistant surveyor, and Philip Gidley King, a fourteen-year-old midshipman whose father, a ship's captain, had been FitzRoy's commander on an earlier voyage. A huge chart table occupied most of the cabin. Lockers and stacks of drawers of the finest mahogany, designed to hold all of one's equipment and personal belongings, were built into the bulkheads and along the sides of the hull and took up nearly every remaining inch. All of our belongings, including my books and instruments, had to be fitted into this limited space. Stokes had his bunk outside the chart room; King and I slung our hammocks above the table. My height was a problem; I had to remove two of the drawers to make room for my feet. The arrangement seemed impossible. Quarters in the rest of the ship were just as tight. Not an inch was lost. Having spent all my life in comfort — even Shrewsbury School seemed luxurious by comparison — I doubted I could bear such confinement.

During our first days at sea as we crossed the turbulent waters of the Bay of Biscay, I was in such a wretched state of nausea and headache I could scarcely leave my hammock. But even more misery was being meted out below, where four seamen were being flogged for drunkenness, insolence, and neglect of duty. The shrieks of the men receiving dozens of lashes of the cat-o'-nine-tails sickened me even more than the pitching and rolling of the ship.

When the horror finally ended and I could bear to stand up and make my way to the captain's cabin, I asked for an explanation of such severe punishment. "Standard naval practise," FitzRoy explained brusquely. "Necessary to maintain discipline. The men would think me weak if I were not to demand and enforce the strictest obedience."

I staggered back to my hammock. Till this incident I had considered FitzRoy the very ideal of the naval captain. Now I began to see another side, dark and intolerable, often deeply morose. Everyone stood in awe of the captain's black moods. John Wickham, second in command, got in the habit of asking me, "Was much hot coffee served out this morning?" meaning, *How is the captain's temper today?*

In the closeness of the chart room my doubts flourished. Following a southerly course, we would soon reach the Canary Islands off the coast of Africa. Our first stop was to be Teneriffe, the destination I had once dreamt of. Now it had become an absolute necessity, a chance to have a break from the relentless seasickness. Once I was able to think more clearly, I could decide whether to continue the journey or to let the *Beagle* and her harsh captain and hapless crew sail on without me.

As the *Beagle* came into port, I struggled out on deck. The sun rose behind the rugged outline of Grand Canary Island and bathed the Peak of Teneriffe in soft, rich colours whilst fleecy clouds veiled the lower parts. Here it was at last! But joy and relief quickly turned to bleak disappointment. Fearing the spread of cholera then making its way into Europe from Russia, officials at Teneriffe refused to allow anyone ashore till we had been quarantined for twelve days. That was too long for FitzRoy. Before I realised what was happening, we'd raised anchor and sailed away, leaving what I believed to be one of the most interesting places in the world. I poured out my despair in my journal.

WE CONTINUED SOUTHWARD, crossing the Tropic of Capricorn, heading towards the Cape Verde Islands. The seas became calmer, and my nausea eased. Shipboard life improved. The air was warm, the night sky starry, and after a few delightful days I decided I would stay on the *Beagle,* come what may.

During this time I began to make the acquaintance of the junior officers and some of the seamen. One of my favourites was Charles Musters, a young gentleman barely twelve years old. His parents lived apart, and his wealthy father, fearing the mother would make the boy too soft, decided his son should go to sea. He entrusted the lad to FitzRoy's care. With the rank of volunteer first class, Musters was expected to rise rapidly through the ranks of naval officers. In some ways the lad reminded me of myself in my school days — curious about everything — and I promised to take him on some of my exploratory walks. George Rowlett, the purser in charge of the ship's stores and accounts, a man in his thirties with a family at home in Falmouth, became Musters's tutor. "Puts me to mind of my own lads," Rowlett said.

This was Musters's first sea voyage, and he seemed to be bearing up well — better, in fact, than I was. Seasickness was always a battle to be fought, more often lost than won. Sometimes I could do nothing but lie flat on the chart table — "taking the horizontal," Stokes called it — leaving space for him to do his work with his charts. Midshipman King, a handsome youth with blond curls and guileless blue eyes, regarded me pityingly. "I'm sorry for you, Mr. Darwin," he said. "But I'm sure you'll get used to it."

"It doesn't bother you at all?" I asked, and groaned as the ship continued her infernal pitching and rolling.

"It's nothing new to me," King replied. "I went to sea with my father when I was but nine years old and grew up on his ship, the *Adventure,* whilst she charted the waters Captain FitzRoy will now survey. I was with her for four years. When my father retired to New South Wales, I signed on the *Beagle.*"

"And shall you stay with the ship?"

"I've studied navigation and astronomy and trigonometry, and after I've passed my examinations, I hope to be promoted to lieutenant. Someday perhaps I shall captain my own ship. Or so my father desires."

"You must have salt water in your veins," I speculated, "and be much better at mathematics than I am."

He smiled and agreed it might be so.

When the seas were calmer, I wrote letters to be posted if ever again I found my feet on blessedly dry land. *I hate every wave of the ocean with a fervour,* I confessed to Fox. *I loathe, I abhor the sea and all ships that sail on it,* I complained to my sisters. Scarcely anyone amongst family and friends in England didn't learn of my suffering. Assuredly nobody on board the *Beagle* cared — except Captain FitzRoy, who sometimes read aloud to me from Miss Austen's novels in an attempt to allay my misery.

Our first stop, after turning away from the beauty and promise of Teneriffe, was the volcanic island of St. Jago, well out into the Atlantic. Happily ashore at last, it was here I first saw the glory of tropical vegetation, heard the notes of unknown birds, and saw new insects fluttering about still newer flowers. Little Musters helped me collect sea creatures in the rock pools — even an octopus that changed colour at our approach and excited us both. Whilst sitting on a beach near a lava rock face that particularly interested me and enjoying a lunch of ripe tamarinds, oranges, and biscuit — that staple of every seafaring man, flour and water baked hard as the rock I was studying — an idea occurred: I could write a book about the geology of this and all the places I was going to visit! That idea changed everything.

After nearly three weeks in St. Jago and the Cape Verde Archipelago we were on our way again. Next port of call: Bahia, in Brazil.

On the 17th of February we crossed the equator, and I was subjected to the traditional shipboard ritual inflicted on anyone making his first crossing of the line. The previous evening the officer on watch reported a boat ahead. The captain ordered the *Beagle* to heave to, in order for him to converse with "Mr. Neptune," who advised that he would pay a visit next morning. A number of us "griffins" — first-timers — were taken to the lower deck, blindfolded, and led up one at a time by Neptune's "constables." My face was "lathered" with pitch and paint and "shaved" with a rough iron hoop, after which I was put on a plank and at a given signal tilted head over heels into a tub of water. Some of the others — the artist and the missionary — were treated even worse and smeared with foul mixtures. A thoroughly disagreeable ceremony, FitzRoy agreed.

THE CAPTAIN AND I established a routine. We breakfasted together every morning at eight and met again at one o'clock for dinner. The meals served to officers and seamen alike were ample: rice and peas, bread, and always pickled vegetables or some sort of cabbage, boiled or made into sauerkraut; vinegar was known to prevent scurvy. At supper, served at five o'clock, we had canned meat, till the cans began to explode, and fresh meat when we were ashore and shot something. I'd brought some specially made fishhooks and often caught our supper. Our meals were prepared and served by FitzRoy's steward, Harry Fuller, but they were drawn from the same stores that fed the junior officers and crew. Ships' cooks, I learnt, were not hired for their talent in the galley, but FitzRoy believed decent food was necessary to good morale and had appointed a man with better-than-average skills.

FitzRoy ran a tight ship, a model of efficiency. His devotion to the paperwork demanded by the Admiralty surprised me; he spent far more time in his cabin, poring over his logbook and writing in his journal, than he did out on deck. Every day at noon he checked his chronometers, maritime clocks essential to determining longitude as the ship crossed the ocean from east to west. Because ordinary pendulum clocks were made useless by the rolling of the ship, the captain had installed twenty-two of these chronometers, some bought with his own money, in the cabin next to his. Each was suspended on gimbals to keep it level with the horizon, no matter how much pitching and rolling the *Beagle* endured, then packed separately in a small wooden box, each box embedded in a thick layer of sawdust to cushion it from shock. The only man on the ship allowed to touch the clocks was Stebbing, the instrument maker, who wound them every morning at nine o'clock.

No one knew just what was expected of me — least of all me — but the captain's example encouraged me to be disciplined, and I set about my self-appointed tasks with methodical rigour, though conditions were cramped. I concentrated on collecting and dissecting specimens and examining them under the microscope, preserving and labelling my little prizes, and recording my observations of plant and animal life. I was much better at zoology than at botany, where I fell woefully ignorant. But I was determined to have a number of specimens ready to ship to Henslow when we reached port. I depended upon the considerable talents of the ship's carpenter, craggy-faced Jonathan May, who had overseen the rebuilding of the *Beagle,* to construct cases capable of withstanding the journey.

The men were always a great help to me, especially the junior officers — First Lieutenant Wickham, thirty-three, serious, intelligent, and ambitious to someday captain his own ship; and Second Lieutenant Sulivan, a ruddy-faced Irishman who showed an impressive knowledge of geology, as well as of verse, which he loved to recite whilst on watch. His favourite was "The Rime of the Ancient Mariner," Samuel Coleridge's long epic poem. Sulivan knew it by heart:

Water, water, every where,
And all the boards did shrink;
Water, water, every where,
Nor any drop to drink.
The very deep did rot: O Christ!
That ever this should be!
Yea, slimy things did crawl with legs
Upon the slimy sea.

And on and on, interminably, till someone bade him stop.

Being the captain's messmate and sharing his table gave me great standing amongst the officers. They called me "sir" till FitzRoy decided I needed a title and a clear function, and designated me "Ship's Philosopher," shortened to "Philos." This amused them and touched me; it was what the schoolboys had once called Ras.

The one officer I took pains to avoid was Robert McCormick, ship's surgeon. He struck me as a bit of an ass, altogether too impressed by his own status. We shared the same interests in collecting, but Dr. McCormick seemed to resent my friendship with FitzRoy, though he never came out and said as much to me.

I tried to fathom FitzRoy's rapidly fluctuating moods. I believed we were friends, but the captain was a volatile man, and upon occasion we disagreed vehemently. The subject that touched off the largest explosion was slavery. I had grown up in a family of ardent abolitionists, all adamantly opposed to the enslavement of one human by another. I was shocked to discover that Brazil was a slave society, and that Portugal was still bringing Africans to that country, chained in the holds of their ships. FitzRoy and I argued about it.

"See here, Darwin, if they're well looked after, what's wrong with it? Doubtless they're better off than in their dirty native villages. I should imagine they're quite happy here."

"Happy?" I exclaimed. I thought of John Edmonstone in Edinburgh and the stories he'd told me as we worked side by side on bird skins. "I sincerely doubt there is any such thing as a happy slave." I thought I'd replied mildly, but my statement infuriated the captain.

FitzRoy shouted, "If you doubt my word, then we cannot live together any longer!"

He stomped violently out of the cabin, leaving me to assume I must leave the ship, or else take my meals in future with the junior officers. Wickham and Sulivan would have welcomed me at their mess, but before the day was over, FitzRoy had sent me a gracious note of apology. We went on being messmates as before, though we avoided the subject of slavery from that time on.

I did a great deal of writing, some of it in my journal, much of it in letters to my sisters, in order that my family could follow my adventures in detail. Given the time it took letters to reach England, they would read of these adventures many weeks after the events had occurred.

My first letters were posted from St. Jago, amongst

them a tender letter to Fanny Owen, and immediately I began another to send her from Bahia. I found myself thinking of Fanny a great deal during the long days at sea, calling to mind the sound of her voice, the remarkable blue of her eyes, the plump roundness of her knees when she lifted her skirt to wade in the stream. I remembered the one or two kisses we had shared and often imagined the delights we might someday enjoy when my adventure ended. I wrote of how keenly I longed for her and for the letters I hoped she'd send me. Though she hadn't promised, I hoped she'd wait.

DUE TO SEASICKNESS I was scarcely able to leave my hammock on my twenty-third birthday. On the last day of February 1832, after twenty days at sea, we dropped anchor at Bahia de Todos os Santos — Bay of All Saints — on the coast of Brazil. FitzRoy planned to spend several months taking measurements along the coast and checking them against the charts. After a few days we left Bahia, and as the *Beagle* made her way south through the rough waters of the coastal shoals, my misery returned again in full force.

As my help was not needed on board, I left the ship soon after we reached Rio de Janeiro on April 3rd. I looked forward to being ashore for an extended period — not just to escape the constant motion of the ship, but to have more space in which to lay out my work. I rented a little cottage a few miles from Rio on Botofogo Bay near a sandy beach at the foot of a mountain and surrounded by beautiful tropical vegetation. No English cottage could compare to it. Like all in the village it was low and painted a gay colour and simply furnished with a plain table and a few wicker chairs rather than our usual dusty velvet-upholstered pieces. My temporary home came with an elderly housekeeper who would shop and cook and wash my clothes, now stiff with seawater. Whilst I was moving my belongings from ship to shore, I suffered a near disaster. Two or three large waves swamped the boat, and soon everything useful to me was afloat — books, instruments, gun cases, etcetera. Nothing was lost and nothing completely spoilt, but most were in some way injured.

After settling in, I rushed to the post office at the British naval station to collect any letters that might have arrived for me. Nearly three months' accumulation was waiting, the first mail we'd received since leaving Plymouth. I took my letters and a cup of coffee out on the cottage verandah, where late-summer flowers still bloomed in this strange reversal of seasons. I had the notion of rationing the letters, perhaps allowing myself to open just one per day, but in the end I could not muster the self-discipline of rationing and plunged greedily into my hoard. There was no letter from Fanny, a sharp disappointment, but others partly made up for the lack.

I began with Henslow's; my mentor had filled pages with gossip about Cambridge. Caroline's held little news but lots of worried affection — was I eating properly, getting enough sleep, taking good care? She and Susan and Catty had agreed to share the letter-writing duties for the Darwins, each to take a turn once a month and make sure a letter was ready to go out on the government packet boat that sailed for South America on the second Tuesday.

Do not expect letters from Ras, she wrote. *He's far too lazy. And we shall write any news from Papa.*

Next, my cousin Charlotte — the beauty of the Wedgwood family, in my opinion — prattled on about her brother Hensleigh's wedding to Fanny Mackintosh, their cousin on Aunt Bessy's side. The sight of the very name Fanny brought to mind Fanny Owen, and I consoled myself that letters were often delayed; perhaps she'd missed the second Tuesday or didn't know about it; I might very well receive some word from her with the arrival of the next packet-boat. It would be too cruel of her not to respond to the tenderness I had allowed myself to express.

I returned to Charlotte's letter and the surprising news that she herself was now engaged — not to my brother, as my sisters had sometimes speculated when they weren't trying to match him up with Emma, but to a Mr. Charles Langton, whose proposal she'd accepted only two weeks after meeting him. The wedding, she wrote, was to take place on March 22nd, a date now past.

The housekeeper came out to let me know a supper was ready for me. She spoke only Portuguese, but somehow we managed to make ourselves understood. I laid aside Catty's letter, unread, and went in to enjoy a stew of beans and pork mixed with greens. Augustus Earle, our ship's artist, and Midshipman King soon joined me. They'd also decided to come ashore and had put up in a small boardinghouse down the road from my cottage; Earle planned to do some sketching, and King offered to perform whatever errands I had for him. I sent them on their way fairly early, eager to get back to my letters. The housekeeper had also gone, saying *"Boa noite"* — good night — and letting me know through gestures that she would return the next day.

With a sigh of contentment I opened Catty's letter, saved till last.

England is gone mad with marrying, you will think, she wrote, going on at length about Hensleigh's wedding and Charlotte's engagement to Mr. Langton, an impoverished parson who did not yet have a church.

Then she broke the stunning news of one more pending marriage: Fanny Owen to Robert Biddulph. *Late in December, Fanny made a secret ride to the Queen's Head inn on the Oswestry Road & met Mr. Biddulph there & agreed to marry him.*

Shocked, I read the lines a second time. There could be no misunderstanding. Headstrong Fanny! Perhaps on the very day the *Beagle* finally left the shores of England behind her, my beloved Fanny had promised herself to Biddulph. My head spun and my stomach heaved, worse than any seasickness I'd yet suffered.

You no doubt remember him: not so long ago he courted

Sally Owen & then dropped her. And that wasn't the first time he had behaved so abominably.

Yes, I remembered him! Biddulph was a cad, we'd all agreed, a monstrous blackguard who'd broken the hearts of at least two girls, a handsome, fair-haired aristocrat who'd danced with Fanny on the same night she'd led me away from her brother's party and kissed me.

My hands were shaking so hard I could hardly hold the paper. Fanny's biggest worry, Catty said, was that Sally would be tremendously angry at her and fancy that Fanny had behaved treacherously, stealing Biddulph away. But now Sally had married Edward Williams and was happy, and had to keep Edward from seeing how upset she was.

Catty went on and on, about how Biddulph had reformed and was no longer dissipated and gambling to excess, and in fact intended to stand for his father's parliamentary seat on the liberal reform ticket. Squire Owen had given his approval to the match, having no reasonable choice after Fanny's secret midnight rendezvous compromised her. Everyone would have thought it a great match, to be Mrs. Biddulph and live in Chirk Castle in Denbighshire, just across the Welsh border. I'd passed by that great grey pile of stones on my geologising trip with Sedgwick.

I hope it won't be a great grief to you, my dear Charley. You may be sure that Fanny will always continue as friendly & affectionate to you as ever & rejoice to see you again, though I fear that will be of poor comfort to you.

I threw down the letter with a cry, relieved that my housekeeper and my friends from the ship were not nearby to witness my distress. I paced the rough wooden floors of the cottage, climbed to my sleeping loft knowing it was futile even to think of closing my eyes, climbed down again, and continued pacing.

Would the story have been different had I stayed in England, returned to Cambridge, and completed my studies for Holy Orders? That had once been my plan, or at least Father's plan for me. But there was nothing to be done. By now, Fanny was no doubt already Mrs. Biddulph.

I talked to myself, pounding my fists on the table. Dogs barked in the distance. The night sky began to brighten. A rooster crowed. Exhausted, I fell at last into a restless sleep.

Earle returned the next morning, ignored my reddened eyes and haggard face, and suggested a sightseeing excursion into Rio. I gladly accepted, though my bones ached and my head throbbed from the tormented night I'd just passed. But surrounded by Rio's fantastic sights and city streets crowded with exotic foreigners, I was able to forget for a short while Fanny Owen's incomparable blue eyes.

Chapter 12

A Great Wanderer: 1832

I WAS STILL GRIEVING when I met an Irishman, Patrick Lennon, who invited me to visit his *fazenda* — coffee plantation — several days' ride up-country. I saw this expedition as a fine opportunity for collecting and gladly accepted. A half dozen of us set off with a guide. I was constantly amazed by the grandeur of the scenery, but there was a decidedly negative side to this excursion. I learnt that I was riding through slave country and listened in revulsion to stories told by the men in our party — of a woman who crushed the fingers of her slaves with a thumbscrew as punishment, of slave hunters who captured runaways and cut off their ears, of a female slave who had thrown herself off a precipice rather than be taken. My companions all seemed to view this as the normal way of things.

"Such treatment is inhumane and unchristian!" I protested, but they laughed derisively and told me I was ignorant and naive, and I soon decided argument was futile.

Worse was to come. When we arrived at the *fazenda* after a week of difficult travel, Lennon got into a disagreeable quarrel with his agent in charge and became violently angry. "I will take all the female slaves and their children to the public market in Rio and sell them to the highest bidder!" Lennon shouted. "And that includes the mulatto brat you fathered!"

The agent turned pale, and I was sure the matter would come to blows. Lennon's nephew and another in our party stepped in and separated the two men, but it was too late for me. I could no longer stay in the midst of such vile behaviour, and as soon as I could I took leave of the man who before this incident had seemed above the common sort. I hired a guide and began the long ride back. Along the way I collected a number of insects, plants, birds, and small animals.

By the time I reached the Botofogo cottage, I'd begun to see my situation quite plainly. It never would have done to marry Fanny. She was made for that draughty Welsh castle in summer, the house on London's Grosvenor Square in winter, and all the gaiety and dancing and parties that went with them. She must have recognised we were wrong for each other, even before I did. But I could not quite get over the fact that less than a month after she'd written to me so tenderly of how much she missed me, she'd agreed to marry someone else. And a blackguard in the bargain! I had a moment of regretting I'd sent her those loving letters but I got over it — at least I had shown my feelings honestly.

The beach at Botofogo and the surrounding forest

were ideal for collecting, a single hour of which kept me fully employed for the rest of the day. Those hours spent hunched over a microscope gave me enormous pleasure. I wrote to Henslow, describing two species of flatworms I'd found. The more I explored and studied, the more I appreciated the complexity of the whole world of nature. It became easier every day to put Fanny out of mind.

THE *Beagle* had come into port, and we'd soon be sailing southward after a few days for painting and repairs in Bahia. I looked forward to new destinations and to being again in the company of FitzRoy and the junior officers, with a single exception: Dr. McCormick, the ship's surgeon. On a visit aboard I learnt that McCormick had left the ship in a great huff, complaining that I was receiving preferential treatment because of my friendship with FitzRoy and insisting that I, an amateur with no official assignment, had taken over the surgeon's traditional position on voyages as naturalist and collector of specimens. In any event, McCormick was no longer with us, and I was frankly glad to have him gone. Benjamin Bynoe, formerly assistant surgeon and a capital fellow, would take his place.

Little Musters welcomed me excitedly. Several of the seamen planned to take a small boat upriver from Bahia for snipe hunting and invited me to join them. "Oh, please do come with us, Mr. Darwin!" begged Musters. "It will be much better for us if you do!"

I was sorely tempted. "The very first bird I ever shot was a snipe," I told Musters, describing that day in the marsh with Uncle Jos when I'd been so excited I could scarcely reload my gun, and I agreed to accompany them. But I still had much dissecting work to do before we sailed for southern climes and changed my mind at the last.

Several days later Midshipman King came to my cottage to bring me the calamitous news: Three of our shipmates had died, amongst them little Musters. Eight had started off together; when they returned to the ship in Bahia, all had fallen ill with fevers. Bynoe found himself faced with an emergency. Five recovered, but within days the remaining three were insensible and raving violently. Bynoe hoped the change in air would help them, but in the end he could do nothing for them. Young Musters was the last to die and was laid to rest in the English burial ground in Bahia.

"Poor little Musters!" King said, shaking his head and nearly sobbing. "Only three days earlier he had learnt of his mother's death and took it very hard. FitzRoy and Bynoe are distraught, and Rowlett is inconsolable. He says it's as though he's lost one of his own."

I, too, felt keenly the loss of the three, but mourned the death of Musters in particular. I also believed my star was presiding over me and had kept me off that fateful excursion.

I MADE ONE LAST call at the naval office to enquire about mail and found two letters from Woodhouse, both dated March 1st. One was from Squire Owen. I recognised

Fanny's scrawl on the other, decided the squire's might be easier to swallow, and read it first.

My dear Charles Darwin, Mr. Owen began. He apologised for the delay in writing, apologised further for the dullness of his letter, and finally reached the heart of the matter:

Fanny, you will perhaps be surprised to hear, has found another admirer in the man who was once rather thought to admire her sister & she is now engaged to marry Mr. Biddulph, & I hope the event will have taken place before this reaches you. Though I am afraid he is now not very rich & indeed probably never will be so, considering the large place he has to keep up & live at, it is certainly what the world calls a very great match for her.

Not very rich? An aristocrat without money didn't strike me as a very great match!

He is very good looking & very gentlemanlike & sensible, though like many others he has been guilty of some foolish acts & I am afraid lost some money at gambling.

Oh, Fanny! Is this what you truly wanted? I had begun to feel quite melancholy, till I reached the squire's next lines: *He has been introduced to your father, who calls him Count Robert of Chirk, though not to his face of course.*

That made me smile, and being somewhat better prepared, I was able to finish Squire Owen's letter and move on to Fanny's.

My dear Charles —

Your sisters tell me they informed you in their last letter of the awful & important event that is going to take place here — My fate is indeed decided — and my dear Charles I feel quite certain I have not a friend in the world more sincerely interested in my welfare than you are, or one that will be so truly glad to hear I have every prospect of Happiness before me.

For heaven's sake, Fanny! On and on she went, such a lot of blather I could scarcely bear to continue reading, but neither could I stop:

I would give a great deal to see you again & have one more merry chat, whilst I am still Fanny Owen. Believe, my dear Charles, that no change of name or condition can ever alter or diminish the feelings of sincere regard & affection I have for years had for you, & as soon as you return from your wanderings, I shall be much offended if one of your first rides is not to see me at Chirk Castle. Remember you will always find me the same sincere friend I have been to you ever since we were Housemaid and Postillion together.

So much for the Lady of Count Robert of Chirk. I packed the letters away with the others and went out determined to enjoy the spectacle of another beautiful sunset. But my wounds had apparently not yet healed. I still could not completely erase beautiful Fanny Owen from my mind or the ache from my heart.

FOR THE FIRST DAY — July 5th, 1832 — it was a joy to be back aboard the *Beagle* and ready for new sights and new adventures. Hundreds of playful porpoises escorted the ship, the whole sea furrowed by them. But by the second day a gale had come up, and I was too seasick to do more than glance at these marvellous creatures before finding it necessary to "take the horizontal."

FitzRoy planned to call at Monte Video in Uruguay and Buenos Ayres in Argentina, and then to continue southward to Patagonia, charting the coastline before sailing on to Tierra del Fuego, "Land of Fire." It was so named three hundred years ago by Magellan, not because of volcanic activity as one might expect, but because of bonfires, built by natives, that burnt along the shore. It was now dead winter in Tierra del Fuego; we hoped to reach it at the start of the brief southern summer.

In mid-August I shipped off my first crate of specimens: a number of interesting rocks, flowering plants I'd pressed and dried, a great many beetles, and several bottles of tiny animals pickled in spirit — alcohol diluted with distilled water. All were carefully described in my notebook and labelled with iron gall ink on vellum, one waterproof label inside the bottle and another pasted on the outside, as Henslow recommended. There were also some bird specimens, skeletons removed and skins treated with preservatives. I worried that the glass bottles would break or the stoppers leak, despite the sturdy packing cases. But May, the ship's carpenter, assured me that whatever he built *stayed* built, and all would arrive safely. It seemed a smallish collection. I hoped Henslow wouldn't be disappointed.

We surveyed the coast as far south as Bahia Blanca — "white bay" — where FitzRoy and I went ashore to visit the *comandante* in charge of an Argentine military fort.

A grizzled old major intercepted our little party and regarded us with extreme suspicion.

"Who are you, sir?" the officer demanded in Spanish, eyeing the instruments I was carrying. I mistakenly tried to introduce myself as *un naturalista*. The major had never heard of such a thing, and his suspicion deepened.

When a member of our party attempted to explain me as "a man who knows everything," all was over — the major was convinced we were spies, and we were forced to return to the ship. Thereafter, when I made forays ashore, I introduced myself as "a great wanderer," which seemed to satisfy the strangers I met. Indeed, it satisfied me as well.

As any great wanderer should, I went exploring — walking, riding, climbing, collecting, and, naturally, shooting. My skill with a gun proved useful in supplying food for myself as well as the ship's crew. The guanaco, a fast runner resembling a shaggy-haired deer, and the agouti, a large rodent, provided the best meat I ever tasted. Armadillo, I wrote to my sisters, tasted very much like duck.

Some friendly gauchos, herdsmen riding across the *pampa* — the plain — on their fast horses, introduced me to the *boleadora*, or bola, two or three wooden balls or stones wrapped in leather and tied at the ends of a rope. They showed me how to whirl the balls round my head, take aim, and let them fly in such a way that the rope wrapped itself round the legs of fleeing guanacos and rheas, large, ostrichlike birds.

"You try, *señor*," urged the gauchos.

I should have practised whilst on foot. Foolishly, I began to gallop across the plain, whirling the balls madly but failing to notice a nearby bush. One of the balls struck the bush, jerking the rope out of my hand and ensnaring the legs of my horse. The gauchos roared with laughter. "Ah, *señor*," they cried, "we have seen every sort of animal caught, but never before have we seen a man caught by himself!"

ONE DAY WHILST SAILING round Bahia Blanca in a jolly boat with Sulivan and FitzRoy, I spotted what appeared to be large bones imbedded in the cliffs above. I pointed them out to my companions. "Could they be fossils?"

"We shall soon find out," replied the captain.

We hauled our boat onto the beach and began digging through the silty soil with our bare hands, uncovering an enormous trove of ancient bones turned to stone. What naturalist would not have been thrilled to discover such a treasure!

The next day I returned with several seamen armed with axes. After six days of excavating, my helpers and I had covered the deck of the *Beagle* with the skeletal remains of long-extinct ground sloths, animals the size of elephants that had once roamed the earth — the *Megatherium,* or "Great Beast." And there was a huge head, something like a rhinoceros, that required hours to dig out, load onto the jolly boat, and hoist onto the ship with ropes and pulleys. I told the scowling Lieutenant Wickham, "The 'dirt' sullying your pristine decks will soon be cleared away — I swear it!" To make room for this enormous find, I promised to disassemble the remains, numbering each bone and fragment; May would build a case for them. Wickham's decks would be tidy once more.

To the seamen of the *Beagle* involved in this operation, I now became known as "the Flycatcher."

THE SURVEYING CONTINUED, but slowly. Realising he needed additional help, FitzRoy hired two small schooners, manned them with members of the *Beagle*'s crew, and despatched them to survey shoals and estuaries. It was high time to head down to Tierra del Fuego. FitzRoy was determined to return the three Fuegian passengers to their homeland and to establish a mission with the help of the Reverend Richard Matthews, the young missionary who was making the passage with us.

I had been amongst these Fuegians, possibly descendants of those fire-builders sighted by Magellan, since we had first sailed from England. After nearly a year as shipmates I cannot say I had got to know them, but Captain FitzRoy's history with the Fuegians dated back several years.

This is the story, as I heard it from Wickham one night when the lieutenant and I had gone ashore together: In 1828 the previous captain of the *Beagle,* deeply despondent, had shot himself whilst anchored in the Strait of Magellan. Some months later FitzRoy was given command of the ship and ordered to continue the survey of this remote and forbidding land. Whilst crewmen were on shore, their boat was stolen from their campsite.

FitzRoy learnt of it and seized several Fuegians as hostages, demanding return of the boat; all escaped except for three men and a young girl. The captain did not recover his boat — badly needed, Wickham said, as six boats had been lost and there was not enough wood left in the *Beagle*'s hold to build another. FitzRoy conceived the plan of taking the Fuegians back to England, to educate and civilise them at his own expense, and eventually to return them to their homeland with the goal of establishing a mission.

"Did the Fuegians understand this plan?" I asked Wickham.

"I think it likely they did not."

At any rate, in December of 1830, FitzRoy had turned over his four charges to the head of a school in a small country town near London where they would be boarded and instructed. Now three were on their way home; the fourth had died of smallpox.

The girl, whom the captain called Fuegia Basket, was about twelve years old, short and nearly as wide as she was tall. Fuegia struck me as quite intelligent. She spoke English rather well, and charmed everyone — she had even been presented to the king and queen of England — romping round our ship, clothed like any English girl in a dress and bonnet. The Fuegian known as Jemmy Button was about twenty, of a good disposition, and vain about his appearance — he oiled his hair, wore gloves, fussily polished his boots. York Minster was several years older than the others, perhaps close to thirty, though age was hard for me to determine. Unlike the amiable Jemmy, York proved sullen and difficult.

The eyesight of the Fuegians was far superior to ours. The two men sighted ships at sea or land on the horizon long before anyone else. But it was clear that York had his sights most keenly set on Fuegia. Everyone assumed they'd become man and wife as soon as they landed at Tierra del Fuego; in the meantime the captain made sure they were kept properly separated.

I saw the group chiefly on Sunday mornings, when all on board the *Beagle* were required to attend divine services conducted belowdeck by Captain FitzRoy. Every week, dressed in full naval regalia — immaculate cream-coloured trousers and a dark blue wool coat with gold epaulettes, gold braid on the sleeves, and a double row of brass buttons down the front — he delivered an overly long and, I thought, overly pious sermon. Even our missionary was permitted only to assist, perhaps with a passage from scripture. The Fuegians sat through it all, their faces unreadable. I wondered what they were thinking and how they would fare once they reached their native land.

WE ENTERED THE HARBOUR at Buenos Ayres, where FitzRoy intended to take on provisions for the long journey ahead that could last six to nine months. We were shocked when a guard ship fired on us; then, adding to the insult, local authorities, fearing cholera, ordered us to turn back. We returned to Monte Video, where more excitement awaited. The local police chief requested our help in putting down an insurrection of local soldiers who had taken over the fort. FitzRoy despatched fifty of our men, who marched through the town fully armed, making a great show of force, and the rebels quickly gave up. It was terrifically exciting, but we never did learn what had sparked the rebellion.

I'd had no letters from England for more than four months, and I was as famished for news as a starving man for food. Once we made our last call, I would have no further word from friends and family for a very long time. Finally I found several waiting for me and devoured every word.

Fanny, who now was only occasionally a cause of some late-night nostalgia and regret, had married Count Robert of Chirk. Caroline, writing in June, seemed to feel I was entitled to details of Fanny's wedding day:

We got to Woodhouse between 8 & 9 & Fanny soon sent for me. She was beautifully dressed in white, of course, with her bonnet & veils. After breakfast all the ladies came upstairs to see her. At 10:30 the procession began. Mr. Biddulph looked very handsome & extremely nervous; during the ceremony Fanny shook so much she could hardly write her name.

My sisters' lives were much tied up in such matters as weddings and engagements, and I was grateful for any news that might have seemed important to them, no matter how dull or distasteful to me. Much better, though, when Caroline wrote about her gardening. But she did include one sentence I found intriguing: *Mr. Sedgwick called for half an hour on his return from Wales & was very pleasant — what a very agreeable man he is.*

That made me smile. But what about Susan? Where was she whilst my old friend the geologist was being so deucedly pleasant and agreeable?

There was also a piece of bad news: My dear friend Fox had been very ill, and been bled so violently that it would be long before he recovered his strength. Caroline, still mothering me, used this as reason to remind me: *Do be careful of yourself dear Charles. I cannot help feeling afraid that you will make yourself ill by overexertion in some scheme which you enjoy.*

Catty, who had received my letter of last April describing my cottage at Botofogo Bay, felt inclined to add a different sort of warning: *Do not let the Cottage put the Parsonage out of your head, a far better thing.* She went so far as to suggest a future occupant for this far-off parsonage. *You will in all probability find Fanny Wedgwood sobered into an excellent Clergyman's Wife by the time you return. A nice little invaluable Wife she would be.* Obviously, I could leave the hard work of finding me a proper spouse to my industrious sisters. *I will not quite promise though that you will find her disengaged, as another Clergyman, Mr. Paget Moseley, is said to be paying her very sedulous attention, but he is such a vulgar, fat, horrid man, I do not think it is possible she will have him.*

Vulgar, fat, and horrid though Moseley might be, he did have the great advantage of being there, whilst I was the great wanderer.

*   *   *

I HAD BUSINESS to transact at the bank in Monte Video. My father had arranged to deposit funds to cover my expenses, which were turning out to be considerable: fifty pounds a year to Captain FitzRoy for my food on the ship, additional funds for rent and food whilst I was ashore, and the hire of whatever horses, mules, and guides I needed for my expeditions.

Finances settled and another case of specimens ready for shipment to Henslow, I passed my days in Monte Video pleasantly. I walked round the city, enjoying the sights and admiring the Spanish ladies in their lace mantillas draped over tall combs intricately carved of tortoiseshells. To my eyes they were exotic creatures gliding like angels through the leafy squares of the town.

On November 27th we boarded the *Beagle*. Nearly every day now FitzRoy spoke of something new added to his plans. I saw no end to the voyage. How I yearned for dear old England! Often I dreamt of green fields, walks round Cambridge with Henslow, visits with Ras in London, shooting with Squire Owen, Christmas at Maer with my cousins. It would be months till I had letters from friends or family. I knew that if I continued to dwell on such things, I should want to bolt.

But there could be no bolting now. We were steering for barbarous regions. I felt hardened by my experiences of the past months and ready for whatever lay ahead. All the officers stowed away their razors and allowed their beards to grow. I did, as well.

Chapter 13

Land of Fire: 1833

"LAND HO!" shouted the lookout from the crow's nest. The fog had lifted. It was December 18th, nine days short of a year since our voyage began.

The tropics that had so charmed me now lay far behind us. I studied Stokes's charts of Tierra del Fuego spread out on the table beneath my hammock, and marvelled at the labyrinth of channels, sounds, coves, and harbours woven amongst dozens — or were there hundreds? — of islands in the archipelago. FitzRoy intended to remain in this desolate area near the bottom of the world for about three months, mapping the waterways and shorelines and devoting a portion of that time to establishing the Christian mission. Experience had taught me his estimates were always too optimistic.

We made the difficult passage through the Strait of Le Maire and found a safe anchorage in Good Success Bay, first visited by Captain James Cook in 1769 on his way to the Pacific. The jagged shore looked bleak and inhospitable, but my attention fastened on a crowd of savages perched on a wild peak overhanging the sea to witness our arrival. Absolutely naked with long tangled hair, they were bedaubed all over with red and white paint; skins of guanaco or seal were thrown over their shoulders. What a fearsome sight these men made! I could only gape at them in fascination. Our three Fuegians on board appeared to be made wary by the sight of their brethren.

FitzRoy despatched a boat with a landing party to make contact with the natives, and I accompanied them. We soon won them over with a gift of bright red cloth, which they placed round their necks, and I willingly entered into the exchange of greeting with an old fellow with long black hair hanging from under a white feather cap who seemed to be their headman. He slapped me on the chest and gestured that I was to slap him in return, which I did, and imitated the noises he made, something like people do when feeding chickens. Their language sounded like a man clearing his throat. I thought him and his fellows friendly enough.

A gale of wind and rain blew throughout the night, and heavy squalls swept down from the mountains. We remained at anchor in Good Success Bay for several days, making more visits ashore. Amongst those who went with us was Syms Covington, the ship's boy who served the poop cabin and was also a tolerably good fiddle player. Covington took his fiddle ashore and struck up a tune, to the utter astonishment of our hosts. And when Midshipman King began dancing with Mellersh, our second midshipman, the Fuegians appeared delighted.

Soon several of them could be seen "waltzing" with several of our officers. As always, I managed to avoid dancing, instead observing the most unusual ball I'd ever seen.

Some of the old men on shore urged Jemmy to stay with them, but Jemmy had as much trouble communicating with them as we did.

"Not my people," he told the captain. "Better to go on."

The captain, too, wanted to move on to March Harbour to the west.

The weather worsened, the most turbulent we'd yet encountered. We made for Cape Horn, veiled in mist, but howling winds drove us out to sea. On Christmas Eve, furiously pelted by hail, we succeeded in reaching a small, protected cove at Hermite Island. There we huddled at anchor on Christmas Day whilst violent squalls raged round us and the williwaws roared down from the mountains — not much of a holiday for the seamen. By the last day of the year conditions were little changed, but FitzRoy was impatient and ordered the anchor raised.

That proved a mistake. For two weeks we made scarcely any headway and were subjected to the worst imaginable misfortunes. Relentless gales threw up enormous clouds of spray, soaking everything with seawater. It was impossible to walk on the decks. For not a single hour was I free from seasickness. I thought it could get no worse, but it did.

On January 11th — the year was now 1833 — FitzRoy sighted a towering rock, leading him to believe we would soon reach March Harbour, only a mile distant. But a sudden gale drove our ship out to sea once more. FitzRoy said it was the most severe storm he had ever endured.

"A gale is not so very bad, if one is aboard a good boat," I remarked, attempting to sound braver than I felt, for in fact I was very much afraid.

"Just wait till we ship a sea," the captain warned, "when a great wave breaks over us."

His warning was prophetic. The storm continued to roar, and throughout the night the *Beagle* rolled helplessly, at the mercy of wind and wave. At noon not one but three enormous waves crashed down on the *Beagle,* one after the other. The first one flooded her decks; the second heeled her over on her beam-ends. Her port railing was underwater, the streaming decks were now vertical, and I found myself flung out of my hammock and sprawled on the hull. The third monstrous wave curled over the starboard side, which was in the air, and spilt its tons of weight into one of the whaleboats. Everything on deck was swept away.

I struggled to gain my footing and held on as best I might to a leg of the chart table, which was bolted down; Midshipman King clung to another leg. His look of terror must have mirrored my own as doors and hatches burst open and water poured through in a great cataract. I was as frightened as I had ever been, certain I was on my way to a watery grave. My life seemed about to end just as my father had feared: I would be drowned, my body lost forever, my family learning of my death only months from now.

Several seamen, led by Sulivan and FitzRoy, struggled to open the wooden ports, the water flowed out again, and the sturdy little ship righted herself. The damage could have been worse: One whaleboat was smashed beyond repair and had to be cut loose, one chronometer was destroyed, and I lost some of my most valuable specimens, a collection of dried plants. But we were alive and all hands accounted for.

"So, Darwin, you've now been officially baptised," FitzRoy commented as I helped him put his cabin to rights. The crisis had passed, but the *Beagle* continued her rolling.

We never did reach March Harbour. York Minster decided that he and Fuegia, his future wife, would go to live with Jemmy Button and the Reverend Matthews in Jemmy's country, Woollya Cove near Ponsonby Sound. Fitzroy and I, Bynoe, Matthews, the three Fuegians, and twenty-seven crewmen boarded three whaleboats and a yawl loaded with provisions donated by the Church Missionary Society for the new mission. We set out through an arm of the sea that connected the Atlantic and Pacific and had been named Beagle Channel by an earlier explorer. Suddenly on a cliff above us four or five naked and painted men appeared out of the mist, springing up and down, waving their arms and sending forth the most hideous yells. York and Jemmy seemed not entirely pleased by the welcome, if that's what it was; poor Fuegia Basket looked terrified.

As we sailed along the coast, fires blazed and the men ran, hour upon hour, naked but for their paint, whilst keeping up a loud, sonorous shout, running so hard their noses bled and their mouths foamed. When we reached Woollya Cove two days later, canoes filled with Fuegians paddled out to meet us, the Fuegians monotonously repeating the word *yammerschooner*. We believed it meant "give me."

We liked the look of Woollya Cove. Rather flat and watered by numerous brooks, it seemed altogether a good place for a settlement. Grass and flowers thrived; timber trees grew in dense stands. Under the curious gaze of dozens of onlookers, including several identified as Jemmy's relations, the *Beagle*'s crew set about constructing the mission. They built three wigwams, small haycock-shaped huts of saplings thatched with twigs and long grasses, like those of the natives. But whilst the native huts were flimsy affairs open to one side where they had their fires, our men secured the newly built wigwams with rope and reinforced them with oiled canvas, making solid-looking dwellings. The Reverend's was provided with an attic above and a crude cellar below for storing his supplies. When the wigwams were finished, our men began to unload the yawl.

I had seldom seen a more unlikely assortment of useless articles: chamber pots, wineglasses, butter dishes, tea trays, soup tureens, fine white linen cloths and napkins, beaver top hats, and a mahogany dressing case. Had anyone given thought to the country and the circumstances to which these items were going? Surely FitzRoy must have recognised the folly. Was he imagining these wild, naked, painted people having a proper English tea together? The means wasted on such things would have purchased an immense stock of really useful articles — knives and tools, for instance. The seamen secured these wholly impractical items inside the huts to discourage thievery, though why anyone would want to steal them was beyond my imagining.

We'd observed that the Fuegians lived mainly on shellfish, mussels, and limpets gathered by the women from the rocks along the shore. But as part of the mission's civilising efforts, the sailors of the *Beagle* turned themselves into English farmers for the next several days. They dug a large garden and planted an assortment of vegetables: beans, peas, carrots, lettuce, potatoes, turnips, onions, cabbages, and leeks. I assisted, laughing to myself at how old Abberley, our gardener at The Mount, would have responded to this enterprise.

In the course of this industrious activity the crowd of Fuegians grew and grew, and the "yammerschoonering" never ceased. We tried to satisfy them with trifling presents — old buttons, bits of ribbon — but whatever gifts we gave them were never enough. They asked for everything they saw and stole whatever they got their hands on.

By the end of January the seamen had finished their

work, and most of the Fuegians had vanished into the forest with their booty. FitzRoy decided to leave Reverend Matthews and our three Fuegian friends alone at the new mission. The remainder of our party moved off a little way and set up camp. But FitzRoy couldn't rest. "I cannot help feeling exceedingly anxious about Matthews," he confided. I shared his unease.

The next day we returned to check on our charges; all seemed well. Reassured, the captain ordered the yawl and one of the whaleboats back to the *Beagle*. The rest of us set out to explore the Beagle Channel in the remaining two whaleboats, long, narrow boats pointed at both ends and easy to manoeuvre by oar or sail.

The sky was bright, the water calm, the scenery spectacular. Enormous glaciers that appeared light blue descended steeply to the edge of water so dark as to be almost black, and fields of white snow surrounded deep green forests. Whales breached and spouted close by. We made camp and set up a watch, still concerned by the motives of the Fuegians who occasionally appeared and behaved aggressively towards us. I took the watch till one o'clock and worried that unfriendly savages might be prowling close by, preparing for a fatal rush, ready to dash our brains out.

The hours passed. Wrapped in an oiled canvas tarpaulin, waiting uneasily for something to happen, I listened to the howling wind. It was deuced cold, the rocks on which I crouched unyielding. A month past the summer solstice, the sky was still light. A brief squall rushed through, dumping a quantity of icy water over my head before it moved on. My thoughts drifted homeward, and I fancied my father and sisters sitting cosily round the fire in our drawing room with Susan perhaps providing some music. Such thoughts were especially vivid now. I was astonished to find I could endure this hard life, but if not for the pleasures of natural history, I never could have done it.

I rose stiffly, stretched, and crept along the perimeter of our little encampment. Detecting no signs of hostile Fuegians, I waited till Bynoe relieved me to take the next watch. There was no trouble that night.

In the morning our two boats continued exploring the channel. We stopped to prepare our noon meal near the foot of a majestic glacier, prompting Lieutenant Sulivan to recite a few more lines of "The Rime of the Ancient Mariner":

The ice was here, the ice was there,
The ice was all around:
It cracked and growled, and roared and howled,
Like noises in a swound!

He would without doubt have continued, but suddenly we heard a thunderous crack. I glanced up as the glacier calved and the whole front of the icy cliff crashed into the sea, sending up a gigantic plume of water. "The boats!" I shouted.

I leapt up and raced for the whaleboats we'd pulled

up on the narrow strip of beach, just as a great, foaming surge roared towards us. We seized the ropes and managed to drag our boats out of the reach of the huge curling breakers that would have smashed them in seconds. I narrowly escaped being carried away by the towering waves, but we had saved the boats and thus saved ourselves. Marooned without food and surrounded by savages, our predicament would have been dire. Later, we climbed again into our boats and entered a large expanse of water that Captain FitzRoy named Darwin Sound — in honour of my courage, he said.

This must have been close to my twenty-fourth birthday, though I scarcely thought of it at the time.

THE RAPIDLY WORSENING WEATHER forced us to turn back. FitzRoy pointed to a crowd of Fuegians gathered on the cliffs above us. "Look, Darwin," he said. "They're in full dress." Red and white paint was the only cover for their nakedness, and they had decorated themselves with ribbons and scraps of the red cloth FitzRoy had given them. We saw a woman wearing a dress we recognised as Fuegia's. That worried us — what was happening to the settlers at Woollya?

Even under sail we had to take turns on the oars, rowing hard and stopping to rest only when the light faded, setting out again an hour or two later as the sky began to brighten. When we reached the settlement, we saw dozens of beached canoes and perhaps a hundred Fuegians, all adorned with bright coloured rags torn from the three returning Fuegians' English clothing. We feared the worst, but our minds were eased when Reverend Matthews came out to greet us with Jemmy and York. All seemed well, till we got Matthews off by himself.

I'd had misgivings all along about Matthews. He was a very young man, about eighteen years old, and though earnest and determined to follow in the footsteps of an older brother who was a missionary in New Zealand, he didn't seem to have the strength and fortitude necessary to such an arduous undertaking.

"Tell us what happened," FitzRoy said.

"They went into a rage when I wouldn't give them what they wanted," Matthews related in a choking voice, "and came back with large stones, threatening to kill me. They held me down and pulled out the hairs of my beard with mussel shells." He rubbed his chin, plainly distressed, and began to weep. "I can't even leave my wigwam," sobbed the poor fellow. "The garden is ruined. They've stolen most of my belongings. Please, take me away from here before they murder me!"

FitzRoy immediately despatched several seamen to collect what they could of Matthews's things and load them into our whaleboats. There wasn't much left, but what there was — tools, knives, and so forth — FitzRoy handed out to the yammerschoonering Fuegians, hoping this generosity would be of help to Jemmy, York, and Fuegia.

"Perhaps they'll be able to effect some changes for the better amongst their countrymen," FitzRoy said with a sigh. "And perhaps Reverend Matthews will regain his courage to try again at a later time. At best, the first steps towards civilisation have been made."

I didn't share his optimism but kept my thoughts to myself.

After an absence from the ship of twenty days and a journey of some three hundred miles, we rejoined the *Beagle*. The weather continued to be abysmal — thick spray whirling across the bay, much rain and hail, wind that howled like a mad thing. Near the end of February 1833, sailing against gale winds and heavy seas, we left the Land of Fire, bound for the Falkland Islands to the east.

THE ENGLISH FLAG was flying in the harbour when we arrived, the Falklands having been taken over from Argentina only weeks earlier. The islands presented a miserable appearance — there was not a single tree — but because of their location in the South Atlantic they were of great importance to British shipping. FitzRoy meant to make an accurate survey, and I began to explore, collecting fossils that differed markedly from those I'd gathered along the coast of South America. The idea occurred to me then to conduct comparative studies of all the plants and animals I'd gathered thus far.

I was not the only collector on board the *Beagle;* Wickham and Sulivan and many of the junior officers were also interested in collecting the rarities they found. The captain's clerk, Edward Hellyer, had a particular interest in birds, and a few days after our arrival he went exploring with one of the sailors from a French whaler that had been wrecked on the island. All aboard the *Beagle* were under strict orders from Captain FitzRoy not to go off alone when on shore. Hellyer, generally a sensible fellow, didn't defy the rules, but he did sometimes bend them. When the Frenchman came back alone, he reported that the clerk had gone on without him.

Time passed, and still Hellyer did not return. A search party went looking for him. First his clothes and gun were found on the beach; hours later his naked body was sighted, entangled in a kelp bed, along with an unusual duck he'd shot and was apparently trying to retrieve. Bynoe did all he could to revive him, but his efforts were useless.

Hellyer's death grieved us. A melancholy procession escorted his coffin to a dreary headland where FitzRoy read the divine service for the burial of the dead as we stood with bowed heads, and a cold and unforgiving wind tore at us.

WE HAD NEVER BEFORE stayed so long in a place with so little worth recording in my journal. But FitzRoy had made a rash decision: to buy another ship. He'd met the master of an American sealing schooner. Due to heavy storms the American had taken few seals, and he was on the brink of financial ruin. Thinking that a second, smaller ship would help shorten our voyage, FitzRoy arranged to buy the schooner, paying for it out of his own funds. He was certain he could convince the Admiralty to reimburse him — it was standard naval practise never to send a lone ship on such a long and dangerous mission. FitzRoy was as excited as a boy in love. He renamed his new sweetheart the *Adventure,* recalling the name of the ship on which he had served at the beginning of his career. He planned to take it to Uruguay for refitting and put Lieutenant Wickham in charge of it.

Whilst FitzRoy and his men completed a thorough survey of the shoreline of East Falkland Island in whaleboats, I explored inland, accompanied under FitzRoy's orders by Syms Covington, the ship's boy who had amazed the Fuegians with his fiddling. Ship's boys were at the lowest rung of the shipboard ladder, assigned the most menial duties. But Covington was a clever fellow and a good shot, and I had been teaching him how to preserve animals and bird skins, as John Edmonstone had once taught me. Covington proved an apt pupil with the nimble fingers and sure touch one could expect of a fiddle player.

I was thoroughly tired of the Falklands, but one thing I never tired of was discussing with FitzRoy what we had observed. I had learnt to avoid his black moods; he always supported wholeheartedly my collecting and lent me whatever assistance I needed, whether it was the ship's carpenter to build packing cases for my specimens or the services of Covington to help prepare them. Though we frequently disagreed in our thinking and our conclusions, the discussions and debates were valuable to both of us. We held entirely different views of a certain kind of fox, the only four-footed animal native to the Falklands. FitzRoy maintained they were related to foxes in Patagonia and had arrived in the Falklands riding on large chunks of ice; I thought they were peculiar to the Falklands. Neither of us succeeded in convincing the other.

There were other debates. The captain was an aristocrat and a conservative Tory to the very marrow of his bones, as well as devoutly religious. I, on the other hand, was not of aristocratic stock, my politics were liberal Whig like my father and uncle, and though I held conventional views of religion, I was not devout. Save on the subject of slavery, which was repugnant to me, our discussions of politics and religion were always civil. And the one true bond was our mutual interest in natural science.

At last we trimmed our wild beards — mine so long I could grasp it in my fist — and made for the warmer latitudes of the mainland.

OVER THE SPACE of two weeks in early April as we sailed northward, I wrote a long and detailed letter to my sisters, covering much of what had happened during the preceding four months and mentioning the vexation of spirit that had infected me and, indeed, many others on the ship. *I can very plainly see there will not be much pleasure or contentment till we get out of these detestable latitudes & are carrying on under full sail to the land where bananas grow.*

At the end of April we dropped anchor in Maldonado on the coast of Uruguay, and I rushed off to post my letter. Several letters were waiting for me, the first I'd had in many months. I retired to my quarters, already chuckling to myself that I would now have the latest news of my cousin Fanny Wedgwood: Had Little Miss Memorandum yielded to the charms of the Reverend Paget Moseley? Or did my industrious sisters still put her forth as the leading candidate for my future parsonage? I settled down with a large hollow gourd of *yerba mate* and a *bombilla,* a silver straw, through which to sip it and opened Caroline's letter, dated September 12th, more than six months earlier.

My dear Charley,

You will I know feel very much for the sad loss Uncle Jos & family have had. In August Fanny Wedgwood was taken ill with a bilious fever. Seven days after she became unwell she expired.

Fanny Wedgwood, dead? Impossible! I felt numb with the shock. This was the first death of someone close to me since my mother had died nearly sixteen years earlier. The news unleashed a torrent of grief, and I found myself weeping. It was some time before I could go on reading. I mourned not only for Fanny but also for Emma, who'd been so close to her, and I remembered that long conversation with Susan, always putting forward Miss Memorandum as a potential wife for me at a time when the only Fanny I could think of was Fanny Owen. Caroline continued with the details of Fanny's illness and death ("mortification of the bowels," according to Father), and how Uncle Jos and Aunt Bessy were dealing with their loss.

ONCE I'D COLLECTED MYSELF, I opened Catty's letter and was relieved to find it a cheery one written in mid-October, sending me news of Father and his pet project, his conservatory. *His banana tree is sent for and a deep hole made for it. Papa means to call it the Don Carlos Tree, in compliment to you.*

Finally, I was able to smile, though my heart was very sore.

I am going to Woodhouse this week, to meet Mrs. Williams & Mrs. Biddulph — that would be the former Sally Owen and Fanny Owen — *as both the husbands will be happily away. Poor Fanny is not said to live a very happy life at Chirk; she has had the horrid old Mother & Sister & Brother staying there a long time, and she dislikes them most cordially.* There followed news of engagements, visits, balls, and so forth. Catty ended her letter, *People here think you will find cruising in the South Seas such uninteresting work, that it gives us some hope you will return before the* Beagle *does.*

Now why on earth would they think that? I wondered. Difficult, demanding, uncomfortable, sometimes miserable, even dangerous — but *uninteresting*? Never!

Chapter 14

The Great Galloper: 1833

WHILST FITZROY was having his new *Adventure* refitted from mast to keel and the *Beagle* proceeded with the survey, I embarked on an expedition upstream from the mouth of the Río Negro in the company of several gauchos and became *un grand galopeador* — "a great galloper."

Tall and handsome with a proud expression, the gauchos sported large moustachios and wore their black hair curling down their backs. Dressed in brightly coloured garments with their great spurs clanking about their heels and knives stuck like daggers at their waists (and often used), they appeared a very different race of men. Their politeness was excessive: They never drank their spirits without expecting you to taste it; but whilst making their graceful bows, they seemed quite as ready, if occasion offered, to cut your throat. I wore a large clasp knife on a string round my neck, in the manner of sailors; the gauchos thought confining my knife in this way was very strange. These men impressed me mightily.

At night we slept under the open sky with the dogs keeping watch. We made our beds of the *recado,* the gaucho saddle, nothing more than leather pads and sheepskins. I thought it more comfortable than the finest feather bed and woke fresh as a lark.

I had been working hard to learn their language, and though I hadn't mastered Spanish, I could by then both understand and make myself understood — and I understood from the gauchos that this was exceedingly dangerous territory.

One day towards sunset as we rode across the pampas, we observed three figures on horseback silhouetted against the western sky. I noticed that the three had dismounted, and one then disappeared. My companions reached for their knives. I had heard the gauchos speak earlier of two of their own killed recently by murderous Indians not far from where we were riding. Now I wondered aloud if the three were preparing an ambush.

"*Quien sabe,*" replied the one riding nearest me. "Who knows? But they don't ride like Christians. Load your pistol."

The gauchos decided we must head for a swamp. If attacked, we would ride into the swamp as far as our horses could go, and then trust to our legs. We all kept our eyes fixed on the horizon, and for some time I feared our lives were about to come to a quick and bloody end. We reached a valley and galloped to the foot of a hill; the gaucho handed me the reins to his horse and crawled up the hill to observe the situation.

Suddenly he burst out laughing. "Women!" he called down to us waiting anxiously below. The "murderous Indians" turned out to be the wives of soldiers stationed at a military post, and the three were out searching for ostrich eggs. We laughed with relief, but I now admit I had seldom been so frightened, except perhaps when in danger of drowning.

I REACHED BAHIA BLANCA, thinking to meet up with FitzRoy and the *Beagle,* but saw no sign of captain or ship. Not wishing to waste the opportunity, I secured another guide and went out collecting again, returning to the place where I had earlier discovered the bones of the *Megatherium.* This fossil hunt was also successful. Wickham would complain of having more petrified bones cluttering up the deck. I wrote enthusiastically to my sisters:

The pleasure of the first days of partridge shooting cannot be compared to finding a fine group of fossil bones, which tell their story of former times with almost a living tongue.

I had another shipment ready to go off to Henslow: some eighty species of birds, twenty four-footed creatures (including a capybara, a large, furry rodent about the size of a pig), four barrels of skins and plants, a number of rocks and fossils, and a few fish, all prepared with Covington's able assistance.

Then, whilst FitzRoy continued to take measurements up and down the coast, I galloped off into the interior for a third time. It was the custom to stop and ask for a night's lodging at any convenient house, and often I enjoyed the hospitality of Portuguese or Spanish settlers. Owners of great *estancias* with thousands of head of cattle sometimes lived in shockingly poor dwellings, with floors of hardened mud, unglazed windows, and only a few rough wooden tables and chairs as furnishings. For supper we were served a huge pile of roasted meat, perhaps some boiled pumpkin, and nothing else — not even bread or salt — save for a mug of cold water.

Differing customs sometimes caused surprise on both sides. My hosts questioned, for instance, why it was that I washed my face every morning; was it some strange religious ritual? In turn, I was put off when the *señora* of the house insisted on feeding me choice titbits from her plate with her own fork. I could imagine what my sisters would think of that, but there was no refusing such a high compliment. My hosts were amazed by such things as my pocket compass and the Promethean matches that I ignited by biting them; they thought it wonderful that a man should strike fire with his teeth.

But my accommodations were not always so humble. On one occasion I stayed at a large *estancia* where I dined with an army captain. After a quantity of good food and wine, the captain said, "I have but one question, my dear Darwin, and I should be very much obliged if you would answer with all truth."

I nodded, preparing for a deeply scientific enquiry.

"Tell me," he said, leaning towards me with great earnestness, "are not the ladies of Buenos Ayres the handsomest in the world?"

"Charmingly so," I replied.

"And do the ladies in any other part of the world wear such large combs in their hair?"

I assured him they did not.

"Look there!" the captain exclaimed to the others at the table. "A man who has seen half the world says it is the case. We always thought so, but now we know it."

My excellent judgement in beauty and knowledge of fashion earned me a most hospitable reception. That night my host insisted I take his bed, whilst he slept on his *recado* like a gaucho.

I ACCOMPLISHED a great deal with my "galloping" — collecting animal skins, mice, fish, plants, insects, seeds, fossils, and a good many geological finds. When I was not living as *un grand galopeador,* I stayed in Maldonado, a quiet village surrounded on all sides by a succession of green hills, and prepared my specimens.

Whilst there I was pleased to receive a number of letters from friends and family. Fox wrote from the Isle of Wight, *I fancy you in the height of entomological happiness & long to be with you.* He felt stronger, he said, but continued to be a good deal of an invalid and blamed his weakness on an affection of his lungs. Poor Fox! I imagined my dear old friend sitting in a chair by the seaside, a blanket over his legs, his face thin and pale, and fretting, *Is there not some danger of your becoming so much attached to wandering that the itch will again become irresistible when you have been home for a year or two?*

I would have only to think of the seasickness that

plagued me every minute I was at sea, and was certain that memory alone would cure any such itch.

Another bundle of letters arrived in June. Susan informed me the "race of Wedgwoods" was fast increasing with the birth of numerous babies to our Maer cousins, and, *Poor Fanny Biddulph is in daily expectation of her confinement.* Who would have ever imagined Fanny, who'd once boldly insisted upon firing a gun, referred to now as "Poor Fanny"!

Caroline, sitting in the old schoolroom where Catty and I had learnt our numbers and letters from her tireless efforts, wrote, *I hope the report we heard was false, the time of the voyage being lengthened, dear Charley.*

The report wasn't false, dear Caroline. I'd often hoped the same, but I was resigned: The time of the voyage was much lengthened, no one knew for how long — certainly not FitzRoy.

During the next several months I would reread these letters many times over, always caught between my yearning for my friends and family and comfortable life in faraway England and my thrilling adventures on the other side of the world.

THE SCHOONER WAS READY by the final weeks of 1833. Certain changes had been made. Stokes, the assistant surveyor, would now be on the *Adventure,* under Lieutenant Wickham's command, and I would have the entire poop cabin for myself. With FitzRoy's permission, I arranged to formally hire Syms Covington as my personal servant and natural history assistant. Covington was an odd sort of person, humourless and with a generally stolid expression, but always meticulous, with a clear handwriting, and well adapted to my purposes.

I wrote to Father, requesting an additional sixty pounds per annum to pay for Covington's services, and in that same long letter sent a list of items I felt I could not do without — books on geology and zoology, some optical equipment, four pairs of strong walking shoes, and more of those Promethean matches that had so impressed the settlers when I struck them with my teeth.

I was sorry to see the departure of Augustus Earle, the ship's artist, with whom I had struck up a great friendship. Earle's health was failing, and he felt unable to face the challenges ahead. FitzRoy found another artist in Monte Video to take his place: Conrad Martens. "By my faith in bumpology, I am sure you will like him," said FitzRoy. Unlike me, Martens apparently had the right sort of nose.

I posted my last letter home from Monte Video on December 3rd, warning my sisters to expect no more letters for a very long while. We had taken on a year's provisions. That day I went on board the *Beagle* for the first night in four months. I luxuriated in my spacious quarters and found it reassuring to have the *Adventure* following along behind us with many of our crew aboard. But having additional space did nothing to ease my seasickness, which returned with a vengeance as soon as the ship was under way. What torture!

Once more we would let our beards grow long as we headed south to Tierra del Fuego.

THE DAY BEFORE CHRISTMAS we sailed into Port Desire, and the following day all hands were sent ashore. By great good luck I shot a guanaco weighing about 170 pounds, providing a holiday feast for the entire crew. FitzRoy sponsored a number of athletic contests with prizes for the winners. Covington brought out his fiddle, and soon many of our seamen were dancing jigs. Everyone was in a buoyant mood when we left a few days later, continuing on south to Port St. Julian. It might have been better named Port Desolation.

Several of us, including Martens, the new artist, accompanied Captain FitzRoy in a search of fresh water to supply an inland exploration. After a few strenuous hours the captain, who was carrying some heavy instruments, suddenly collapsed. Exhausted and painfully thirsty, he could go no farther. Hoping to find water at a lake we thought we saw in the distance, I left him resting with the others on the treeless plain whilst I pushed on for another ten miles. But what we'd seen was not a lake, as we'd desperately hoped, only a field of snow-white salt. I made my way back to find the captain still unable to go on. We tried to devise a way to carry him, but all of us were too tired to attempt it.

"Leave me here," he ordered weakly. "Go back to the ship and send water."

We looked at one another. "I command you," he gasped.

We obeyed with great reluctance. One man volunteered to stay with the captain, the rest of us continuing back to the *Beagle* and despatching a party with water to find FitzRoy and revive him. By midnight we were all safely on board again and thankful for it. For two days I lay in my hammock, ill with fatigue and suffering a fever.

I was eager to leave this depressing place, but not before I had added a certain rare bird to my collection. I'd often heard the gauchos speak of a bird they called *avestruz petise,* an ostrich so rare that perhaps it didn't even exist. I knew that a French naturalist named Orbigny had recently explored in this area, and I was selfishly afraid he would get the cream of all the good things before I did, including that ostrich. My blood was up; I wanted to bag that rare bird!

One day whilst we were out hunting, Martens shot an ostrich that appeared to be one of the common sort, about two-thirds grown. We gave the bird to the cook to roast. My mouth full of the succulent meat, I told Martens the story of the Glutton Club at Cambridge and the tough old brown owl we'd once had roasted and tried to eat. In the midst of my story I suddenly realised what the gauchos had been talking about: *avestruz petise* meant "little rhea." The little rhea, that rare specimen of ostrich I'd been looking for, was now mostly devoured. I leapt to my feet, insisting that every last scrap of skin and bone — all the inedible bits — be handed over to me without delay. Covington was despatched to rescue the head, neck, legs, wings, and feathers from the cook's waste pile.

"The Flycatcher wants it," the seamen said, rolling their eyes.

Properly preserved and labelled, the remains of *avestruz petise* went off with my next shipment to Henslow.

WE SET OFF once more, the *Adventure* on an eastward course for the Falklands whilst the *Beagle* sailed on to the familiar waters of the Strait of Magellan. It was March 1834 when we arrived at Woollya Cove. Every man aboard was curious to learn the fate of Jemmy Button, York Minster, Fuegia Basket, and the little settlement we had left with misgivings many months earlier. No one was more curious than our Reverend Matthews, who expressed his willingness to try again to establish a mission.

Three canoes paddled out to meet us, but we were in for a shock when we recognised Jemmy Button amongst the canoeists. He was a stout lad when we'd left him, hair neatly cut, particular about his clothes, afraid of dirtying his shoes, scarcely ever without gloves. It was painful to behold the poor fellow now: thin, pale, squalid, and naked excepting a bit of blanket round his waist, his matted hair hanging over his shoulders. I never saw so complete and grievous a change.

We brought Jemmy on board, got him some clothes, and sat down with him to dine in the captain's cabin. He used his knife and fork correctly and behaved as properly as though he'd never left us. FitzRoy offered to take him back to England, but he refused; offered a second time and was refused even more adamantly. We could not understand why he wanted to stay in this godforsaken place. He'd been robbed of all we'd left with him, the wigwams still standing but deserted, the garden a trampled ruin, York Minster long gone back to his own tribe with all of Jemmy's clothes, taking Fuegia with him.

Later that evening a boat pulled alongside with a woman in it weeping piteously — his wife, Jemmy told us. Pleased for him, we sent her gifts of a pretty shawl, a dainty handkerchief, and a gold-laced cap. But all she really wanted was Jemmy.

It was hopeless. Even Matthews agreed there was nothing left with which to work here. We gave Jemmy clothing and accepted some gifts from him — two spearheads and some arrows he'd made for the captain — shook his hand, and said farewell. Not one of us was free of sadness, and FitzRoy was uncommonly despondent, his experiment at civilising a complete failure.

WE LEFT Tierra del Fuego and sailed for the Falklands to join the *Adventure*. The best thing about that visit was the arrival of a packet boat from England with a bundle of mail. The letters, mostly from my sisters and written the previous October, were as always filled with titbits of gossip about friends, cousins, and the inhabitants of Chirk Castle. First, Catty:

The odious old Mrs. Biddulph & Miss Biddulph are come there, whom poor Fanny perfectly hates & who are intolerably proud and disagreeable to her. Fanny does lead a melancholy life with her old mother-in-law.

The Lady of Chirk Castle, I thought uncharitably, was getting exactly what she deserved.

On the subject of my beautiful cousin Charlotte Wedgwood, now Mrs. Langton, Catty continued:

Charlotte seems extremely happy, full of scrattles & household care (so unlike her). Mr. Langton is rather a chattering man who governs most absolutely in all trifling concerns. Susan attributes this to his having been one year on board ship when a boy. If this is the case, what will become of your poor wife, after so many years of your apprenticeship in the art of governing?

At my current rate of progress on a two-year voyage that was soon to enter its third year with no end in sight, the issue of a "poor wife" over whom I would supposedly have "absolute authority" seemed a remote possibility indeed and, in fact, one to which I gave little thought. We seafarers lived in a masculine world and the officers, at least, rarely spoke of wives or sweethearts.

Nevertheless, my heart did interrupt its regular rhythm when I came upon a letter in Fanny's own scrawl. *I do flatter myself you have not quite forgotten me altho' I am become a steady stupid old matron, and the pleasant times we have passed together in the good old times of the Housemaid & the Postillion at the Forest. My little daughter (how odd it sounds) is 6 months old, & a nice little creature she is. How I should like to see you here, my dear*

Charles. I long for you to return & hope this next year will certainly bring you back. I assure you I still look forward to some pleasant times again with you when you are cured of your roving turn and settle quietly with the little wife in the little parsonage.

What was it about ladies, I wondered, that kept them from moving on? They married, they bore children, they visited friends and family, but their minds seemed frozen at some point in the past. Despite my lengthy time away and all I had seen and experienced, they assumed I, too, was exactly the same as I was when I left England. I didn't want to hear any more about the girl I had once loved but who had pledged herself to another within weeks of my departure, married and given birth to a child, and was now plagued by an astoundingly selfish beast of a husband and a shrew of a mother-in-law. Yet, I confess, the sight of her handwriting was itself enough to make me long for the end of this never-ending voyage.

As I sat down to dine with FitzRoy in his cabin, this was much on my mind. "So, Darwin, I see that you made a great haul of letters today," said the captain.

"Indeed," I replied.

"Nothing unpleasant, I trust, my dear Philos? You look a trifle perplexed."

I hesitated. Could I speak to him of this? What advice would he have to offer? I had no notion of his own personal circumstances; we had never spoken of anything bearing on our lives in England. "No, no," I said reassuringly. "Nothing unpleasant at all." And I turned the conversation to other matters.

ONCE WE'D SAILED WEST again from the Falklands to the Patagonian shores, FitzRoy ordered the *Beagle* hauled up on the beach at Port St. Julian for repairs to her keel; she had struck rather heavily on a rock, tearing off some of her copper. FitzRoy was eager to do some exploring on land, and he now had in mind a glorious scheme: to reach the other side of the Andes. If we were successful, we would be the first Europeans to go so deeply into the country. Whilst the ship was being repaired under Wickham's charge, FitzRoy, Bynoe, Martens, Stokes, I, and a number of others set off in three whaleboats to explore the Rio Santa Cruz leading west towards the mountains.

The current proved much stronger than we expected, and we could use neither oars nor sails to move upstream. For eleven days we labouriously hauled the boats along with ropes. Temperatures dropped well below freezing. In the extreme cold our guns would not fire to bring down game when we were lucky enough to sight it. FitzRoy put us all on half rations of dry, hard ship's biscuit. Most of the men clearly wanted to turn back — cold, tired, hungry, and frightened, too, by the hostile Indians we believed were watching quietly, perhaps preparing to attack. Finally, FitzRoy called a halt to the expedition. We needed only three days to get all the way downstream.

It had been a rugged undertaking, but nevertheless I was thrilled by the geology, seeing with my own eyes proof in the rocks that the Biblical story of the Flood could not be literally true. I believed that the cliffs of the river valley and of the Andes Mountains had slowly over an immense period of time risen above sea level. Clearly, these stony layers had been laid down over a much longer period than the forty days and nights described in Genesis.

By the first week of May we were aboard the newly repaired *Beagle.* Martens and I had shot several of the deerlike guanaco, and our water barrels were brimming. Then I made one more expedition on this inhospitable land and nearly came to regret it.

On a relatively calm day I went ashore with a few sailors to collect what might be my last geological specimens from that area. But when the time came to return to the ship, the sea was too rough for the jolly boat to fetch us. We would have to spend the night on the beach.

It was very cold, but by huddling together we could make the best of it. I yearned for the shingle beaches of England, where little pebbles make a much more comfortable bed than the hard, frozen ground. Then the rain began, and we were all sufficiently miserable. I never knew how painful cold could be. I shivered so much I was unable to sleep for even a minute. A second night passed with no rescue; we had consumed our supply of biscuit, and now we were hungry as well. How the men must have blamed me for a misery that lasted two days! Never was I so glad to be on board the *Beagle,* even as she tossed and rolled and my stomach tossed and rolled as well.

*   *   *

IN JUNE WE SAILED through the Strait of Magellan, past towering icebergs and glaciers, past the magnificent sight of Mount Sarmiento, past the East and West Furies — a rocky group of small islands that seemed a death trap — and out into the Pacific Ocean. Every inch of the way we were punished by gale winds, lashing rain and sleet, and monstrous waves. The southern hemisphere was now heading into winter.

A little farther to the north in an area FitzRoy called the Milky Way, so many breakers crashed upon the rocks that one sight of it was enough to make any mortal dream for a week about shipwrecks, peril, and death. With that safely behind us we felt supremely grateful to have left Tierra del Fuego and the detestable southern latitudes forever.

Chapter 15

Earthquake & Volcano: 1834

SURVEYING ALONG THE COAST of Chili, the *Beagle* and the *Adventure* dropped anchor June 12th at Chiloé, a bleak island where the rain never ceased. We stayed for some days in order to replenish supplies — pigs and potatoes were as plentiful as in Ireland — and sailed on. Presently we had a grievous matter to attend to: George Rowlett, the ship's purser, had succumbed to a complication of diseases. He was a good friend to many and well respected by all. I thought he had not been the same since the death of poor little Musters.

Mr. Rowlett's body was prepared for burial by his messmates and sewed up in his hammock by the sailmaker. A bag of sand was attached to the dead man's feet and his body laid out on a plank. The tolling of the ship's bell summoned officers and crew to the main deck. We stood with our caps held over our breasts as Captain FitzRoy read from the Book of Common Prayer in an unsteady voice.

"Forasmuch as it hath pleased Almighty God of His great mercy to take unto Himself the soul of our dear brother George Rowlett here departed, we therefore commit his body to the deep, to be turned into corruption, looking for the resurrection of the body, when the sea shall give up her dead."

"Amen," we murmured. FitzRoy nodded to the seamen standing next to the body. I thought the captain himself did not look well; his hands were trembling. As Covington played a sombre tune on his fiddle, the men tipped up the plank, and the body plunged into the sea, the splash of water over the body of an old shipmate an awful and solemn sound. It was the fifth death we'd experienced on the *Beagle,* and it exacted a heavy price from us all.

WE ENTERED THE HARBOUR at Valparaiso. The climate was delicious — the sky clear and blue, the air dry and the sun bright. The pretty whitewashed houses were picturesque, the views of the distant mountains sublime. Compared to any place we had visited, Valparaiso seemed almost a sort of London or Paris. FitzRoy planned to stay for an extended time, whilst the *Beagle* was again put up for repairs.

A box had arrived from Shrewsbury with the boots I badly needed, and there was a packet of letters from my sisters. As usual there were none from Ras, who didn't like to write, though I thought him a capital fellow for sending me boots and books and whatever else I asked for. I arranged the letters by date and prepared to enjoy each one.

Catty reported that Father's trip to visit Winchester and Salisbury cathedrals had been spoilt by the gout, the worst he'd ever had, and he was laid up for seventeen days. That was in November, almost a year earlier. How was he now? Better? Worse? She added a bit of rather shocking gossip about Ras, who was spending entirely too much time with Hensleigh Wedgwood's wife, the former Fanny Mackintosh. Everyone in the family believed Ras was in love with her, Catty said, and Father fumed that an affair was likely to become public knowledge at any time.

We're continuing our efforts to pair him off with Emma Wedgwood, scarcely a new idea. They have a great deal in common and most agree would make an excellent couple.

But Caroline's letter, begun December 30th and offering best wishes for a happy new year — it was mid-October of 1834 as I read this — had this to say: *Erasmus is become quite a grand man. He has a cabriolet & a few weeks ago my father gave him a beautiful grey horse, a hunter. I think you will hardly know Ras, he is become such a happy person.* Imagining Ras running about the streets of London with his cab and grey amused me, but what about his love affair with Hensleigh's Fanny? And the matchmakers' attempts to marry him to Emma Wedgwood? There was no mention of that.

A second letter from Catty written at the end of January delivered good news: Fox was getting married.

He appears to be much in love with Miss Fletcher, and it appears that his bad health has been partly caused by his anxiety about her feelings. Now it is happily settled, I do hope he will become stronger. I could not imagine Fox sick with love, but I was glad to hear his health had improved.

In the last of the letters, written on February 12th, my twenty-fifth birthday, Susan sent birthday greetings. She also set about improving me, as she had done nearly all my life. *How very much we enjoyed your journal and what a nice amusing book of travels it would make if printed, but there is one part I shall take in hand as your Granny, namely several little errors in orthography. It is my duty to point them out.*

I couldn't dispute Granny's corrections. I confess that I did spell *quarrel* with a double *l*, omitted the *d* from *landscape* and the second *h* from *highest*, spelt *cannibal* with an *a* instead of an *i*, and wrote *peaceable* as *peacible*.

⁓

ON MY SECOND DAY ashore in Valparaiso I paid a visit to an Englishmen's club and was startled to hear my name: "Darwin! I'll be deuced if it isn't Gas!"

There, grinning broadly, stood my old school chum, Richard Corfield. Soon we were tucking into a fine dinner of fresh roast beef and catching up on our lives. A year or two older than I, Corfield had come out to Valparaiso soon after university. "I courted a lady, but she rejected my suit," he explained. "As good a reason as any for settling halfway round the world, wouldn't you say?"

He'd gone into the import business and made a success of it. His older brother, a friend of Ras, had written to him about my voyage, and before the meal was finished Corfield invited me to make his home my headquarters for as long as I was in Valparaiso. I accepted, and the next day I moved with my servant into Corfield's delightful house, one story high with all the rooms opening onto a pretty courtyard. Over the next fortnight he introduced me to a number of Englishmen who had settled in that city, and soon I was enjoying a satisfactory social life.

But I could not remain at leisure for long. Fine views of the mountains fired my curiosity, and in August I left the seductive comforts of Corfield's house to set out on horseback with Covington. We travelled north a short distance along the coast before turning inland towards the Andes. I stopped at a gold mine, the rage for mining having left scarcely any area untouched. I was aghast at the poverty of the labourers. Naked except for cotton drawers, they carried loads of ore weighing over a hundred pounds up rickety ladders from the bottom of mineshafts 450 feet deep. These men were not slaves, but may as well have been. They were paid next to nothing, allowed only rations of bread and beans, and treated worse than any horse by their taskmasters.

Now riding south with the idea of making a great loop, we visited several small villages, the names of which

I could scarcely spell or even pronounce. In St. Jago, the capital of Chili, a lively city surrounded by majestic snow-topped mountains, I stayed for a few days in a little English hotel. Continuing south and then west towards the coast, and finally north again to Valparaiso, I planned to complete the circuit in six weeks. But the final two weeks of my expedition were of such great misery that I thought I should soon be having the captain's sombre words read over my body. I blamed my wretchedness on some sour wine that did violence to my stomach and sent me into dreadful fevers.

Too weak to sit on a horse, I sent Covington to hire a wagon and make up a pallet in it for me for the remainder of the journey. I was near collapse when Covington half carried me into Corfield's house and summoned the ship's surgeon. For the first time in my life I was seriously ill. Bynoe came and dosed me with calomel, a purgative, to rid me of fever. But that failed to cure me. For a month I lay in bed, unable to conquer the weakness or loss of appetite. During those long, fretful days, it was all I could do to hold a book or put pen to paper. My thoughts were disordered. I considered returning to England, but the notion of enduring months of seasickness in my present condition was unthinkable. It was a grievous loss of time, as there was much more exploration and collecting I wished to do.

FitzRoy came to call, hovering over me like a worried auntie and making sure I was well cared for. He saw to the shipment to Henslow of specimens I had spent many hours preparing with Covington's assistance: bird skins, pillboxes filled with insects, small parcels of seeds, plants gathered in Patagonia, a sealed bottle of water and *gaz* collected from a hot springs at the foot of the Andes. FitzRoy promised to delay sailing till I was fully recovered.

Lieutenant Wickham was another frequent caller. Though he often complained I brought more dirt on board than any ten men, I had missed him greatly after FitzRoy placed him in command of the *Adventure*. Aside from FitzRoy, Wickham was by far the easiest man amongst the officers with whom to converse, and I welcomed his visits.

One pleasant afternoon as we sat in Corfield's lovely English garden with birds trilling and roses just coming into full blow in the southern spring, I sensed the lieutenant's unease. After some delicate prodding he at last confided that FitzRoy was considering a return to Tierra del Fuego. I groaned. It was the last place in the world I wanted to go.

"The captain feels he has not yet finished the survey to his complete satisfaction," Wickham said. "But he is keeping this plan very secret, lest the men should desert. Everyone so hates that confounded country."

I believed something more was afoot here, and Wickham confirmed it. "The captain believes he is going mad."

The lieutenant raked his fingers through his thinning hair and fixed his gaze on the ground. I knew, as he surely did, that FitzRoy's predecessor as the *Beagle*'s captain had died by his own hand, blowing his brains out with a pistol; that former captain's depression and rash act were a result of the pressures to chart these extreme southern waters. FitzRoy was under similar pressures. Wickham must have known, too, that a strain of madness ran in FitzRoy's family, his uncle having slashed his own throat.

"Do you agree he's going mad?" I asked.

Wickham hesitated. "It's possible, but I don't believe he is." He recounted what had happened whilst I was ill. "The Admiralty dealt him a bitter blow by refusing to approve his purchase and refitting of the *Adventure*."

FitzRoy had paid for all of it out of his own pockets — he was the descendant of a wealthy family and his fortune was large, but perhaps not large enough for this. He had been sure the Admiralty would approve what seemed an excellent idea and reimburse him, but his request was turned down. "They have criticised him for investing so much time and money in the survey of Patagonia and Tierra del Fuego. He is exhausted in body and mind, and his funds are rapidly becoming exhausted as well."

A servant brought us tea and sweet biscuits on a silver tray, and for a time we sipped our tea in silence, our eyes on the far-off mountains but our thoughts on FitzRoy.

"He has sold the *Adventure* and laid off her crew," Wickham continued. "This has grieved FitzRoy badly, especially since he got for the *Adventure* far less than he had invested. For days on end he refused to leave his cabin. When he did come out, he was extremely thin and showed a morbid depression of spirits. He asked Bynoe for his medical opinion. Bynoe said overwork was to blame and encouraged him to rest and regain his strength. The advice did no good. FitzRoy resigned his command."

FitzRoy resigned? I was stunned. "What is to happen now?" I asked.

The lieutenant shrugged. "FitzRoy appointed me to take command of the *Beagle,* though it's the last thing I want — not under these circumstances. The Admiralty has instructed FitzRoy to finish the survey of the southern parts and then return to England by way of the Strait of Magellan and the Atlantic. I've tried to persuade the captain it would be better to continue his survey of the west coast, and then to proceed across the Pacific, as the original plan called for."

"And have you been successful in your persuasion?"

Wickham shook his head sadly. "He has already written out his resignation and posted it."

I BEGAN TO CONSIDER my own options. Illness does make one long for home. For weeks I had made use of Corfield's library, often immersing myself in the poetry of William Wordsworth. I was drawn particularly to his Tintern Abbey poem:

> *Five years have passed: five summers, with the length*
> *Of five long winters! And again I hear*
> *These waters, rolling from their mountain springs*

With a soft inland murmur. — Once again
Do I behold these steep and lofty cliffs . . .

I read the lines again and was so overcome with home-sickness that I determined to take leave of the *Beagle,* make my way to Buenos Ayres, giving the Andes a thorough examination en route, and then sail directly for England. By that plan I could be home in little more than a year.

But no sooner had I made my decision — which wavered whenever I thought of what I would certainly be missing — than Lieutenant Wickham returned with a fresh report: He was now convinced the captain was quite sane, and he had succeeded in persuading FitzRoy nothing could be gained by his resignation.

"I swore I could not be induced under any circumstances to return to Tierra del Fuego," the officer explained. "I told him we must finish surveying the coast of Chili, and when that was done, head out into the Pacific and complete our circumnavigation of the world."

"What does FitzRoy say?" I asked.

"He is won over. He withdrew his resignation — it had not yet left with the mail bound for England — and has resumed command."

I breathed a grateful sigh. I would not leave the *Beagle.* I would continue with her to the end of the voyage.

WHEN I RETURNED to the ship soon after, it was clear to me that the captain, gaunt and hollow-eyed, was far from recovered from his melancholy state. Perhaps I wasn't fully recovered from my illness either, for the two of us immediately had a furious argument.

We were dining in the captain's cabin when FitzRoy began to complain. "What a deuced nuisance, Darwin! I'm apparently expected to entertain all the supposed 'important people' in town, bring them on board, give them food and drink and amusement, answer their ignorant questions . . ." He trailed off wearily.

Trying to be helpful, I said, "Perhaps it's not really necessary, FitzRoy. A note of thanks, perhaps some small gift, might be a sufficient gesture."

FitzRoy instantly turned on me, dark eyes blazing. "You, sir, are an ingrate!" he shouted. "Precisely the sort of man who would receive any sort of favour and make no return!"

Amazed by this outburst and rather injured by his unjust accusation, I got up and left the cabin without a word.

I returned to Corfield's house and allowed a few days to pass before I again boarded the *Beagle*. FitzRoy welcomed me as cordially as though nothing unpleasant had happened between us. On November 10th we were under way again. Our destination was rainy, forlorn Chiloé, but our mood was hopeful. Nevertheless, home remained many months in the future.

For the remaining weeks of 1834 we worked along the coast of Chili, often admiring the range of mountains gleaming in the distance. At Christmastime the white-topped cone of Mount Osorno began to spout volumes of smoke as Martens sketched the event. Shortly after the beginning of the new year, the volcano erupted, putting on a spectacular show of light and colour.

The entire crew remained on deck throughout most of the night, taking turns at FitzRoy's telescope as the mountain heaved up enormous boulders and the sky was bathed in a great red glare. This was not nature as Wordsworth described it, peaceful groves and copses and hedgerows, but a force of immense power and ferocity.

The rumbling continued, but the *Beagle* crew went on with its assigned tasks. Some of the men gathered the abundant oysters and fish from the sea and birds and geese from the air, and we all dined well.

In early February we dropped anchor in Valdivia, a congenial place where the residents extended their hospitality, even inviting us to a ball where dark-eyed señoritas in bright satin gowns smiled and flirted behind their fans with our officers.

Valdivia was memorable for more than comely smiles and blushes. Covington and I had been walking along the shore and stopped by a wood to rest. Stretched out on the ground, I felt the earth tremble beneath me. An earthquake! I leapt to my feet. I had no difficulty standing upright, but the motion, like a ship in a little cross ripple, made me giddy. The world moved beneath our feet like a crust over a fluid.

Valdivia was little harmed, the houses being made of

wood and able to survive the motion. But days later when the *Beagle* sailed up the coast, we found Concepcion in ruins. The town was nothing but heaps of brick, tiles, and timber, and not one house left habitable. A tidal wave had further buried the ruins with all sorts of wreckage — chairs, tables, bookshelves, whole roofs of houses, various merchandise scattered about. The front of the great cathedral was now a pile of rubble, leaving only the two side walls standing. Everywhere was desolation. FitzRoy used his instruments to measure the elevation of the area and determined that it had been raised up about eight feet.

On March 10th I wrote to Caroline, describing the earthquake and advising her of our determination to continue the journey round the world. Assuming all went according to plan, I was now eighteen months from my homecoming. Still, I couldn't refrain from imagining it, down to the last detail: *I am beginning to plan the very coaches by which I shall be able to reach Shrewsbury in the shortest time. The voyage has been grievously too long; we shall hardly know each other.*

At four o'clock the next morning I started on a second expedition to the Andes with a string of hired mules, two peasants, and a trusted guide. On my first Andes journey I had suffered badly from the ill effects of sour wine, or perhaps the bite of some malevolent insect. The dangers I confronted on this second journey were much worse: the possibility of death by freezing in a snowstorm; death from *punado,* altitude sickness;

death by tumbling into a crevasse. But the views were so magnificent, the colours so intense, the air so crystalline, that I shut the dangers out of mind. Eventually I found myself on the eastern slope of the Andes, the side I'd once viewed from Patagonia but had been out of my reach.

By the end of this expedition I had concluded that the area had been undergoing continuous uplift little by little over millions of years. What's more, the elevation was still continuing, even to the present day. The entire area was not solid but was constantly in motion and constantly changing. The more I explored, the more of the whole field of geology I understood. One small thing led to another, and then another. It was like learning a new language. I knew I'd need plenty of proof to convince anyone, and I had collected a mule's load of rock specimens revealing deposits of seashells far from any ocean. Who would believe me if I didn't carry evidence?

AFTER A MONTH of exploring with a great deal of geologising and no disasters, I arrived back in Valparaiso in the best of moods. Since leaving England I had not made so successful a journey — or such an expensive one. I would have to ask Father for additional funds. I was sure he would not begrudge it if he knew how deeply I had profitted from it.

Several letters had arrived in my absence. Here was Caroline writing last September to say they'd received my letter sent a year ago from the Falkland Islands.

Charlotte's husband was in poor health, Fanny Biddulph looked exceedingly thin but exceedingly pretty, my dogs remembered their training and had not chased off after a hare when ordered not to, and the old laboratory where Ras and I had performed so many interesting experiments had been turned into a laundry. A laundry! It seemed more like a lifetime than just a few years had passed.

Preparing for one more expedition in South America — my last, I felt sure — I wrote to my sister, begging her to remind Father to have funds available for me in case of emergency and to assure him I would spend scarcely a penny whilst crossing the Pacific. Privately, though, I did believe I could manage to spend money on the moon.

At the end of April Covington and I travelled northwards through miserable countryside, mountains as bare as turnpike roads. I carried my bed, a kettle, a pot, a plate, and a basin. We bought corn or grass for the horses and food to cook for ourselves and slept in the open air, as it was impossible to sleep in any of the houses on account of fleas. What a torment those ravenous little beasts could be in a hot, dry climate! But then, when we journeyed to the Cordillera de la Costa, a mountain range parallel to the Andes, the temperature plummeted, and it was most piercingly cold. For the next ten weeks I rode, explored, and collected, and was glad when it was over. FitzRoy picked us up on July 5th and we proceeded to Lima, in Peru.

Three stern letters awaited me there, each sister taking her turn to sound the same theme. January: *Papa wishes to urge you to think of leaving the* Beagle *& returning home. The time of the voyage goes on lengthening every time we hear of it* . . . February: *I wish with all my heart you would be sufficiently homesick as to proceed no farther with this endless expedition* . . . March: *It will end by your wasting the best years of your life on shipboard.*

I wrote to assure them I truly *was* on my way home, future letters must be directed to Sydney, and they would not hear from me for upwards of ten months.

Then I took time to send a letter, long overdue, to Fox. My dear friend with whom I had shared so many delightful breakfasts at Cambridge was now a clergyman with a wife and a child on the way — how strange that seemed!

Returning to dear old England is a glorious prospect. Five years is a sadly too long period to leave one's relations & friends; one returns a stranger.

Finally, I acknowledged to Fox the question that continued to trouble me: *What I shall ultimately do with myself* — quien sabe? *Who knows?* My friends were mostly married and settled — Ras was an exception — but I still had no idea of what my future life would be. Was I wasting the best years of my life, as my sisters seemed to believe? I didn't think so, though I could not say to what end these years were being spent.

I am very anxious to see the Galapagos Islands, I wrote my friend. *I think both the geology & zoology cannot fail to be very interesting. We sail within the week.*

Chapter 16

Enchanted Lands: 1835

EARLY SAILORS CALLED the archipelago the Enchanted Islands, perhaps because they were uncommonly difficult to navigate. Ocean currents were strong between the ten principal islands and countless very small ones, and winds blew fitfully or fell calm in this area known as the Doldrums. The skies were almost always too misty or blanketed with clouds to steer by the stars. FitzRoy's assignment was to fix the exact location of the Galapagos once and for all. Not an easy task, but I harboured no doubts he was up to it.

We sailed from South America on September 7th and reached Chatham Island eight days later. Instead of the silky tropical beaches I had envisioned, I saw only black lava, broken into forbidding heaps of slag. But the bay swarmed with fish and turtles popping their heads up, and soon we were having a merry time of it, dropping lines overboard and hauling in a plentiful catch. Later in the day I went ashore with Covington and Bynoe to observe the sleepy-eyed tortoises that gave the chain of islands its name: *Galapagos* is the Spanish word for tortoises.

These clumsy creatures lumbering slowly over the rocks appeared to be animals from antiquity or even inhabitants of some other planet. I could walk close behind one whilst it was quietly pacing along and it took no notice of me, but as soon as I passed by, it would draw its head and legs into its shell, utter a deep hiss, and fall to the ground as though struck dead. I managed to measure one old fellow at seven feet in girth; others looked even larger. When I tried riding on its back, it made no objection, but I found it hard to keep my balance.

After a few days of exploration, we found a source of fresh water to replenish our supply and took on board a number of tortoises. Turned on their backs and stacked below decks, they could remain alive for weeks on end without food or water and would provide many a good meal of fresh meat for officers and crew after long days at sea. I thought the meat delectable when fried in its own oil or roasted in its breastplate. The young tortoises made capital soup, a heartier dish than the clear broth I'd enjoyed at Maer Christmas dinners in my boyhood.

At Charles Island I met the governor, an Englishman named Nicholas Lawson. He showed me round his compound, ornamented with flowerpots made of tortoise-shells. Lawson pointed out that the tortoises differed from island to island, and he could tell from which island any one of these creatures originated by the shape of its shell — some domed, some saddle-shaped, some in between.

We observed an astonishing variety of birds — doves, hawks, and flightless cormorants with small wings but large webbed feet suited to ocean swimming. Boobies waddled about on feet so brightly coloured they might have been painted, and plummeted from great heights straight into the sea to catch a fish. Red-footed boobies fished in different waters from their blue-footed cousins, and all were so tame you could catch them easily in your hands.

I industriously collected all the animals, plants, insects, and reptiles I could, labelling, cataloguing, and preserving with Covington's assistance. Though all living creatures on those islands interested me, not all forms of life were beautiful in the way one might ordinarily define beauty. Most repulsive were the iguanas — big, ugly black lizards two or three feet long that scrambled over the rocks, dove into the sea to feed, and quickly scrambled out again; "imps of darkness," I heard them called. On Albemarle, the largest of the islands, I encountered an even more hideous type, orange and yellow with brick red on its hind parts and a row of spines down its back. They sat on tree limbs, chewing on leaves and gazing at me with singularly stupid-looking faces.

FitzRoy left me on James Island with Bynoe and several others, and we spent nine days gathering specimens. Mockingbirds, doves, and an array of finches darted amongst the verdant growth. Of the finches, each type was slightly different. Some nested near the ground and fed on cactuses or seeds; some nested high in the trees with a diet of insects or leaves; each had a beak suited to its food. I was struck by the many kinds I observed, all differing from island to island. The mockingbirds I collected from Chatham Island were not like those on Charles Island, and neither of those were like the mockingbirds on Albemarle. I could not have imagined that islands only fifty or sixty miles apart, most of them within sight of one another, formed of precisely the same rocks, located in a quite similar climate, rising to a nearly equal height, would have been populated by such different kinds of the same species. I could think of no explanation for such differences.

We came back to our camp, sunburnt, hot and thirsty at the end of a day of collecting to find that a breaking wave had spoilt our source of fresh water from a small well. We had brought no other water with us.

"We're in trouble, lads," said Bynoe. "If the *Beagle* doesn't fetch us by tomorrow, we're likely to expire."

Obtaining a supply of water fit to drink had been a problem throughout the voyage, and the water stored in barrels on board the *Beagle* had often been foul, but this was the first time I realised I was in real danger of dying of thirst.

As we sat on the beach gloomily pondering our fate, I remembered lines from Sulivan's favourite poem:

Water, water, everywhere
Nor any drop to drink.

Suddenly, out of the blue, an American whaler dropped anchor nearby. We waved our hats, and a jolly boat soon came to meet us. We explained our situation, and in an hour's time they'd brought us three casks of water and a gift of onions that pleased our ship's surgeon, one of the foods that prevented scurvy. We agreed that the Americans were much more obliging than any of our countrymen would have been.

AFTER LITTLE MORE than a month, with thirty tortoises on board (plus two small turtles as pets) and our water barrels filled, we were under sail again, bound for Polynesia. Our destination lay 3,200 miles to the west, nearly four weeks of boundless ocean. Trade winds blew steadily round the clock, carrying us along at the rate of 150 to 160 miles a day. The sun shone brightly in a cloudless sky, and FitzRoy and I spent many a pleasant hour on deck, reading and talking, as the deep blue ocean passed swiftly beneath our bow. We arrived in Tahiti, the largest of the Society Islands, in mid-November, a Sunday on our calendar but already Monday on theirs.

Tahiti was the sort of tropical paradise one reads about and dreams of, and I was immediately charmed. A crowd of people with merry, laughing faces gathered to welcome us and accompanied us to the home of the missionary, Mr. Wilson. The manners of all were entirely faultless, banishing at once the idea of savages. I had never seen finer-looking men, tall, broad-shouldered, and strong, wearing little more than a coloured cloth tied round the waist. Most were tattooed with elegant designs. The women decorated themselves with flowers in their hair or behind their ears, but they were dressed from neck to feet in long, shapeless gowns brought by the missionaries — a disappointment to some of our seamen, who had heard stories of half-naked beauties.

Wishing to make a short expedition into the mountains, I hired two guides to accompany me and my servant. We set out the next day through a lush, green valley with an abundance of tropical fruit trees — banana, orange, breadfruit, and pineapple. Cocoa-nut trees grew everywhere, and I found that nothing tastes more delicious than the milk of a young cocoa-nut after hours of walking under a burning sun.

The valley soon narrowed to the width of a stream with high, precipitous walls, and we began to climb, cautiously making our way along ledges so narrow I had to cling to the walls. As we climbed higher, we resorted to ropes to haul ourselves up the vertical wall of rock. Higher still, our guides propped a notched log against a wall as a ladder, the notches to serve as footholds. The abyss beneath the ledge on which we perched must have been five or six hundred feet deep. Had this extreme drop-off not been partly concealed by overhanging ferns, my head would have turned giddy and nothing should have induced me to attempt the ascent.

I looked up at the makeshift ladder and then glanced at Covington. He was pale and sweating, but he said nothing, no doubt cursing himself for having agreed to work for me. I nodded and began climbing. Covington followed.

"Well done, Covington!" I cried heartily once we'd reached the top.

"We'll have to go down again, sir," he said, his pallor now even more noticeable.

"It won't be nearly so bad," I assured him, trying to convince myself as well.

We came to a small, flat area, and our guides deftly erected a shelter of bamboo stalks tied with strips of bark and covered with banana leaves. That done, they built a fire by twirling the end of a blunt pointed stick in a grooved log, an art I finally managed to master. They wrapped meat and fish and fruit in banana leaves and roasted the parcels on a bed of hot stones, producing a meal so delicious it nearly made up for the terror of getting there.

ONE NIGHT during our stay in Tahiti FitzRoy invited Pomare, queen of Tahiti, to dine aboard the *Beagle*. He ordered the ship decorated with flags and sent four boats to fetch the queen and her court. The queen was a large, awkward woman entirely lacking in grace and beauty and wearing a perpetually sulky expression. Once we succeeded in hauling our guests aboard, Covington brought out his fiddle and our sailors did their best to entertain this royal person with song. FitzRoy ordered sky rockets fired off into the ink-dark night, bringing the evening to a satisfying end.

After ten peacefully enjoyable days — though decidedly frightening at times — we weighed anchor and steered a course for New Zealand. Beside me on the deck with a gentle land breeze at our backs stood our own missionary, Richard Matthews. I'd spent little time in his company since we'd retrieved him from Tierra del Fuego some twenty-one months earlier. I believe he felt a great despair for his failure to establish a missionary colony with the Fuegians, and since then he'd kept mostly to himself, avoiding our expeditions ashore. But now his pallid face was alight with eagerness.

"Ah, Mr. Darwin, I am convinced I shall find fulfilment with the good people of the Church Missionary Society," he said with more enthusiasm than I had ever heard him express. "My brother serves in a New Zealand village, you know." He was like a man transformed.

THE JOURNEY to New Zealand occupied three weeks with the usual ill effects on my stomach. Though relieved to be ashore again, I was sorely disappointed in the country, much of it uninhabited and useless, and disappointed, too, in most of the inhabitants.

FitzRoy and I decided to visit Kororarika, the island capital. Besides a considerable native population, unattractively tattooed and dressed in dirty blankets, we saw English residents of the most worthless character, many of them convicts who had escaped from the penal colonies of New South Wales. This town seemed the very stronghold of vice with spirit shops everywhere and a whole population addicted to drunkenness. Their houses were filthy, and the idea of washing themselves or their clothes appeared never to have crossed their minds. Though many tribes in other parts had embraced Christianity, in Kororarika the greater part remained heathens. Compared to the Tahitians, these men seemed utter savages.

Not all of our sojourns were so depressing — quite the opposite when we accompanied Matthews to call on the missionaries in the village of Waimate. The sudden appearance of an English farmhouse and its well-dressed fields, placed there as if by an enchanter's wand, lifted my spirits. There were three large houses in which the missionaries — Mr. Richard Davies and two others — resided with their wives and children; nearby were the huts of the native labourers. After we had tea with Mr. Davies and his family, he took us on a tour of the farm.

Large gardens and orchards were planted with every fruit and vegetable that England produces as well as many belonging to a warmer clime: asparagus, kidney beans, cucumbers, rhubarb, apples and pears, figs, peaches, apricots, grapes, olives, gooseberries, currants, and many different kinds of flowers, in addition to fine crops of barley and wheat and of potatoes and clover. Round the farmyard were stables, a threshing barn with a winnowing machine, a blacksmith's forge. A little rill had been dammed and a water mill erected. In the middle of all was the happy mixture of pigs and poultry that may be seen in every English farmyard.

"Five years ago nothing but the fern flourished here," said Mr. Davies with a well-deserved note of pride. "Native workmanship taught by me and my fellow missionaries has effected this change."

We passed the night in this English Eden, and the next day, Christmas, found a merry group sitting round a table at tea — in the centre of the land of cannibalism, murder, and other atrocious crimes. Here we said farewell to Matthews, looking more cheerful than he had in many months, and left him to stay at the farm where his brother was expected to return soon.

A few days later we sailed away from New Zealand, all of us glad to leave, for — except for that small paradise — this was not a pleasant place. It was worth remarking that we first departed the shores of dear old England four years earlier. I never dreamt I would still be so far from home — halfway round the world.

On January 12th, 1836, we dropped anchor in Sydney, New South Wales, Australia. It was a new continent and the beginning of a new chapter in our voyage.

SYDNEY WAS A CIVILISED city, entirely different from all I had witnessed in New Zealand. Here were the things one could expect to see in a bustling capital: superb villas, a fine museum, a splendid botanic garden, handsome carriages rolling through the streets. For a time I even thought it might be a decent place for one such as myself to settle; one could grow rich very quickly. On the other hand, many of those well-dressed citizens were men who had come out from England as convicts, sent some years earlier to serve their sentences. I suspected that a good many of those I passed on the street were still somewhere between a petty rogue and a bloodthirsty villain, and that convinced me to give up the idea of living there permanently.

I paid a call on Conrad Martens, the ship's artist, who had settled in Sydney after he'd left the *Beagle* to travel the previous year.

"Come, Martens, show me your pictures," I said after we'd drunk a bottle of wine and I'd regaled him with tales of my adventures in the Galapagos and Polynesia. I was unable to resist buying two watercolours, one of the Rio Santa Cruz, the river that had so taxed us in Patagonia when we set out to reach the Andes; the other was of the *Beagle* in Tierra del Fuego. I had to write to Father asking for additional funds — again.

The next day I hired a guide and two horses and set out on a ride into the interior. During the two-week expedition I observed a great deal of the geology of the land and the plants and animals unique to it. On my return I stayed a night at Woodbridge, the estate of Captain Phillip Parker King, father of Philip Gidley King, the young midshipman who had been my cabin-mate for much of the voyage. The elder King, nearly bald and with a booming voice, had commanded the original *Adventure;* FitzRoy had served under him. He seemed eager to make me welcome. FitzRoy had called on his former commander just days earlier, and King was much distressed by FitzRoy's appearance.

"What on earth has happened to FitzRoy?" King asked, appearing genuinely anguished. "He's but thirty, yet he looks years older."

It was true: FitzRoy's handsome face had grown haggard, his cheeks sunken, his once thick, dark hair now lank and thin. But the most drastic change, I thought, was in his eyes; though acutely intelligent, they seemed haunted.

"Captain FitzRoy has suffered greatly," I told his former commander, and explained what had happened. "I fear for his health."

King shook his head sadly. "Perhaps a good rest once he's back in England will set him right again. He is an excellent fellow, I'm sure you agree."

And I did agree, though privately I believed our captain still suffered many demons. He was of noble character, but was unfortunately affected with strong peculiarities of temper. No one was more aware of this than he. I often doubted what would become his end.

Captain King and his son, Gidley, took me to call on their relations at their country house — a handsome place, but not so grand as the great English estates like Maer and Woodhouse. We sat down to luncheon with their other guests, who included a bevy of pretty Australian girls, their blond hair, blue eyes, fair complexions, and modest manners so deliciously English-like one might have fancied oneself in England. (The food, too, was deliciously English, especially the trifle.) Being in such company reminded me of all that I missed.

I was surprised to learn that Gidley King had elected to leave the *Beagle*. I found an opportunity to speak with him before I left. "What shall you do now?" I asked the young man.

"My father wants me to sit for the examination in

order to be promoted to the rank of lieutenant," he said, "but I have no wish to do that. I would much prefer life as a farmer than as a naval officer, and I believe that's the life for which I'm best suited."

"So you don't have salt water in your veins after all?"

"I once thought I did. But I've become convinced otherwise."

"And what does your father say to that?" I asked, thinking of my own father's plans for me.

"He disapproves. But my mother does not. She says that no woman in her right mind should ever marry a seagoing man."

I thought Mrs. King's opinion was a highly intelligent one, and I wished Gidley well.

WE MADE THE SIX days' passage to the island of Van Diemen's Land, and I found I liked Hobart Town, the capital, even better than Sydney. Our next port was King George's Sound at the southwestern tip of the Australian continent — eighteen hundred miles of stormy sea. Heaven protect and fortify my poor stomach! The object of this part of the voyage was simply to take measurements of longitude with FitzRoy's chronometers. That work completed, we crossed the Tropic of Capricorn and made for the Keeling Islands in the Indian Ocean.

These islands were made up of reefs, beautiful formations of delicate coral polyps, and the clear water was shallow enough for me to wade from island to island. I splashed along waist-deep, brightly coloured fish darting round me, and thought about the infinite number of organisms with which the tropical seas teemed.

Then it was on to Mauritius, farther to the west. We were now most definitely homeward bound. The closer the day came, the more insistent was my desire to be back amongst friends and family. But what was my life to be, once this voyage was over? Certainly not what I'd once imagined. But *what*? For several years the picture had been blurred, shifting and changing.

I was past my twenty-seventh birthday. I had spent enormous amounts of my father's money. I had laboured for so many months — years, in fact! — with every ounce of energy I possessed, doing the hard work of science. The proof was in my notebooks and case upon case of specimens. Now, every day, I saw myself more clearly as a scientist, immersed in geology and natural history.

I looked forward with no little anxiety to the time when I should walk again with Professor Henslow, who, putting on a grave face, would decide the merits of my work. If he shook his head in a disapproving manner, I would know I'd better at once give up science, for science had given up on me. I would soon have the verdict.

It wasn't just Henslow whose approval I needed. I hoped Father would not be disappointed to see that I was not cut out for a life in the church. But would he understand that science was a useful life? Could he see me now as I saw myself — a scientist?

The *Beagle* sailed on towards home, and I prayed to my guiding star that he could!

PART III
Charles

Chapter 17

Towards Home: 1836

THERE NEVER WAS a ship so full of homesick men as the *Beagle*. Mauritius was a pleasing place, but with home on our minds almost constantly, no place would have been entirely charming.

Whilst at sea in fine weather my days passed smoothly. I was very busy, rearranging my old geological notes and, in fact, rewriting them and had begun to discover the difficulty of expressing my scientific ideas on paper. The task was pretty easy, as long as it consisted solely of describing what I'd seen, as I did in my journal, but when reasoning came into play, making the proper connections and explaining them clearly, the difficulty increased.

Covington sat with me at the chart table, helping to organise my papers — and such a lot of papers there were! His clear handwriting proved useful in translating my scribbled lists into something legible. In the captain's cabin FitzRoy was occupied in writing his account of the voyage, and he proposed I join him in the venture, mingling my journal with his. He was daily becoming a happier man.

My observations in geology had put me in high spirits, and I began to hope real geologists would consider them useful. To be near experts who could help identify my specimens — geological, zoological, botanical — I thought I'd need to live in London for a year. The prospect was not altogether pleasing to me. I disliked the idea of giving up walks in the country for life in the teeming city. Nevertheless, at the end of a year of hard work, I would have made greater sense of my materials and could decide the next step.

CONTRARY TO THE RULES of the universe, time had become elastic, stretching out long and longer. After what seemed an interminable month anchored near Cape Town, the *Beagle* rounded the Cape of Good Hope in mid-June, the start of winter below the equator, and we learnt our route was not certain after all. Quite possibly we would cross the South Atlantic and stop briefly at Bahia de Todos os Santos, then point our bow to the northeast and sail over the Atlantic once more before a final landing at Plymouth. Four months might become five. But what if five months stretched to six, and six turned to seven? The thought was more than I could bear.

We were bound for St. Helena in the middle of the South Atlantic sixteen hundred miles from the Cape, the British Crown colony where Napoleon had been exiled. As remote a spot as one could imagine, this speck of an island rose from the ocean like a huge castle surrounded by a great wall built of streams of black lava. I took lodgings high in the clouds, at an altitude where the weather was cold and the rains frequent, and for five days I geologised to my heart's content.

We proceeded next to Ascension, another dot on a map of the British Empire, a wasteland of volcanic lava flows surrounded by a raging ocean. A packet boat had left mail for us there, including nearly a year's worth of letters. Caroline's assured me of the arrival of my journal as well as numerous boxes of specimens I had feared lost.

I will say just what I think as to your style. I thought that you had, probably from reading so much of Humboldt, got his phraseology & occasionally made use of the kind of flowery French expressions which he uses, instead of your own simple straightforward & far more agreeable style.

Too much like Humboldt? It was Humboldt's book that first inoculated me with the desire to travel to exotic and distant places. I had not quite expected that kind of reaction from Caroline.

I turned to a letter from Susan, once again performing her role as Granny:

We are now reading your journal aloud, and Papa enjoys it extremely except when the dangers you run make him shudder. I cannot think how you could write such a collected account of your travels when you were galloping so many miles every day. When I have corrected the spelling it will be perfect.

She included an extract from a letter written by Professor Sedgwick to my old headmaster at Shrewsbury School, Dr. Samuel Butler, who had in turn forwarded it to Father:

It was the best thing in the world for Charles that he went out on the voyage of discovery. There was some risk of his turning out an idle man: but his character will now be fixed, & if God spare his life, he will have a great name amongst the naturalists of Europe.

I reread that passage several times over with considerable relish. So I had not turned out an idle man, or a pococurante! I would not be a disgrace to the family after all.

And then another from Caroline:

You must now hear how your fame is spreading — a note came to Father on Xmas day from Professor Henslow speaking most kindly of you & rejoicing you would soon return "to reap the reward of your perseverance and take your position amongst the first naturalists of the day." He sent along copies of extracts from your letters he had printed for private distribution & read at a meeting of the Cambridge Philosophical Society on 16th November.

I rushed down to FitzRoy's cabin with the letter and found him absorbed in a letter of his own. I thought I glimpsed a miniature portrait of a lady on his writing table that I had not seen before, but I was too excited by my news to remark on it.

"Yes, what is it?" he asked gruffly, plainly interrupted in the midst of important correspondence.

I read him part of Caroline's letter: *"amongst the first naturalists of the day."*

FitzRoy's sharp features relaxed, and he smiled

warmly. "Of course, my dear Philos," he said. "The world is thine oyster. Now if you would be so good as to pardon me? I have a letter that absolutely must be posted before we sail."

TILL FITZROY ISSUED the order fixing a westerly-southwesterly course from Ascension, every man aboard hoped we might now turn to the north and home. However, the captain had become convinced of errors made in his earlier longitudinal measurements, and he was determined that his voyage round the world that had begun in the South Atlantic must also end there. On August 1st we dropped anchor once more in Bahia de Todos os Santos on the coast of Brazil.

It had never occurred to me that I would again be in "odious South America," as my sisters described it, but once ashore I enjoyed tramping through the tropical forests as I had several years before, fixing forever in my mind the thousand beauties of the orange tree, the cocoanut, the mango and banana. On August 17th I boarded the ship. Now there could be nowhere to go but home.

We lay close-hauled to the wind, and the considerable pitching motion thrust me again into the grip of seasickness. Four days later we crossed the equator and on September 9th the Tropic of Cancer, stopped in the Cape Verde Archipelago for just five days — how interminable the days seemed! — and reached the Azores on September 20th. I hired a horse and guides and went in search of a volcano I'd heard of but found it hard to concentrate, so much was my mind on The End of the Voyage.

FitzRoy produced his handsome blue dress coat with the gold trim and cream-coloured trousers. He'd worn that uniform — perhaps he had two or three of them — every Sunday when he conducted divine services and any time he'd gone ashore on official business. Covington brushed my one decent set of clothes, made by an English tailor in Valparaiso, and trimmed my hair without commenting that my hairline had lost considerable ground to my forehead in the past five years. When he held up a mirror, I plainly saw baldness in my future.

The final amen to the voyage, four years, nine months, and five days after the *Beagle* had set sail from Plymouth in the last days of 1831, was a terrific storm in the Bay of Biscay, one last reminder of the miseries of sea travel. As we docked at Falmouth late on October 2nd, 1836, and the ropes were made fast, I swore a solemn oath never again to set foot on a ship.

I WAS PACKED and ready, carrying with me only my notebooks, a few personal items, and some ragged bits of clothing. I had arranged for storage of my equipment, books, and my most recent specimens till I could decide where to have them shipped. I had already said farewell to the crew, most of whom I would likely never see again, and to Covington, who would continue on to Plymouth and Portsmouth with the *Beagle*. I planned to retain Covington as my servant and assistant once I'd settled somewhere; he'd said he was agreeable.

The moment the gangplank was lowered, FitzRoy and

I shook hands and promised to remain in close touch. I was once again on English soil, but to my surprise and shame, I experienced no warm feelings. I could scarcely believe myself really there. Perhaps I was only dreaming and would soon awaken. That same night, a Sunday — and a most dreadfully stormy one it was — I set off by mail coach for Shrewsbury.

Through the dark, wet hours we rolled from stage to stage, stopping only long enough to change horses. By morning the rain had lessened, then ceased, and a few rays of sunshine pierced the iron grey clouds. I could not take my eyes from the English countryside, so gloriously green and richly cultivated. I marvelled, believing I had never seen anything so beautiful, whilst my fellow passengers seemed to take no notice of it whatsoever.

I arrived in Shrewsbury late on Tuesday, and the coachman let me down at the Lion Inn — the very same Lion Inn from which I had commenced my journey so long ago that it seemed another lifetime. It was raining lightly. I walked along the gleaming wet cobblestone streets and crossed the Welsh Bridge, pausing to gaze down at the rain-pocked waters of the Severn. Night had fallen, and as I made my way up to The Mount, I was reminded of the times I'd run breathlessly from school when I was a child and ached for the comfort of home.

The house was dark when I arrived, everyone doubtless asleep, and I thought it best not to disturb them. Instead, I turned and walked slowly back down the hill, crossed over the river, and wandered through the town, past the school and the old castle now veiled in fog, and finally to the Lion Inn, where I spent the night.

The next morning, five years and three days after I'd left, I retraced my steps, anticipating the welcome I knew would greet me. My family had always been predictable in their habits, and I timed my arrival for the minute they would be sitting down to breakfast. I let myself in by the side entrance I'd used on my unlawful runs from school and stepped quietly into the dining room.

The first to notice me was Nancy, my old nursemaid who still made her home at The Mount and had never failed to send affectionate greetings in my sisters' letters. She stared and then threw up her hands, crying, "Thanks be to God! It's Master Charles!" and burst into tears.

Conversation ceased, forks dropped. Mayhem ensued.

Immediately surrounded by the best and most loving family a man could wish for, I gave myself happily to their fond caresses and endless questions. Susan noted that I had, indeed, grown thinner — too thin, in fact; Cook would remedy that, she promised. Soon every maid, stable hand, and gardener — even old Abberley, now toothless — had rushed in to greet Master Charles.

But it was Father's amazed comment that I found most striking. "Why," he said, "the shape of his head is quite altered."

IT WAS NOT JUST the shape of my head that was altered. Everything seemed different, and yet the same. I was five years older, but so was Father, even more massively heavy, gouty, and short-winded, satisfied to sit in his library with his books or in his conservatory with his exotic plants. Marianne's husband, Dr. Parker, had taken over most of Father's medical practise. The yellow phaeton was long gone.

The sisterhood had done admirably in keeping me informed of events of their lives, both large and small. But I was surprised, even a bit shocked, to find that they, too, were five years older. Caroline was now thirty-six, her thick, black hair no longer so thick or so black, but streaked with grey and pulled into a matronly bun. Susan was thirty-three, more Granny-like in manner than ever, her brow often furrowed with disapproval at somebody or something. My dear little sister, Catty, who had once played Friday to my Robinson Crusoe fantasies, seemed to have kept some of that playfulness, though now twenty-six. My sisters were all still unmarried. There was no mention of Adam Sedgwick, and I dared not ask. All three were rapidly approaching spinsterhood, but apparently content with looking after Father. Marianne, they reminded me, had five children; when I'd left, she had but two.

I STAYED IN SHREWSBURY for just ten days, though once again time was playing its elastic trick on me and seemed longer. For the first three or four days I was happy to sleep, eat the fine roast beef dinners that Cook prepared, and wander round the property in the company of Abberley, who leaned heavily on his cane and seemed deeply interested in my observations of plants collected in my travels. In the evenings I sat by the meagre fire and drank tea whilst my father and sisters plied me with questions about the voyage, Captain FitzRoy, and whatever else they could think of.

During those days and nights when I'd yearned so intensely for home, I had not recognised the difficulties I'd encounter once I was actually there. The questions my family asked were about some hair-raising event that had taken place several years earlier — my adventures with the gauchos of Patagonia, for example, or our encounters with the Fuegians — and I was hard put to recall the details. Now I was far more engaged by the geological discoveries I'd made, but my sisters merely listened politely to what I had to say and then moved on to some other subject in which they were interested.

Inevitably, that subject was my "plans."

"You expect to stay in Shrewsbury, I suppose?" Caroline asked, more a statement than a question.

"We can understand that you might not wish to return right away to studies for Holy Orders," Susan broke in, her needle darting in and out of a piece of linen embroidery. "There's ample time for that."

"And you might even wish to consider something different," Catty said, continuing the line of thought it seemed they'd discussed for months and possibly years.

I muttered something about "pursuing a life in science."

"Well, of course, Charley! That's quite possible!" Caroline cried enthusiastically. "Many of the men you most admire are Anglican clergymen as well as respected scientists."

"Mr. Henslow," Susan suggested, glancing at Catty

for agreement. "And that lovely Mr. Sedgwick. Surely you could have no objection to that?"

"It wouldn't take long to finish the required studies," Caroline assured me, "and then you could settle down to an orderly life, doing all those things that seem to fascinate you. Somewhere in the country — perhaps right here in Shrewsbury! How splendid that would be!"

"We do so regret that somehow Ras has managed to slip away from us," Catty complained. "He has his place in London and hardly ever comes to see us."

They had quite a lot to say about Ras — I was grateful to have the subject of the conversation veer away from me and fasten onto my unsuspecting brother — and a woman he seemed interested in, or who at least was interested in him.

"Miss Harriet Martineau," Susan advised, lips pressed in a disapproving line. "She writes books," she added. "A feminist. We understand she moves in exalted intellectual circles. We could name others better suited."

My sisters didn't speak then, or in any of the evening chats that followed, of the little wife and the children they expected me to acquire, once I'd settled into a cosy parsonage somewhere nearby. But I knew they were thinking of it.

Nor did they mention the Lady of Chirk, the former Fanny Owen, now Mrs. Biddulph, but I knew they were thinking of her, too.

"Squire Owen always enquires so kindly after your welfare," Catty said. "He is most eager to see you."

"And the Wedgwoods, particularly Uncle Jos and

Charlotte, never fail to ask after you," Caroline said. "You must plan a visit to Maer as soon as possible."

"I long to see them all," I said. "But it's essential that I see Henslow almost at once. I've sent him a great many of my specimens, enough to fill a museum, and we must go over everything."

I didn't tell my sisters on any of those evenings there was no way on earth I could now study for Holy Orders and confine myself to the life of a country parson. Or even of a Cambridge fellow, like Sedgwick.

Nor did I mention to them my plan to live in London, and to begin thinking and writing about all I'd seen, everything I'd learnt.

Father listened thoughtfully to the conversations and said nothing. He was plainly relieved to have me home again, safe and sound. There were no questions about my plans, for the immediate future or for the years beyond. Unlike his attitude when I was a boy and then a young man who appeared bent on disappointing him, he now seemed content with who I was, and for that I felt the deepest gratitude. Both of us had changed.

After ten days of my sisters' solicitude and my own growing restlessness, I packed my notebooks and boarded a coach to London to see Ras. From there I planned to visit Henslow in Cambridge. And then I'd get to work.

Chapter 18

The Scientist: 1837

RAS PROUDLY SHOWED ME round his handsome new lodgings in Great Marlborough Street, six spacious rooms and a pretty rear garden.

"It was dreadfully difficult to have it all set up as I wished," he said, waving a languid hand at a houseful of polished mahogany tables, fringed draperies, velvet-covered settees, ornate silver candlesticks, and Wedgwood china. "You're most welcome to stay here as often and for as long as you like."

In the midst of the noisy tumult of London, Ras lived a resolutely tranquil life. To my eye, though, he looked thinner, paler, less energetic.

"You haven't yet seen what filthy specimens I've brought back with me," I warned, "or you'd quickly withdraw your invitation. But I'd be grateful if you'd help me find a place and put my name up for membership at your club."

"Gladly, dear fellow," Ras promised. "You're not planning to linger in Shrewsbury, then?"

"I have work to do here."

Ras smiled knowingly. "No doubt the sisterhood has already complained to you that I positively refuse to venture to Shrewsbury more than once a year. It's a perfectly dreadful journey, as I'm sure you know from experience."

I nodded. "They did mention it."

Ras still spent much of his time with Hensleigh and Fanny Wedgwood and their children — their daughter Julia, nicknamed Snow, was his pet, according to Caroline — and they were frequent visitors whilst I stayed with him. There was no hint of any improper affection for Hensleigh's wife. As the sisterhood had advised, he did appear quite taken up with Miss Harriet Martineau, famous as an author and lecturer on economics and politics. At the snap of her fingers Ras drove her round town in his cabriolet without complaint. She had recently returned from a long visit to the United States, where she had sharp things to say about the plight of women and slaves and was not at all reticent to express her strong opinions. I wondered if Ras might be considering marriage to this formidable creature. She had already lectured him about his idleness, he confessed.

"Perfect equality of rights is part of my doctrine," the lady informed me in her unpleasantly loud voice the first time we met. "I mean equality between men and women as well as between the races." I found her ideas interesting but the lady herself exceptionally unattractive.

"I'm not sure Harriet envisions any sort of actual

equality between herself and Ras," Hensleigh later murmured. "It seems she has the upper hand and intends to keep it that way. She has announced her intention to speak to him one day soon about her notions on marriage."

I STAYED WITH RAS for a fortnight, and whilst there I received a cheery letter from Captain FitzRoy. Since the *Beagle* had put in at Falmouth in October, FitzRoy had taken her on up the English Channel to Plymouth, by order of the Admiralty, and finally to Portsmouth, where the crew was paid off. At every port the ship, famous for her long voyage, attracted a great deal of attention. His letter concluded with astonishing news, sprinkled with exclamation points:

Indeed, Charles Darwin, I have been very happy — even at that horrid place Plymouth — for that horrid place contains a treasure which even you were ignorant of! Now guess — and think & guess again. Believe it or not, the news is true — I am going to be married!!!!!to Mary O'Brien. — I had decided on this step very long ago. Now all is settled & we shall be married in December.

FitzRoy, married? No, I would not have guessed it — until I recalled the miniature portrait I'd glimpsed on his writing table. I supposed now that he had met and admired her before we set sail. For five years — how unbearably long it must have seemed to both of them — they had corresponded, thought of each other constantly, longed for each other. He had never let one hint drop about this, just as I had never spoken a single word to him of Fanny Owen. But Mary O'Brien had waited for him, and once they'd met again, it was done!

Half of me envied him — but only half. The other half felt dismay. I could not imagine I would ever have such good fortune, or that it was even the kind of fortune I desired.

HENSLOW, NOW SILVER-HAIRED, greeted me warmly when I arrived in Cambridge. "What a great lot of science you've done, Darwin!" he exclaimed, thumping me repeatedly on the back. For the next few days we talked, often far into the night. "I have put all of your specimens into storage, and I should be most happy to assist you in whatever ways I can."

"I'll take rooms nearby. We'll get to work as soon as I'm free." I winced, thinking of the demands on me, and added, "Family visits, you know."

Tearing myself away from Henslow, I stopped briefly in Overton on my way to Shrewsbury at the home of my eldest sister, Marianne, where a quartet of nephews stared at their uncle Charles in round-eyed wonderment and I was introduced to their infant sister. Then I returned to The Mount.

Those first weeks back in England were far more difficult than I had ever imagined. There were constant invitations, all from people I cared deeply about: Fox and his wife and baby daughter on the Isle of Wight; good old Herbert, founder of the Glutton Club, who had given me the first really good scientific instrument I'd ever owned; Uncle Jos and the Wedgwoods at Maer; Squire Owen at Woodhouse. I felt I could not possibly see and talk sensibly to all those people, or meet all their expectations. They would anticipate greeting the same old Charley who'd gone off and had a number of adventures since they'd seen him last. But I was not the same old Charley; I felt I'd become an entirely new man.

I did make a brief visit to Maer. Uncle Jos greeted me like a long-lost son. Emma and Elizabeth had hurriedly read a book by some earlier explorer about his gallop across the pampa, and my cousin Harry asked intelligent questions, all listening attentively to what I had to say. But I daresay I disappointed them. I felt deeply the absence of their sister Fanny, Miss Memorandum, and I found myself tongue-tied. Maer — Bliss Castle — was the place where I had once felt most at home, and now it was as though I were amongst complete strangers.

All I could think about was the vast amount of work I wanted to accomplish. I could not afford to lose any more precious time calling on friends, no matter how old and dear.

I did not ride over to Woodhouse, though I would have enjoyed a tramp across the heath with Squire Owen. No doubt he would have found me odd, compared to his former young and eager hunting companion. I no longer believed in shooting living creatures simply for the sport of it, and that would have surely surprised him. It surprised me, too. One day after a massive shooting spree in

Argentina that had ended with dozens of dead animals, I felt nothing but disgust. From that day forward the only reason for killing an animal was for food or for a specimen to be studied — not for the pleasure of adding to my tally.

As soon as I decently could, I left Shrewsbury and rushed back to London. There I met with Charles Lyell, a geologist whose theories had provided the basis for my own ideas. We spoke the same language. I saw in him a man who was neither parson nor university lecturer but a man of science free to follow his natural inclination — to think.

I wanted to settle my jolted brain into some sort of order. In January I rented lodgings in Cambridge across from the Fitzwilliam Museum where, I imagined, Titian's *Venus* still reposed behind a velvet curtain, and I despatched an urgent message to Covington in nearby Bedfordshire, asking him to join me.

"When we were at sea, I thought I could not wait to see my mother and sisters," he remarked in his usual flat voice as he was unpacking. "But after a fortnight I'd had enough of their endless questions and worried looks." That was all he had to say about his family visit, and I understood completely.

We set to work. Most of the floor was crowded with plant, animal, rock, and fossil specimens, the results of five years of collecting, to be sent off now to various scientific experts for identification and classification. A dining table, several chairs, and one threadbare sofa held papers that would become the source of my books and articles. All of this lay within reach of the writing desks Covington and I maintained at opposite ends of the room. The two of us could work for hours without exchanging a word. The only other person I spoke to was Henslow.

At the same time I was occupied with my journal of the voyage, which I had agreed to publish with Captain FitzRoy's official description of the expedition. Heeding Granny's criticisms, I tried to rework the journal in a more accommodating style. Perhaps in rewriting my journal I would begin to make some sense of the ideas bombarding me from every side. But the work went well, and by the spring of 1837 I no longer felt I had to stay shut up in my Cambridge rooms. Covington packed up my papers and specimens, and we moved to London.

LONDON WAS AN ODIOUS, dirty, smoky city, and yet nowhere else could I be so near the very things I needed most — museums, libraries, scientific organisations, the scientists themselves. I took rooms in a house at No. 36 Great Marlborough Street, quite near Ras's house at No. 43.

Ras stopped by as I was settling in, stared at the barrels and boxes and piles of books and papers stacked randomly on the floor and every available surface, and shook his head. "I am both impressed and appalled by the amount of materials you've got here, Charles," he said, and drifted away.

My brother took charge of my socialising. Many diverting intellectuals attended Ras's frequent dinner parties; amongst those usually present were Hensleigh and Fanny, of course, and Harriet Martineau. She made herself very agreeable and held forth on a most amazing number of subjects. She may have had her marital eye on Ras, but thus far nothing had come of it.

The life of a bachelor was not an easy one, though Ras had apparently decided it was easier than the alternative. If one were an eligible man, neither too poor nor too ugly, then one became fair game. I found I had a certain social appeal as both bachelor and traveller returned from exotic climes. Everyone, it seemed, had an unmarried sister or daughter I simply must meet. But I found this exhausting. I had always felt awkward in the presence of the fairer sex, and five years in the company of men — from the charming and aristocratic captain to the crudest gaucho — had not made these meetings any easier for me.

Charles Lyell, the geologist whose work deeply influenced my thinking, was married to the eldest daughter of Leonard Horner, also a geologist. Horner had five unmarried daughters, all of them brilliant, educated, talented, and accomplished: one was a botanist, another a linguist as well as a watercolourist, a third a collector of ferns and shells. I was always made welcome at the elegant Horner house in Bedford Place, across from the British Museum and a short walk from my cheerless rooms, and I often broke my vow of unstoppable work to visit that amiable family. The temptation was too strong to resist.

It seemed I had my pick of the "Horneritas," as Ras called them. Did I favour Katherine, the collector of shells? Susan, the artist and linguist? Or Frances, with her impressive botanical collection? The two youngest, Joanna and Leonora, not yet twenty years old, were not considered candidates. Lyell and Professor Horner himself, as well as my brother and Hensleigh's wife, kept up a steady murmur of encouragement. To make sure I got the hint, Aunt Sarah — my mother's elderly sister — sent me forty pounds as an advance wedding gift. No bride was specified, but clearly everyone expected me to choose one, and soon.

THE CARE AND LABOUR involved in preparing, preserving, cataloguing, and shipping my specimens, from the smallest insect to the mighty *Megatherium,* had begun to pay off. But the one place where I had not been as careful and methodical in my work as I should was with my bird specimens from the Galapagos Islands.

Perhaps I'd suffered from some sort of enchantment, like the early sailors, for I had not kept separate the specimens I'd collected from each island. At the start of 1837 I turned over my bird skins to John Gould at the London Zoological Society. Gould, considered the leading ornithologist in Britain, set aside his usual work to examine the skins.

Within a week he reported that the birds I'd identified as blackbirds, gross-bills, and finches were actually all finches, so peculiar that they formed an entirely new group of a dozen separate species. He speculated that the three mockingbirds I'd collected from three different islands (but hadn't labelled which island) weren't simply variations, as I'd thought, but three distinct species of mockingbird, each originating on a different island and unknown beyond the Galapagos archipelago.

An affable fellow with a cherubic face, Gould showed me through his laboratory. Dozens of stuffed birds appeared to watch us intently. "See here, Darwin," Gould said, "I need additional bird skins, properly labelled, if at all possible, if I am to ascertain whether these are separate species or simply varieties of the same species. I haven't enough evidence to make a determination."

I promised to try.

Covington volunteered to lend some of his bird skins — he had four in good condition and knew precisely where he'd got them. Another source was Harry Fuller, the captain's steward, also an enthusiastic collector of birds. FitzRoy, too, agreed to let Gould have a look at his collection, after which he would turn it over to the British Museum.

In the end I accepted Gould's conclusion that all these birds, including some I'd labelled as wrens, were separate species of finch — not just different varieties, but separate species. That was important.

In mid-March I was seated in the audience when Gould rose before the members of the London Zoological Society and began to speak. His subject was the small rhea — the *avestruz petise* — I'd shot in Patagonia and on which my shipmates and I had heedlessly dined till all that was left was skin and bones. Gould had studied the remains I'd managed to retrieve and had given our bird a name: *Rhea darwinii*. Blushing, I rose from the audience to accept the congratulations of the members of that erudite body.

But why two different kinds of rhea, a small one in the south of Patagonia, a large one in the north? Why different species of finches on neighbouring, nearly identical islands of the Galapagos? What did it all mean? I'd be deuced if I could imagine how it had happened. I had no idea that yet made any sense to me. I filled a notebook with ideas, questions, musings, then bought several more notebooks and gave them letter names: *A* for geology, *B* for species that seemed to change, and so on. I didn't want to let anything slip away. My mind never rested.

RAS INVITED ME to another of his elegant dinners. "Caroline is coming up to London for a few days," he said. "She and Emma Wedgwood will stay with Hensleigh and Fanny. They'll come here for dinner, of course."

"Is the sisterhood still nudging you towards marrying Emma?" I asked. Ras and I had grown closer since I'd become his London neighbour, and I felt easy asking him questions of a personal nature. "I think they'd prefer our cousin over Miss Martineau as a possible sister-in-law. Harriet's political leanings are too extreme for Shropshire sensibilities."

"I've learnt to ignore our sisters, Charley," Ras said with a slight smile. "Best if you do the same. It will make life easier for you."

Ras's dinners were leisurely affairs with plenty of time for conversation between courses. After we'd made our way through the cream of carrot soup, the baked salmon, and the roast chicken with prunes, I told the story — I'd already told it many times — of the rare specimen we'd eaten for dinner in Patagonia.

"And now," I said as the butler refilled our wineglasses, "that poor unfortunate bird has been named for me."

Emma, seated across the table, smiled brightly. I noticed, not for the first time, that Emma was quite pretty. She was twenty-nine, a year older than I, and wore her auburn hair drawn up in shining loops; her gown of blue silk showed off the flawless skin of her neck and shoulders. I wondered that Ras could have preferred Harriet Martineau, who ordered him about as though he were her footman. Miss Martineau seemed ready then to hold forth in stentorian tones — she was rather deaf and used an ear trumpet, and therefore often spoke too loudly.

But before she did, Emma said in a clear voice, "Charley, please do tell us about the Fuegians."

I obliged her, creating a vivid picture of the naked savages with painted faces and sealskins thrown over their shoulders. "They ran and shouted until they foamed at the mouth and blood streamed from their noses," I said.

But this wasn't the kind of story the other young ladies wanted. Caroline looked a little pale. "Charley, please —" she said weakly. "Not at the dinner table!"

"Perhaps not anywhere," Miss Martineau said severely. "Perhaps we'd rather hear about something botanical."

I realised I'd have to be careful of the anecdotes I produced in mixed company.

After we'd finished the meal — the trifle, the savoury, the glasses of port — Emma came to sit beside me. "I liked your story, Charley. I don't think you should try to make it more palatable for the ladies." She glanced at Miss Martineau.

"I see," I said, feeling suddenly awkward. Why on earth was Ras not pursuing our charming cousin?

"Do you remember the time we were together at Maer, before you went away?" she asked. "You upset the boat, and we both fell into the pool!"

"My dear Emma," I said, remembering the moment well, but not as she described it. "I believe it was you who upset the boat. In any case, that is one of my best memories of being on a boat. I was dreadfully seasick every minute the *Beagle* was at sea, and I shall never again repeat the experience."

"But you would not object to taking me boating on the pool?"

"I should find it a pleasure," I said.

Ras interrupted, summoning us to the parlour. "Emma, my dear, I've just purchased the most exquisite little spinet pianoforte, and I should be honoured if you'd give it a good thumping, so we can consider if I've done well in buying it."

Emma excused herself and rose, obeying Ras's summons. "I've been studying the music of Frédéric Chopin," she explained. "I heard his music in Paris, and I do think it quite lovely."

Lovely, indeed. Emma's playing had become much more controlled than when all of us were younger and spent our holidays at Maer. She had a polish now and an elegance that had been missing before, but a little of the exuberance was gone.

THE SUMMER OF 1837 brought unaccustomed excitement. The whole country was going mad for the accession to the throne of our new queen, eighteen-year-old Victoria, with all the accompanying pomp and ceremony. But much closer to home and our hearts in Shropshire was the marriage of Caroline.

Emma's brother Joe surprised everyone by proposing to my sister in July. Caroline was thirty-seven, and Joe was forty-two. I had long ago assumed she would not marry, believing silent Joe would never be able to bring himself to utter the words that must have been locked up in his heart for at least a decade or more. I did not go down from London for the wedding at the little Maer church on August 1st. Even my other sisters had little to report. Knowing the principals, I suspect there was no more than a quiet exchange of vows, Joe probably just nodding his head when required.

Covington and I had fallen into a predictable daily

routine. He slept in the small room we used for storage, rose early, and prepared a breakfast of sausages and eggs whilst I dressed. We worked till hunger began to gnaw at noon, Covington hurried out to purchase a meat pie or some other item for a hasty midday meal, and we resumed our work. Late in the day I sometimes joined Ras at one of his dinners or, more often, went alone to the Athenaeum, the private club to which I'd been admitted. This routine carried us through day after day of unstoppable work, week after week, for months on end.

I felt driven. I hated giving up even a small amount of time for social events, convinced that if I didn't get things organised and written as quickly as possible, I would never finish. I took on more and more projects, fueled by my excitement for the ideas tumbling through my head. The understanding of what I was demanding of myself made me positively dizzy.

Ras expressed disapproval. "Slow down, Charles," he said.

I could not.

I was in an ill humour — I disliked London, the dirt that sifted into my wretched rooms above the noisy street, the abominable murky atmosphere. I needed to get away from the city, to walk in the country. I wanted to visit Henslow in Cambridge for quiet talks, and I'd even thought of making a dash to the Isle of Wight to see Fox, but the time, the time, where would I get the time? I had to inform my sisters that I could probably not visit till the next summer. I knew they'd be disappointed. They wanted their "dear Charley" back in their lives, the way it had been before. But I wasn't that boy anymore. I scarcely recognised him.

I was thinking constantly, and some of my ideas were so startling I scarcely knew how to deal with them. These ideas had to do with species that were not unchanging, as God had created them and the Bible described them, but had somehow changed slowly over long periods of time — as slowly as mountains lifted up, as slowly as coral reefs grew in the sea.

"Transmutation," I scribbled in my notebook. I was pretty sure it did happen, but I didn't have any idea how. The idea of transmutation was radical. It would disturb people who believed in the six days of Biblical Creation. It would upset my sisters — though probably not my father or Ras — and most everyone I knew.

At the same time a different kind of radical idea had crept furtively into my mind, slyly shouldering aside the others, refusing to be ignored or to go away.

The idea was this: *Perhaps I should marry.* Perhaps as much as I needed a walk in the country, I needed a wife.

Chapter 19

Questions & Answers: 1838

I HAD BEEN BACK in England for some eighteen months, and my brain was in turmoil.

On my fingers I ticked off the names of friends who had embarked upon the sea of matrimony since I'd first set sail on the *Beagle:* Lyell had married the eldest of the Horneritas and now regularly encouraged me to follow his example. My cousin Fox, with whom I had first glimpsed the voluptuous Venus on the wall of the Fitzwilliam Museum, had become a husband and father. Hensleigh had married the lovely and amusing Fanny, and they'd recently produced a third child. Moody Captain FitzRoy, now the father of a daughter, seemed content with the deeply religious lady who had waited five years for him. Cameron, the school chum who used to help with my experiments, had acquired a splendid helpmeet for his life as a country parson. Even silent Joe Wedgwood had summoned the courage to marry my sister.

Now Covington reported that Lieutenant Sulivan, who by turns amused and irritated his shipmates with his lengthy recitations, had married an admiral's daughter apparently fond of poetry. Most surprising, she intended to go on voyages with him, and they would sail for the Falklands shortly, if they had not already. (As an admiral's daughter, perhaps she was immune to seasickness.) That brought the number to seven. If I counted Charles Langton, who'd married my cousin Charlotte, the total rose to eight.

Obviously still not members of that elite society: my brother Ras and I.

Sitting in the library of my club one evening after dinner, I seized a sheet of stationery, drew a line down the centre, and began to scribble two columns: on the left, a column in favour of marrying, and on the right, the opposite view. I paid no attention to grammar and punctuation (this would have upset Granny, but she would never see it) and sometimes failed to keep the pros and cons strictly separated. Generally, though, the argument went thus:

MARRY	NOT MARRY
Children – (if it please God) – Constant companion & friend in old age who will feel interested in one – object to be beloved & played with. – better than a dog anyhow. – Home & someone to take care of house – Charms of music & female chit-chat – These things good for one's health – but terrible loss of time. My god, it is intolerable to think of spending one's whole life like a neuter bee, working, working & nothing after all. – No, no won't do. – Imagine living all one's day solitarily in smoky dirty London house. – Only picture to yourself a nice soft wife on a sofa with good fire, & books & music perhaps – Compare this vision with the dingy reality of Grt. Marlbro' St.	Freedom to go where one liked – choice of Society & little of it. – Conversation of clever men at clubs – Not forced to visit relatives, & to bend in every trifle. – to have the expense & anxiety of children – perhaps quarrelling – Loss of time. – cannot read in the Evenings – fatness & idleness – anxiety & responsibility – less money for books &c – if many children forced to gain one's bread. – But then it is very bad for one's health to work too much. Perhaps my wife won't like London; then the sentence is banishment & degradation into indolent, idle fool.

Marry – Marry – Marry

By the end of this exercise, I had nearly convinced myself what I should do. I continued scribbling on the back, determined to consider the subject methodically and rationally, without allowing myself to be swept away by emotion.

Supposing I accepted the arguments favouring marriage, there were more questions to be considered. First and foremost: *When? Soon or late?* My pen raced across the page.

If I married tomorrow, there would be an infinity of trouble and expense in getting and furnishing a house — morning calls — loss of time every day, unless my wife made me keep industrious. Then how should I manage all my business if I were to go every day walking with my wife. Eheu!! I should never know French, or see the Continent, or go to America, or go up in a balloon, or take a solitary trip to Wales. I'd be no better than a poor slave. — Never mind my boy — Cheer up — One cannot live this solitary life, with groggy old age, friendless and cold and childless, staring one in one's face, already beginning to wrinkle. Never mind, trust to chance — keep a sharp look out.

There was yet another, larger problem: I considered a wife the most interesting specimen in the whole series of vertebrate animals, but only Providence knew whether I could ever capture one. So there was the torment: What lady would think me an acceptable husband? Suppose she, whoever she was, found my nose objectionable, as FitzRoy once said he had, believing I lacked sufficient energy and determination to endure an arduous sea voyage round the world. And how much more arduous was a voyage on the sea of matrimony! And if a specimen in a white petticoat actually found me acceptable, could I then provide a means of feeding her? Father had promised me a generous allowance if I were to become a clergyman and had a modest living in the church. But since I was no longer on the path to becoming a clergyman, would my father continue the allowance he'd once promised? I had come into shares of an inheritance from my mother on the Wedgwood side, but that would scarcely be enough to house and feed a large family. The whole notion of existing in poverty on the fringes of London or Cambridge whilst pursuing my scientific investigations put me entirely out of sorts. My stomach churned, and my head ached till I finally consulted a physician about ailments that included heart palpitations.

"I strongly urge you to knock off all work for a time," the doctor recommended. "Go live in the country for a little while. Ride, fish, shoot, rest. That's my prescription."

I decided to follow the physician's advice. I made an excursion to Scotland, visiting old haunts in Edinburgh and walking along the beach at the Firth of Forth, the site of my first serious collecting. Then it was on to the Highlands and a tramp through Glen Roy for some serious geologising. On my way back to London I stopped for a fortnight in Shrewsbury for a long-delayed family visit.

Father and I sat in his library, the scene of a number of uncomfortable conversations in the past. Nothing about the room had changed — the same book-lined walls, the same leather chair built to accommodate his girth — but at least one of the two people now seated in that room, and perhaps both, had changed a great deal. Over the next few days our discussions ranged across a broad spectrum of subjects, medical, scientific, metaphysical. For the first time in my life I felt completely easy with my father — so easy that I soon found myself candidly describing my dilemma.

"I have been contemplating the idea of marriage," I said, adding hastily, "but with no one in mind. I'm worried about how I'm to live and support a wife and children. Is it better to be married and live in near poverty in London, where I would be like a prisoner, or be married and live in poverty of a different sort in Cambridge, where I would be cut off from the scientific circles so important to me?"

"You needn't make such a choice, Charles," Father said, puffing as though he had climbed a flight of stairs; he had become quite short of breath. "I can promise to keep you at a decent level of comfort. I am a much wealthier man than you had perhaps imagined — not, I hasten to add, made wealthy by the practise of medicine, but from years of investments."

He reached for an accounts book, bound in black and red, opened it and pushed it towards me. On one double page were entered the companies in which Father had invested — canals, railways, property — and the income from each. It was a considerable amount.

This revelation cast my dilemma in a different light

but still left important questions unanswered. I confessed then that I had drawn up a balance sheet: to marry or not. "Sometimes it seems that Ras has the ideal life," I said. "He is able to do precisely as he wants, but for me the yearning for feminine companionship sometimes outweighs that."

"Quite understandable, my dear Charles," Father said. "And should be undertaken sooner rather than late, especially when one has children. One's character is more flexible when one is young and one's feelings are more lively, and those are good things." He was silent for a moment, gazing off at some distant memory, and then added quietly, "You'll soon be thirty. And you know, Charley, if you don't marry soon, you will miss so much good, pure happiness."

I knew he must have been thinking of my mother when he spoke of that kind of happiness, and I was deeply touched.

SOON AFTER THE CONVERSATION in the library at The Mount, I made a short visit to Joe and my sister Caroline, who confided the happy news that a baby was expected in the winter. From there I moved on to Maer. It wasn't entirely true that I had no one in mind: Emma's sweet face had come into my thoughts with disturbing regularity. But I had not formulated any sort of plan.

Emma and her sister Elizabeth managed to dragoon me into helping them organise a charity bazaar, an enterprise that consumed most of the day. Such a vast assortment of treasures — embroidered handkerchiefs and purses, painted trays and similar items, each one uglier than the last — all of which must be sold to uphold someone's family honour. And so we purchased each other's trinkets.

"The Fuegians would clamour for this," I said of a particularly garish hair ornament, but we did succeed in finding a pretty little wax doll for Hensleigh's daughter, Snow.

That evening after dinner, I followed Emma into Uncle Jos's library, where we found ourselves alone. "Foul weather," I observed, staring witlessly at the rain sheeting off the windows.

Emma, looking less uncomfortable than I felt, rose easily to the occasion. "If it weren't, Charley, I should invite you to take a boat out onto the pool, and we could try very hard not to capsize and drown each other. Maybe it will be fair tomorrow."

"I leave tomorrow for London," I said.

"But you've hardly got here!" Emma complained. "I never have a chance to ask all the questions I've been storing up for you. And Miss Martineau isn't here to tell me that my questions are not appropriate."

"You can ask some of them now," I assured her.

Emma's blue eyes widened behind the little gold spectacles perched on her nose. "Tell me about the tortoises," she said. "And the iguanas."

I was so distracted by her physical presence, so close, and the slight whiff of scent from her hair, and her fetchingly bare arms, that I could hardly speak about the creatures that had so fascinated me on the Galapagos Islands. Here was enchantment of a different sort.

"The tortoises are enormous," I said. "And the iguanas are truly hideous, inhabitants of another universe. You'd like the blue-footed boobies, though — they are quite comical."

Soon I found myself conversing with her easily, and the thought came that I might well speak now the words already formed in my mind: *Emma, will you consent to be my wife?* The words may have even been on their way to my lips, but I hesitated too long, the moment passed, and the words evaporated, leaving a throbbing headache and a turbulent stomach in their wake. I excused myself and fled from the library, fighting back the nausea.

The next day the Wedgwood groom drove me to the new train station at Whitmore. My last glimpse of Emma's face, puzzled and disappointed, haunted me. I wondered if I'd ruined my chances with her forever.

THE TRAIN RIDE to London was my first experience of this newly established mode of travel, and it was a great disappointment, rough and much plagued with many changes and lost luggage. We were late getting into Birmingham on account of high winds, and the London train would not wait five minutes. The indignation of all of us unfortunates was immense. One passenger sought revenge by taking the night horse coach to London, at his great inconvenience. I comforted myself with beef-steak and tea whilst waiting many hours for the next train. Everyone said this was the way of the future. I could only hope for improvement.

By the first of August I was back in my dreary rooms on Great Marlborough Street, having been away for nearly a month. In my absence Covington had done what he could to improve our lodgings, adding shelves, putting things in order, using household money to buy a few items, like matching plates and cups, in the event that we should have visitors.

I decided to write to Emma, something in a light-hearted vein about the problems of travel by rail, and suggest that I might soon visit Maer again. When I read it over, the letter seemed shallow and foolish, but I sent it off anyway and once more retreated into my work. I had nearly finished rewriting my *Beagle* journal, and Covington copied the untidy pages in his meticulous hand. I seldom went out, unless it was to visit Ras when he was at home and not off somewhere with Hensleigh and Fanny, and I continued to take my evening meals alone at the Athenaeum.

I had a long list of books, which I read methodically, making detailed notes. Amongst them was an essay by Thomas Robert Malthus on *The Principle of Population*. His idea was simple: Population growth, if unchecked, always exceeded the means to support it. The result was famine and death. In nature, he observed, all plants and animals produced far more offspring than could survive. At least some did survive, if not starved, killed by predators, or destroyed by natural events. But why did those manage to live and to carry on whilst others did not? I thought some survived by mere chance. But others must have been bigger, stronger, faster, tougher, or cleverer than the others and managed to stay alive long enough to produce the next generation.

Since the Galapagos visit I had been pondering the question of transmutation — changing forms — and how new species came into being. After reading Malthus, I was struck by the notion that favourable variations — size or strength or speed or some other advantage — would tend to be preserved. Over time, this would result in the formation of a new species.

At last then I had a theory by which to work. My ideas were starting to come together.

ONE NIGHT, as autumn was settling damply over London, Ras and I dined together. After finishing a plate of baked oysters, I put my question bluntly. "Catty and Susan insist that you are in love with Emma Wedgwood. Is that so, Ras?"

Ras touched his napkin to his lips, looked away, and then met my eye directly. "No, Charley, I am not in love with Emma, though a dear, sweet thing she is. I thought it would be as obvious to you as it is to everyone else: I'm in love with Fanny Wedgwood. I have been in love with her since she first moved to London with her father. I may have been in love with her even before that. Certainly before she married Hensleigh, who often treats her brutishly. The sisterhood tried vainly to marry me off to Charlotte, before she met Langton, and then to Emma, and they've nearly convinced themselves I'll marry Harriet, though she frightens them half to death with her outspoken opinions on nearly every topic. But the only woman I have ever loved, and the only woman I shall ever love, is Fanny. It's hopeless, of course. I take what I can get — the few scraps of attention she can spare me."

His frankness shocked me. So it was true, what Catty had written many months ago whilst I was on my voyage and Father had feared a scandal. "Does she love you as well?"

Ras shrugged. "Perhaps. She doesn't say. She knows how I feel, and I believe she cares for me, but I have never heard the words I long to hear." Ras sighed deeply and sank into a dark mood. Then he seemed to rouse himself. "And you, Charles? Are you in love?"

"I don't know," I answered truthfully. "I'm not sure I know what it is to be in love."

"Let me restate my question, then. Are you thinking of asking Emma to marry you?"

I hesitated. "I suppose I am."

"You *suppose* you are?" One eyebrow raised, the other frowned, an odd quirk of his.

"I don't know," I repeated. "I believe I need a wife; I believe marriage would be a good thing. I've known Emma all my life, though now it seems I scarcely know her at all. Perhaps it's all a huge mistake."

"Someone else, then?" Ras asked. "One of the Horneritas? Katherine is plainly in love with you, and

Mrs. Horner is determined she shall have you as a son-in-law."

"She is? But why me?"

"You are being a trifle thick now, aren't you? A bit of a blockhead? Perhaps because you are much in demand as a scientist with a promising future."

"And more than a bit of a bore, I'm afraid," I said. "The Horneritas are 'excessively brilliant,' as Susan would say, and I'm certain would give me scarcely an evening's peace, always wanting to engage in an intellectual discussion when I simply wish to stare into the fire. I worry that Emma will expect balls and parties and going out in society, and I just can't bear —"

Ras cut me off. "That's Fanny Owen you're describing, Charles. Now *that* marriage would have been a mistake of great magnitude. But our cousin at Maer Hall is not like Mrs. Biddulph. Emma has a serious side, if you'll allow her to show it, and I think her the perfect wife for you. She turned away any number of suitors whilst you were off in pursuit of the wild *Megatherium*. Please don't waste any more time with your useless dithering — as soon as you possibly can, ask her to marry you and be done with it."

I took Ras's advice to heart — not immediately, but after a few more weeks of useless dithering. I gathered my courage and decided to travel once more to Maer Hall, determined to speak to Emma about my feelings, though I was uncertain exactly what those feelings were. I rehearsed the words over and over and braced myself for rejection, or at least a request to give her time to think it over. Then I would have to endure the agony of waiting for an answer, which could as well be no as yes.

Fanny and Hensleigh planned to travel to Maer at the same time, and the three of us arranged to go together. The sun glowed weakly behind a thick pall of smoke and fog as our train left London. I said nothing of my plan to speak to Emma but managed to spend most of the journey in what must have seemed morose silence to my companions. I was not morose; I was merely marshalling my forces. It was a Friday, November 9th.

We arrived at Maer Hall close to midnight and retired at once. When I awoke the next morning, the ground was carpeted with frost, the air fresh and clean. But I had an evil headache, and my stomach was again in turmoil. My sister Catty arrived, as did Emma's aunt Fanny Allen. After lunch I begged time to read and rest in my bedroom whilst Catty, Emma, Elizabeth, and Hensleigh's Fanny took a walk round the pool. Late in the afternoon I heard music, someone playing the pianoforte. Chopin, I thought. I roused myself and went down to the drawing room, knowing the pianist must be Emma.

She was alone. I stood listening and rehearsed again what I planned to say: *Emma, will you do me the honour of becoming my wife?*

Emma stopped playing, and when I cleared my throat, she turned. "How nice of you to come for a visit, Charley," she said. "We've all been longing to see you!"

"Emma," I began. "W-w-w-w —" I stopped, horrified. My stammer, after a long absence, had returned. I couldn't get out even the first word of my proposal. And I would never be able to manage to say the most crucial word: *wife*.

Emma gazed up at me, smiling. "That was a Chopin prelude — my favourite." She paused, examining my face. "What is it, Charley?" she asked sympathetically.

"Marry me, Emma!" I blurted, and for once in my life I stopped thinking and *acted*. I dropped to one knee, took her hand in mine, and looked into her eyes, clear and blue and startled behind the smudged lenses of her spectacles. "Marry me, Emma. I want you to be my wife" — this time I managed it without stammering — "if you'll have me."

"Yes, I'll marry you, Charley," she replied. No hesitation, no request for a little time to think it over, just a firm, unequivocal "Yes," as though I'd asked her to play Mozart instead of Chopin.

I wondered if I should kiss her, but at that precise moment the bell chimed to announce dinner. I got up off my knee, still holding her hand in mine. We took another long look at each other, a little stunned by what we had just agreed to do. I let go her hand and we walked, separately, to the dining room, not daring even to glance at each other.

Both Emma and I remained uncommonly quiet throughout the meal, which seemed a merry dinner for everyone else. I found it impossible to swallow more than a few bites, though as always the table was well provisioned with several brace of pheasants roasted to a golden brown, no doubt shot by Uncle Jos, and followed by a baked tart made of apples from the Maer orchard. I saw the others stealing furtive glances, first at Emma, then at me, as the conversation continued to bubble round the two of us, sitting mute as statues.

After dinner Emma's father asked her to play, as he usually did when there were guests. That evening she seemed subdued. "Just one piece," she said. "A nocturne."

What she played was so lovely, so haunting, so sublime, that my throat swelled with deep feeling.

I had a desperate wish that everyone would retire, and soon, so that Emma and I might have a little more time to talk, though I wasn't sure what more I had to say. Uncle Jos eventually helped Aunt Bessy to her bedroom, and one by one Aunt Fanny Allen and Elizabeth and Catty excused themselves. Hensleigh and Fanny Wedgwood stayed just where they were.

As soon as the others had gone, Fanny eyed both of us and demanded sharply, "What's happened? It's plain that *something* has."

Emma glanced at me, a question in her eyes. "I have asked Emma to marry me," I said hoarsely.

"And I have accepted," Emma added quickly.

"Oh! Oh! Oh!" Fanny cried, leaping up and rushing to embrace Emma, and Hensleigh stepped forward to slap me on the back and then to kiss his sister.

Though my head was throbbing and I longed to lie down and sleep for hours, that was plainly going to be impossible. Fanny, exuberant, kept us up, asking questions that neither of us could answer — *When is the*

wedding? Where will you live? How did this all begin? —
till Emma announced that she had eaten scarcely a
mouthful at dinner and was now on the verge of starva-
tion. Hensleigh was sent to forage in the pantry, returning with a loaf of bread and a dish of butter. Fanny
routed Elizabeth and Catty from their beds, and we
were subjected to more shrieks and embraces. "We have
wished for this for such a long time!" Catty announced,
and Elizabeth rejoiced. A celebration was taking place
all round us, but neither of us seemed able to partici-
pate. I felt numb. Emma looked pensive.

Finally, so exhausted I could scarcely think, I swore
the others to secrecy till I would speak to Uncle Jos in
the morning, bade them all good night, and stumbled
off to bed.

Still I couldn't sleep. I had not yet kissed my intended
bride. I didn't know how she really felt. I didn't quite
know how *I* felt. Perhaps we were making a dreadful
mistake and Emma sensed it.

EMMA HAD ALREADY GONE up the hill to teach her Sunday
school class at St. Peter's when I went down to breakfast.
Uncle Jos, Aunt Bessy, and Bessy's sister, Fanny Allen,
were still innocent of the major event of the previous
evening, but the others seemed about to burst with their
secret. After breakfast — I could manage only toast and
tea — I followed Uncle Jos to the library. He looked at
me keenly whilst I nervously clasped and unclasped my
hands.

"Well, my boy? Something on your mind? Out with it!"

"I've come to ask you for Emma's hand in marriage." I must have sounded as though I were being strangled.

Tears sprang from his eyes and poured down his weathered cheeks. "Oh, my dear Charley!" he sobbed. "You have my permission and my blessing. Nothing could make me happier. Have you spoken to her?"

"I have. She has accepted." I couldn't help noticing that Uncle Jos showed considerably more emotion than Emma had. Or, for that matter, had I.

The old gentleman pulled out a handkerchief, dabbed at his eyes, blew his nose heartily, and beamed. "Let's go tell the world," he said, "in the event they haven't heard it already."

Emma returned from her class, looking cheerful — at least she had not changed her mind. Lunch turned into a celebration with toasts to our future whilst Emma and I sat side by side, smiling but saying little, though I felt much needed to be said. There might have been an ocean between us that neither of us seemed able to cross. As soon as the meal was over and I could decently leave, I said my good-byes to the Wedgwoods, promised Emma to come back in a few days, and rode off with Catty for The Mount to tell Father what I had done.

What I had *not* done, though, was to take Emma in my arms and kiss her.

Chapter 20

Emma: 1839

THE WHEELS WERE SET in motion. Emma accepted my proposal of marriage on Saturday, everyone at Maer Hall was told on Sunday, and soon everyone else would know. I hardly knew where to begin to sort out all that lay ahead. How on earth would I manage to accomplish my work and to take care of the practical matter of setting up a household for myself and *a wife?* It was daunting, and my stomach reacted badly, as always.

As Catty and I bowled along towards Shrewsbury in a cold drizzle, I extracted a promise that she would not run screaming through the neighbourhood with the news till I had spoken to Father and received his permission to marry Emma. Catty agreed, though I'm certain she immediately told Susan and the two of them mapped out an efficient strategy to spread the word.

Father was pleased, as I imagined he would be. "You have drawn a prize!" he said, not once but several times. We talked at length — there would be no financial worries, he said, so long as we were prudent — and before letting me go, he gave me a piece of advice.

"Charles, listen to me well, for this is not a bit of idle chatter. In recent months you and I have spoken rather openly about our religious ideas, and I saw clearly that you are not suited for the life of a country parson I had once had in mind for you. I do not fault you for this in any way. However, I would caution you never to let Emma know the extent of your rejection of traditional beliefs. Conceal your doubts as best you can, for they can only cause heartache."

I thanked him for his concern and promised to be very careful indeed with what I told or did not tell Emma.

MY SISTERS REJOICED; they had apparently been hoping for just such an outcome. Letters flew in all directions. Over the next several days I wrote to inform family and friends of this turn of events and received their congratulations on my extreme good fortune in securing such a lovely, intelligent, and agreeable young lady to become my wife. Ras replied:

I feel very glad in what I am sure will give you so much & such certain happiness. It is a marriage which will give almost as much pleasure to the rest of the world as it does to yourselves.

He was about to go out driving Miss Martineau, he said, and they would take the opportunity to look for suitable houses for Emma and me. The debate over suburbs versus central London had already begun to rage round the fire at The Mount. I planned to return to Maer on Saturday for a day or two before leaving for London and wrote to Emma:

We must have a great deal of talk together. Do have a fire in the library. The date of the wedding needs to be set-tled, and we must talk seriously about where we shall live.

I worried, I told her, that after living a life with the kind of large and agreeable parties to which she was ac-customed, Emma would find our quiet evenings dull, and she would find me a selfish and solitary brute and our life together "a great hum."

Before I could send off this letter, the first in which I addressed her as "my own dear Emma," Catty marched into my bedroom waving a letter from Emma herself, but directed to Catty, not to me. "Here, Charley," Catty said. "You must read this."

Emma had written it the previous day. *Since Charles left I have been rather afraid of his being in too great a hurry, so I hope you will all hold him in a little.*

Too great a hurry? Hold him in a little? The reason, Emma went on, was that her marriage and departure from Maer would be very hard on her older sister, Eliz-abeth, who would be left alone to care for their aging parents. This was especially difficult now that Aunt Bessy had become frail and forgetful. Aunt Fanny Allen had added a note at the bottom of Emma's letter:

Tell Charles to be a good boy & take things leisurely. How I do wish he would wait till Spring & fine weather! Do dear Catty clog the wheels a little.

Clog the wheels a little? The old auntie wanted us to

wait two more months to marry! I had taken quite a longish time, I realised, to come to the decision and even longer to speak the right words, but now it was decided, the words spoken and accepted, and I wanted the wedding to take place with all possible speed. I remembered a letter I'd received from one of my sisters some four years earlier whilst the *Beagle* was in South America: *It will end by your wasting the best years of your life on shipboard*. I did not believe then, nor did I now, that my years on that voyage were wasted. But I could not tolerate the loss of any more time.

I returned to the letter I had just written to Emma and, acknowledging her concerns about Elizabeth, added this:

Do, dear Emma, remember life is short, & two months is the sixth part of the year, & that year from which things shall hereafter date and I am part of you, dearest Emma.

I could state my feelings no more plainly than that.

I RETURNED TO MAER as promised, and such a different time this was! Alone in the library before a dancing fire Emma and I discussed plans for our future life together.

Emma agreed to a wedding on January 29th, two months distant, but reminded me of all that needed to be accomplished in what, to her, was a very short time. We had still to decide where we wished to live, acquire furnishings, hire servants, etcetera, etcetera. There was no further talk about clogging the wheels.

I had promised myself I would always be open and honest with Emma and would not pretend to be someone I was not — someone who enjoyed dancing (I hated it) and dinner parties (unless with good friends) and attending the theatre (I thought it generally a great hum). I readily confessed preferring solitude to society. With each confession dear Emma nodded sympathetically and murmured, "Of course, my dear Charles, I understand," or "Yes, Charley, I agree."

Emboldened, I decided to go a step further. "I think you should know, Emma, that my religious beliefs may be somewhat different from yours. They are not traditional, and perhaps they never were exactly so." I rushed on impetuously, "Since the voyage and my opportunity to observe so many interesting phenomena, be they geological or botanical or zoological, I've begun to think seriously about the way our world has evolved since its earliest beginnings, and I see that I cannot look to the Bible for infallible answers —" I stopped abruptly, seeing Emma's sweet face grow pale and her look of dismay. "I'm afraid I'm giving you pain, dear Emma. I'll speak no more of it."

But Emma shook her head. "I thank you from my heart for your openness with me. I should dread the feeling that you were concealing your opinions from fear of giving me pain. My reason tells me that honest doubts can't be a sin, but I do feel it would be an aching void between us."

We had been sitting cosily, half turned towards each other, her knee sometimes brushing my leg, her hand lying trustingly in both of mine. But now I stood up abruptly and began pacing. I had made a serious error in judgement. Father had been right! Why had I not listened to him?

I tried to soften what I had just said. "Yes, Emma, merely certain doubts, that's all, sure to be resolved in time, nothing that should concern you."

She was surely unconvinced but chose then not to press me further. I tried, clumsily, to change the subject. "My dear Emma, let us speak of other matters. Surely it's more important to solve the practical problems and leave the metaphysical questions till later?" Taking her hand again, I tried not to notice that her eyes were bright with tears.

"You're right, Charles," Emma said with a gallant smile. "Perhaps we should talk about where we shall live."

After some little discussion, we agreed that renting a house in a central part of London, where my work would keep me, was the sensible thing to do for at least the first year or two.

This time, before I left Maer, I did not fail to take Emma in my arms and kiss her. And in her warm and affectionate response I was reassured that we should always be able to resolve whatever difficulties we encountered.

I HAD SIMPLY not given any thought to the Horneritas. But back in London I found a kind note from Lyell congratulating me, with a chastening postscript added by Mrs. Lyell, the former Mary Horner: "Your letter caused us *some* surprise." And when Ras met Mrs. Horner a few days later, she reportedly exclaimed, "So this is the reason Charles would not come near us of late!"

I wondered uneasily if I owed the Horners an apology for not marrying one of their daughters, but I was not sure how to go about that, and so I did nothing.

Captain and Mrs. FitzRoy received my letter and invited me to tea. "My dear Darwin," the captain said cordially, "you shall not know what real happiness there is in a man and a woman living together till you have tried it for at least six months." Not wishing to contradict him, I refrained from saying I felt sure Emma and I would require much less than six months to discover happiness. Nor did I take the opposite view when he insisted vehemently that the suburbs were the only fit place to live.

Ras agreed with Emma and me that we should look for a house in the city; so, too, did Father, and Susan also cast her vote for the city. Thus encouraged, I conceived a plan for taking systematic walks through every suitable neighbourhood in hopes of finding a good house at no very great cost.

By Wednesday, November 21st, I had received my first letter from Emma since our engagement. I had already managed to make my future wife unhappy.

When I am with you all melancholy thoughts keep out of my head, but since you are gone some sad ones have forced themselves in, of fear that our opinions on the most important subject should differ widely.

I had no doubt what she meant by "the most important subject," though I had no reply that would satisfy her. To my relief she moved on to a discussion of cooks and kettles and so forth necessary to establishing a household and let the religious question slip away. She had begun addressing me as "you old curmudgeon" and "tiresome toad" — the Wedgwoods had always indulged in such loving insults — and I felt her affection for me growing, as mine grew for her.

The question of a suitable location for our home continued to occupy us: the back lanes of Regents Park? Bayswater, perhaps, or Kensington? Houses were very scarce, and it seemed to me the landlords had all gone mad, asking such outrageous prices that I was becoming discouraged.

I have seen no one for these two days; & what can a man have to say who works all morning describing hawks & owls & then rushes out & walks in a bewildered manner up one street & down another, looking out for the words "To let."

My letter had scarcely gone out when I received Emma's announcing her decision to come up to London to help with the search.

It is very well I am coming to look after you, my poor old man, for it is quite evident that you are on the verge of insanity & we should have had to advertize you "Lost in the vicinity of Bloomsbury: a tall thin gentleman, quite harmless, whoever will bring him back shall be hand-somely rewarded."

"SCRATTLE" WAS THE STAFFORDSHIRE word for the tedious

details of housekeeping, details that as a bachelor I had always managed to escape or ignore completely. Now housemaids had to be hired, as well as a cook and a manservant; linens for beds, towels for washing up, pots and pans and kettles and knives had to be assembled, and a supply of coal for heating and cooking ordered, and who knew what else needed doing to keep one's life moving along in a somewhat orderly fashion. It all occupied far too much time, thought, and energy. But "Little Miss Slip-Slop," as Emma's mother used to call her, was proving a capable scrattler after all.

Emma came to London by train with her brother Harry — she quite enjoyed the experience — and stayed with Hensleigh and Fanny for two weeks. We looked at houses and dined often with Ras. Good Fanny offered to take over the tedious business of engaging a housemaid, and Ras's housemaid promised to recommend a cook. Whilst I attempted to work, Emma shopped for a wedding dress and trousseau and was back in Maer in time to celebrate a last Christmas with her family as Miss Emma Wedgwood.

Within the week it was my pleasure to inform Emma that I had at last negotiated for a house we had both liked. No. 12 Upper Gower Street was unpretentious but had rooms ample for our needs: four floors with servants' quarters and the "museum" for my specimens on the top floor, more servants' quarters and the kitchen on the ground floor, and drawing room, dining room, bedrooms, and a quiet room where I could work on the middle floors. There was even a long, narrow back garden, however weedy and desolate it appeared on the day of our visit. Fanny, who had been with us that day, had pronounced the furniture hideous, and none of us could ignore the appalling decorating scheme — azure walls, bright yellow curtains, and red velvet upholstery on the hideously carved settees. It was such a tropical combination of colours that we called it "Macaw Cottage."

Emma wrote back, expressing her satisfaction and delivering an affectionate scolding: *I do not like your looking so unwell & being so overtired. Leave London for Shrewsbury to get some rest and then to come to Maer to be idle.*

I may have wished to follow her advice, but I had far too much to do. I could not seem to settle down to work in earnest, just at the time I most wanted to. New responsibilities as secretary to the Geological Society took up much of my week. My *Beagle* journal was ready to go to press but required an appendix. Papers on botanical subjects had to be written and presented. I had written sixty-five pages of my paper about the geology of Glen Roy and thought I had only fifteen more to do. I was determined to finish before the wedding.

I COULDN'T SLEEP — nerves, I suppose. On a Sunday morning I rang for Covington. "I am very sorry to spoil your holiday, but I must begin packing up, as I cannot rest."

Covington, who had been in the dark about most of

my plans excepting the fact of my engagement, gaped at me in astonishment. "Pack up, sir? For what?"

I explained the situation. "I'm to be married in a few weeks," I said, "and I'm determined to move into the house on Upper Gower at once. Tomorrow, if possible."

"Shall you be needing my services after you move, sir?" he asked, his expression impassive as always.

"I've made enquiries to find you a new position. Nothing has turned up, but it should not be excessively long till it does."

Covington nodded without comment, and we began sorting through a multitude of papers, a chore that occupied us through Sunday evening. By Monday afternoon everything was carefully packed, and I despatched Covington to hire two large vans and several porters. The porters were displeased by the weight of the geological specimens that had to be shouldered up the narrow stairs to the "museum" on the top floor. By six o'clock all my goods had been transported to Upper Gower Street.

Soon everything was settled. I thanked Covington for his excellent service over the past seven years, presented him with a gift of money — two guineas, which I thought ample — and wished him well, promising to maintain contact with him. After Covington had left to pack his own things and spend a last night at Marlborough Street, the elderly housemaid cooked me a supper of eggs and bacon and tea before she, too, left me alone. I carried my supper into my study, marvelling at its quietness, and when I'd finished, climbed to the "museum." Gazing round at the attic room full of boxes of specimens, I was reminded of the cabinet where I'd kept the treasures I'd collected as a boy.

The physical work of moving proved a rest for me. My papers and specimens were much better organised and arranged than ever before. I could now look forward to my country holiday — and to my wedding — with a clear conscience.

"GOOD HEAVENS, CHARLES!" Fanny Wedgwood cried when she toured Macaw Cottage soon after I'd moved in. "Do send those odious yellow curtains to the dyers at once and have them stained some very pale colour, drab grey or slate, to balance the eyestrain induced by the azure walls."

"But is that what Emma would want?" I asked, wishing I had not to make such difficult decisions.

A decision I did make on my own was on the choice of new clothes. My tailor tried to convince me I needed a blue coat and white trousers, which I thought highly impractical for travelling in stormy winter weather. I settled instead for tobacco brown with a waistcoat of pale ivory, all of fine quality.

Emma and I continued to exchange letters every two or three days, our letters often crossing in the mail. I again visited Shrewsbury and Maer to make final plans for the wedding, which would be as small and simple as possible.

"Don't you wish you could be married like a royal

prince without being at your own wedding?" Emma asked me, and I realised, not for the first time, that this dear sweet girl must be able to read my thoughts.

I had proposed a brief wedding trip to Warwick Castle, but Emma scotched that idea. "I don't find the steam much up for that," she said. "It's too cold for the beauties of nature or art, so we may as well go straight home after the ceremony. Papa has already reserved places for us on the train." So that was settled — I was agreeable — and I would instruct the housemaid to have a fire built before we arrived.

I assured Emma I'd bought the ring. "And we've received a most interesting wedding gift from my good old friend Herbert — he who gave me my first excellent microscope."

"Something of scientific interest?" asked my bride.

"Cherbury calls it a *Forficula,* the Latin for earwig, an insect identifiable by the forceps at its posterior end. This, however, is a massive silver weapon that Ras has explained is intended for serving asparagus."

With such matters to discuss, I did not again find myself uncomfortably dealing with Emma's concerns about my unbelief and the state of my eternal soul.

BENEATH A LOWERING SKY on a cold and blowy Tuesday morning, January 29th, 1839, a small party climbed the hill behind Maer Hall to St. Peter's Church. If I could not be absent from the wedding like a royal prince, as Emma had suggested, our actual wedding was the next best thing. Elizabeth tried hard to conceal her sadness that Emma was leaving. Poor Caroline was so worried about her frail young baby that she prepared to rush away immediately. Emma's mother was too ill to be brought up to the chapel, and my father declined to make the trip from Shrewsbury. Ras was greatly comforted when I told him his presence was not required. Uncle Jos was there and weeping happily. Catty and Susan were present and in fine spirits, and Charlotte and her husband, Charles Langton, were perhaps the brightest sparks in the chapel.

I shall always remember Emma in the greenish grey silk gown she'd ordered in London and a white bonnet trimmed with some sort of lace and flowers. I suffered a pounding headache and felt unwell, but somehow made it through the ceremony, conducted with all due solemnity by our clergyman cousin, John Allen Wedgwood. Within twenty minutes we were making our way down the hill from the church to Maer Hall. There was barely enough time to eat a mouthful of the small wedding cake and to drink a bit of punch. Emma changed out of her silk gown and into a plain travelling costume, kissed her sisters and her parents, and was handed into the carriage. I climbed in beside her. Before we left for Whitmore station, Charlotte remembered to pass us a basket with sandwiches and water Elizabeth had packed for our journey to London.

We arrived that evening at Macaw Cottage rather tired from the nervousness of the morning ceremony and the long hours on the train. It was snowing and very cold, but fires blazed cosily in every room. Emma removed her bonnet and pelisse and laid them aside. She looked extremely pretty. *You've drawn a prize,* I thought to myself, just as Father said.

There was enough food left in the basket for a late supper — we'd eaten scarcely any of it on the train. But now we were ravenous, and we sat at our ugly dining room table and like children on a picnic solemnly finished whatever remained, to the last crumb. I watched Emma bite, chew, and swallow. She concentrated on her sandwich and wiped her lips with one of the napkins Elizabeth had thoughtfully included.

She folded her napkin, turned to me, and smiled. "Well, *Mr. Darwin,*" she said, "here we are."

Here we were, indeed. I reached for her hand. It was surprisingly warm — warmer than mine. So many decisions had been made and actions taken since the day ten weeks earlier when I had first proposed to Emma and she had accepted. My life had been transformed, turned on its head. I had longed for this moment — but I confess that I was now very unsure how to proceed.

"It's warmer in the drawing room, *Mrs. Darwin,*" I said.

We rose, Emma tucked her hand in the crook of my elbow, and I escorted her, rather awkwardly, to the grotesque red velvet settee. We sat down, our fingers enlaced. I rubbed her fingers nervously with my thumb.

Emma drew her hand away and gently cupped my face. "It's all right, Charley. I've spoken with Charlotte, and she's told me what I need to know. I think the thing for you to do now," she said, smiling, "is to kiss me. But first let me take off my spectacles."

Emma brought her face close to mine and touched my brow, my chin, my nose with infinite tenderness. "You know, my dearest Charley," she said, "I have always been exceedingly fond of your face. I've always seen kindness there, and intelligence, and a gentle sort of strength. But your nose, Charley — I do very much love your nose!"

I kissed her then, again and again and again, awakening an ardour in both of us that took us by surprise and swept us away together.

The Rest of the Story

CHARLES DARWIN was a rising young naturalist — but not yet a famous one — when he and Emma began their married life together in the winter of 1839, two weeks before Charley's thirtieth birthday. Six months later his *Beagle* journal was published, starting him on the road to fame, not only in the scientific community but also among well-read people throughout England. And their first baby was on the way.

The Darwins lived quietly, as Charles preferred. After a few years they tired of the noise and filth of the city and bought a house large enough for their growing family in Kent, sixteen miles south of London. At Down House Charles found the privacy he needed to think, write, and pursue his studies of a variety of living creatures. The family increased and thrived; Emma gave birth to ten children in fourteen years, and Charles was a kind and devoted father. When Annie, their second child, died at the age of ten, it nearly broke her father's heart. Seven Darwin children lived to be adults.

As the years went by, Charles continued to fill notebooks about everything that interested him, as he always had. He made progress on his books about geology and zoology — birds, reptiles, fish. He scribbled notes on his ideas about how species changed through a process he called natural selection — notes not yet for publication, not even to share with colleagues, but to explore in his own mind. Painstakingly he expanded these ideas; still he kept them to himself. His theory not only contradicted the story of the Creation told in Genesis but also implied a universe in which God was no longer the sole creator of all that was or would ever be. His ideas were bound to be upsetting — not only to his beloved Emma, but to his friends and family and to Victorian society in general. So he waited, accumulating evidence, wanting to be sure.

Year after year Charles Darwin put off writing the "big book" that would explain and support his radical theory. Meanwhile, he continued to publish books about coral reefs and the geology of South America and of volcanic islands. He bred pigeons and observed how their characteristics changed. He wrote several articles based on eight years of studies of barnacles. Still he held off. In 1858 a young British naturalist, Alfred Russell Wallace, living on a remote island in the South Pacific, sent Darwin an article describing similar ideas of evolution. Only then did Charles realize he had to make his own ideas public.

Darwin was fifty when *On the Origin of Species* was published in 1859. Describing how transmutation takes place (he didn't call it evolution) by means of natural selection in pigeons, dogs, and other life forms, it immediately became a bestselling book and touched off a storm of controversy that rages to this day.

Origin was followed eleven years later by another "big book," *The Descent of Man and Selection in Relation to Sex*. In it, Darwin advanced his idea that humans were like other life-forms and developed according to the forces of natural selection. *The Expression of the Emotions in Man and Animals,* published in 1882, the last year of his life, carried his groundbreaking theories even further.

SINCE BEFORE HIS MARRIAGE Charles had been suffering from constant headaches and stomach upsets. Within a short time afterward he became seriously and continuously ill. His condition was never diagnosed. For the rest of his life, Charles's chronic poor health plagued him, often reducing him to the state of an invalid. Emma cared for him lovingly, and he depended on her completely.

Charles Darwin, whose theory of evolution is one of the greatest contributions ever made to science, died April 19, 1882, at the age of seventy-three. He had wished to be buried in a plain, unpolished coffin in the village of Down where he had lived most of his adult life. But Parliament insisted that Charles Darwin was too important a figure for such a quiet funeral, and convinced his family to allow him to be laid to rest at Westminster Abbey with full pomp and ceremony. Emma, who had looked after him loyally for so long, lived another fourteen years; she was eighty-eight when she died. Erasmus — Ras — long considered "of a delicate frame," had died only eight months before Charles, aged seventy-six and still a bachelor. Soon after his cousin, Charlotte, died in 1862, his sister Catty married the widower, Charles Langton. Of the sisterhood, only Susan — Granny — remained unmarried and lived on at The Mount until her death. Another important figure in his life, Captain Robert FitzRoy, had committed suicide in 1865 at the age of fifty-nine.

CHARLES DARWIN'S BOOKS FILL A SHELF. Books *about* Charles Darwin fill libraries. An online search of his name turns up about 3,340,000 results.

But who was *Charley Darwin*? — I mean the schoolboy who preferred to catch beetles and hunt for newts in the old quarry rather than study Latin and Greek, the young man who was more comfortable on horseback galloping across the pampas of Argentina than he was sipping tea in an English drawing room. Charley's early struggles to discover who he was and what he wanted to do with his life led me to write his story as a novel, to see his world through his eyes, experience his life as he felt it, and describe his adventures, his successes, and his disappointments in his own voice.

Charles Darwin's brief *Autobiography,* his *Beagle* journal, and his voluminous correspondence have all provided windows into Charley's world. In this book I've written his story as he might have written it in nineteenth-century England, down to the English spellings that look so odd to an American: *whilst, amongst, neighbour, meagre, travelled, learnt, titbit,* and many more, and spelled (*spelt!*) place-names as they were then: *St. Jago, Chili,* for instance, has become *Santiago, Chile.*

As he had suspected when he first wrote out his debate with himself on the subject of marriage, Charley never did "know French, or see the Continent, or go to America, or go up in a balloon." But his remarkable, wide-ranging imagination, his powerful intellect, and his patient observations of the world around him carried him far beyond the wildest adventures of his voyage around the world.

Bibliography

Browne, Janet. *Charles Darwin: Voyaging*. Princeton, N.J.:
    Princeton University Press, 1995.
Darwin, Francis, ed. *The Autobiography of Charles Darwin and
    Selected Letters*. New York: Dover, 1958.
Healey, Edna. *Emma Darwin: The Inspirational Wife of a Genius*.
    London: Headline, 2001.
Nichols, Peter. *Evolution's Captain: The Dark Fate of the Man
    Who Sailed Charles Darwin Around the World*. New York:
    HarperCollins, 2003.

Online sources:

University of Cambridge. "*Beagle* Diary." *The Complete Work of
    Charles Darwin Online*. **www.darwin-online.org.uk**
University of Cambridge. *Darwin Correspondence Project*.
    www.darwinproject.ac.uk

For British spellings:

Shorter Oxford English Dictionary, 6th ed. 2 vols. New York:
    Oxford University Press, 2007.